GAME FOR THE MIDDLE KINGDOM

JACK KING

This is a work of fiction. All of the characters and events portrayed in this novel are either fictitious or are used fictitiously.

Game for the Middle Kingdom / Jack King
(Previous title: Quest for the Middle Kingdom, September 2014)
2nd Edition Paperback: Spring 2016

ISBN 13: 978-0-9973471-2-8 (Paperback)
ISBN 13: 978-0-9973471-3-5 (eBook)

Editor: Amy Nedrow
Interior Design: Susan Veach
Cover Design: Richard Turylo

Other books by Jack King:
Time Rider - Wildertrek
Time Rider - Red Attack

Readers may contact Jack King at:
www.Jack-King.com
authorjackking@gmail.com
@authorjackking (Twitter)

Printed in the United States of America
Published by Author (PBA)

Important Note

At the time of the story, the newly invented sport of basketball was named Basket Ball, and the capital city of China was called Peking or, more commonly, Beiping.

Dedication

To those who ventured all to bring their faith to the great people of China...
This story is gratefully dedicated.

Acknowledgements

Thanks to a number of reviewers of the original manuscript. Your excitement about the story and diligence encouraged and propelled me toward the final version.

Part I
The Highlander and the Harem

Chapter One

Born at home in late spring, 1882, in the midst of a sudden thunderstorm so severe that locals remembered it years later, David Adam MacDougall emerged from his mother's womb bawling loud enough to match the tremendous thunder claps outside, his red splotchy face an angry welt against the whiteness of the blanket. For all that, he was still a fine looking baby boy, his features well formed, symmetrical, and strong.

"Aye, tis a handsome wee laddie you have here, Claire." Old Doc Black hiccupped, his enthusiasm as much bolstered by the strong spirits he kept imbibing from the flask inside his vest pocket as the attractiveness of the newborn in front of him. The old man's bleary eyes viewed the new infant with a fair amount of pride. Having delivered most of the newborns in the sleepy little village for the past forty-seven years, the latest baby was always the best, in his opinion.

"He's got a magnolious pair o' lungs on him, he has." Cradling the screaming infant in the crook of one arm, the old man stuck his finger in his ear and twisted vigorously at the blasts of noise echoing inside the little room and out. He laid the howling boy in the waiting mother's arms. Immediately the baby quieted, finding and latching on to the exposed breast. The woman softly cooed to the infant as little David began pulling in strong mouthfuls of the warm nourishing milk.

"Och, you did verra good this time, Doc. And you, too, sweetheart." Standing by his wife's side, Jonathan MacDougall let go of the hand he had been holding throughout, and clasped her shoulder. He beamed with pride at the happy sight. His third born, a second brawny son.

Exhausted but pleased, Claire looked up at her husband and gave him a reassuring smile. "Aye, he be a fine beautiful boy, Johnny."

"'Another MacDougall he is, in the long line o' our clan." Watching his wife tenderly care for the newborn, Jonathan reflected on the lineage of his clan.

Though he knew it not, the baby came from a long, twisting, yet unbroken line of somewhat respectable forebears, all descended from a doughty Highland Scottish clan who had once ruled Lorne, the Isle of Mull in Argyll, and the surrounding lands in the thirteenth and fourteenth centuries, with an iron fist. The Hebridean Island chain that formed a major part of the ancient MacDougall fiefdom were a widespread and diverse archipelago off the western coast of northern Scotland of which the Inner Hebrides contains Mull itself.

Little coastal fishing villages dotted the many bays and inlets to the west of the MacDougall place. Ancient farming towns abounded on the inland side and all across the landscape of the Highlands of which Jonathan's hamlet was only one. His community had its own high street running down the central of the village, just like all the others.

Jonathan, kind-hearted to a fault, was a modestly wealthy landowner who, true to his good nature, was generous and forgiving of the hard-shell crofters who farmed his scrappy-hilled acres. If he'd told one, he'd told them all, "Och, no, Ernest, you can be a waitin' till the next time to pay me your due. I be in no hurry, man."

He cared for his tenants as human beings. He knew most of his fellow landlords were greedy men who thought nothing of uprooting starving crofters for more profitable uses of their property.

Over the years, David learned compassion and quiet humility from watching his father as he grew up. He also witnessed the increasing poverty and anguish among many within his village. Even as a boy, he perceived the widespread hardship, and it gave him a lasting desire to help those less fortunate.

Scotland was a land in cruel transition. Jonathan had inherited his acres from his father and grandfather MacDougall, but too many countrymen owned nothing but the rags on their back. Even then, some of the clothes were stolen. In Jonathan's adulthood and David's childhood, they witnessed a ruthless shift.

One day, Jonathan's young sons found him outside,

staring sadly toward the distance beyond their unplowed fields into the grayness of the hills. "Ah, boys," he sighed. "Tragic tis. Seeing farms a disappearin'. Watchin' entire villages becomin' ghost towns. Good folks a starvin'. Poor men forced to seek work elsewhere to feed their families." He shook his head.

"A horrible thing."

Over time, David saw so many friends leaving, he asked, "Why do they all have to be a going, anyways, father? Gee willikers, I miss playing the football with Gordie and Mungo and Blane, and fishin' with Breannan. Every time I turn 'round, more bodies are gone."

"Och, son, tis verra heartbreakin', tis. They all be a leaving here 'cause they be desperate. The poor souls canna make a decent living anymore around here, I'm a feared. Tis the same all over. They all be wishing for greener pastures. Some are sailing off to America or Canada. Some to Australia or South Africa. Some, I've heard, are goin' as far as Chiny or South America. Others are a moving to the south lands, a hoping to get work in the plants n' factories in the big cities there."

Indeed, of the MacDougall tribes still in Scotland, nearly half had already moved south to the great industrial towns in the Lowlands to seek a better life and steadier work.

One snaggle-toothed patriarch on the lower rung of clan prosperity had lamented to David's father, "Fire and damnation. We canna live anymore on this God-forsaken half acre of soil that wadna produce enough to eat even if the Saint Andrew hisself crapped holy manure on it."

Jonathan didn't reply, but instead shook his head with empathy and put his hand on his third cousin's shoulder.

At that, Gillis turned and gave his kin a furtive jealous glance. "Some MacDougalls has a softer bed than others, they do." He stared bitterly one last time at the unforgiving stony fields around him, his steel-bristled eyebrows jutting over his watery eyes in a look of surrender.

There was a moment of silence before the old man scowled and shook his gray head. "Ah, Jonathan, it's bin a cruel life, it has. It's taken me first two wives of me youth." Gillis MacDougall sighed deeply. "Bin the ruin of me oldest son and his dear sweet family, too."

"So you be a going soon, Gillis, would you? Is there anything I can do for you?" The younger man looked over at the older man, compassion etched in his lean face.

"Aye," the old man replied. "You can be a lending me some money, if you will, to tide us over 'til Mason can git a job in the factory. We'll pays you back as soon as we're able."

Jonathan stared down at the ground for a minute. He had offered, after all. "Well, sir, things be tough all over. 'Tis, even for us." He lifted his head and smiled gently. "Och, let me check with the wifey and see what we can squeeze out for you. I'm sure we can do something."

At that, the two kinsmen turned their gaze back to the rock-strewn fields and the distant hills where the green-topped patches were slowly changing from late summer hues into the mottled browns of fall.

David knew of some distant clansmen who resolutely

eked out a bare existence for themselves and their families as fishermen in the struggling coastal hamlets. Admittedly, a few MacDougalls in Scotland were well off. "Aye, me first cousin Kyle is a part owner in a small shipbuilding company called Archibald Ferguson & MacDougall down in Glasgow," Jonathan had once told David. "They've had their struggles, they have, but I believe they're a goin' to make it now."

Another uncle and three other relatives, including David's second cousin, Michael, had trained or were training as engineers. Jonathan MacDougall himself was wealthy enough for his two sons, Robert and David, to attend their choice of university or seminary. After all, Jonathan's grandfather and one great uncle had been ordained ministers. But on the other side, Jonathan's oldest brother, one uncle, and another great uncle had been ferocious street fighters, turning to lives of petty crime and constant brawling.

David had heard the stories many times.

His father said, "Me big brother Alan once killed a man with one punch. They say he drove the jawbone into the poor fella's brain. He fled the law, he did. Skipped the country. Just wild like the wind, he was."

"Is he still alive?" asked David, as his big brother Robert walked up beside him.

"Och, boys, I've not heard or seen o' him for goin' on eighteen years. We dinna know."

David glanced up at his father. Jonathan MacDougall was lanky, but his father, Murray, David's grandfather, had been a large man, thick as well as tall, muscular, and naturally athletic. It was said he was able to lift two huge cotton bales by himself, one on each shoulder, where a normal man could barely tote one. As David grew older, it became obvious to everyone he had inherited his paternal grandfather's muscles and strength, combined with his father's kind nature. That was a most fortunate thing for others because he had also inherited fists of fury, a condition his father labored long and hard to moderate in David as a child.

A stern Presbyterian by belief, Jonathan MacDougall imbued in his two boys a devout reverence for the kirk, or church, and God from an early age. David, especially, grew up loving the brown-bricked single-story building that stood near the center of the village. He loved the smell, look, and feel of the old smoothly-worn wooden pews, the way the sunlight danced through the stained glass windows on either side, the way the pastor's heavy melodious voice rumbled and reverberated within the tightly boxed sanctuary space. He revered his father, whose basic goodness he hoped to match as a man. But, sitting in his starched Sunday clothes next to his big brother and sister Andrina sandwiched between their parents in the second to the front left pew, he was awed by the sound and fury of the words of Reverend Hennessey. The cadence of his sermons captivated him, though he understood little or nothing of the theological import of the man's speech. Listening intently, he sometimes repeated the words to himself, if a particular phrase sounded splendid to his ears.

"What are you doing?" Robert would catch him moving his lips, and give him a sharp elbow to the side as Andrina snickered under her breath.

"Leave me be," mumbled David, rubbing his side, but keeping his eyes focused on the minister with the wondrous voice.

Yes, David loved the old church. Unlike his brother and sister, he also paid close attention during the evening Bible readings led by Jonathan.

The father made a point of inculcating Biblical truths at every suitable opportunity, while his children were home from school, when chores were being done, or as they shared a moment together outside watching the land and sky and other proofs of God's creation.

"The Heavenly Father above loves all his children. Ne'r forget that, laddies," he repeated often, tousling David's thick hair and playfully thumping Robert on the side of his head in the process. "You ought be respectful of others, no matter where they be from, or how little 'tis they have in earthly goods and possessions. Remember, the Good Book says our Lord had nowhere to lay down His precious head whilst He was here on the earth.

"Also, ne'r start a fight. Remember that. Always run from it if you can. You ought to defend others if needed. No greater love has any man than to lay down his life for another. But turn the other cheek if someone offends you. You ought not defend yourself 'less your own life be in danger. Do you understand?" Jonathan looked down at children with a grave expression.

Robert simply nodded, his attention focused instead on a particularly large blackbird flying overhead. He watched the big bird land on a twisted tree off in the distance, strut along a limb and call *chook, chook* to warn off would-be intruders. Andrina beamed brightly up at her father, knowing the words were meant for her boisterous brothers only. She was the sweetheart of the family.

But David replied with shining innocent eyes, "Aye, father. I understand."

Chapter Two

Mindful of his father's admonition, as a youth David tried hard to be good, and especially not to get into any fights, though it seemed fate pressed many more temptations across his path than it did with his brother. At school and playtimes, he turned the other cheek when it came to the personal taunts, shoving, and insults. He even avoided taking up for Robert once or twice, who he figured was big enough to handle his own fighting. But when it came to his sister, and particularly his beloved mother, there came a day when he couldn't avoid confrontation.

The two bigger boys crowded around David, pushing and shoving him, their loutish faces drawn into snarls. Their breaths stank to high heaven. The nasty McConahay twins were nearly two years older and notorious playground bullies. They had waited until recess to pounce. Robert MacDougall had gone home sick that morning, so they didn't have to worry about him. Old Mr. Reilly and the watery-eyed Mr. Douglas along with the other teachers had gone to the threadbare lounge to smoke, talk about the women, complain about the misfortunes of life, and share a few pulls of cheap whiskey. As long as they stayed sober enough to teach the brats and maintain order in the classroom, the mutton-chopped Headmaster Mr. Gordon C. Watts didn't give a donkey's ass what they did. He himself stayed in his sparse little office to take his usual nap during the break time, head tilted against the high-backed chair, snoring away.

The other kids playing around the shabby weed-infested schoolyard immediately stopped what they were doing to watch, but were afraid to get too close. Pretty Rose McDonald bravely started to come over to his aid, but David grimly waved her off.

He could feel the heat rising in his face but stayed calm, looking from one boy to the other, gauging their reach, coolly determining who he should hit first. Though he'd kept his promise to his father until now to never fight, he knew deep inside he'd always had the ability. The angrier he got the more detached and intense his concentration became to inflict punishment, as he coldly viewed the two taunting twins circling him.

"Yer ma is nothin' but cheap trash and a hoor, she is!" spat Brian.

"Yah, and 'cause she's a hoor, that makes you, yer big brother, and yer little sister unholy brats, it does, MacDougall," snarled Toby, the other one, pointing his thick index finger right in David's face.

"Andy O'Henry beat on yer Ma 'cause she's nothin' but a worthless h—"

Jack King

A fast right cross rocked Brian McConahay flush on the side of his jaw, dropping the dazed and surprised older boy to his knees. Before Toby could react, David hit him with a flurry of hard jabs, breaking and bloodying his huge nose and splitting his lip. Toby backed away, cursing and cupping his hand over his bleeding mouth and nose. He stood staring, unbelieving, then pulled his twin roughly by the collar. Enraged now, he screamed, "Get up! Get up, Brian. Och, me fuckin' nose! He broke it. The little bastard broke it. Come on, Brian, let's take this sonnabitch."

Once the fight started, the crowd of spectators broke into raucous cat-calls, some toadies urging the twins on to victory because they feared retribution, others urging David on because they despised the McConahay brothers.

Unperturbed by either the sudden noise or his two opponents, David took a sudden step forward to get inside Toby's reach. He ducked under one haymaker and blocked several wild swings. The bigger boy got lucky once and caught David a glancing blow to his cheek. But then his luck ran out. Bobbing and weaving, David landed six sharp punches into Toby's lower abdomen and center chest, right over his heart. Toby suddenly gasped for air, leaning forward and clutching his stomach in pain. David finished him off with a left to the chin. Brian, standing up now, started to swing, too, but thought better of it. He hurriedly backed out of reach, holding his hands up in surrender.

The bullies had made the unfortunate mistake of

assuming David was the weaker fighter of the two MacDougall brothers simply because he was the younger and smaller.

"What the devil is a goin' on out here!" Mr. Reilly had heard the growing commotion from the opened lounge window and because he had given up the most comfortably cushioned armchair to go investigate the noise, he was furious and out for blood.

Brian immediately exclaimed, "MacDougall started it, sir! He knocked me down, then attacked me brother, he did. Just vicious, he is! I dinna know what came over him, sir. We was just havin' a little chat with him when he went crazy." An innocent look was plastered on Brian's countenance. His twin rushed to his side, vigorously nodding in agreement and pointing to the smears of blood clotted in his nostrils and over his mouth and chin.

"MacDougall, is this true? Did you attack these boys?"

"Aye, because they were calling me mother bad names, sir, and wouldn't stop."

"Sticks and stones, Mr. MacDougall, words dinna hurt you. Or yer Ma, either. Lad, you canna be a using your fists every time someone says a word o' two you dinna happen to agree with. Do you understand?" He looked sternly at David for several moments. "Do you understand me?" he repeated, harshly.

"Yes, sir," David finally mumbled, staring at Reilly's lump of an Adam's apple that bobbled up and down as the man spoke.

Reilly kept glaring at the boy. "Aye, I grew up with Alan MacDougall, yer uncle. He was a hothead, too. A bad seed, all around. Wound up killin' a man, he did, over some trifling thing." He folded his arms, tapping his chin with one hand, deep in thought. "Aye, we need to teach you a hard lesson, laddie. I'll be askin' the Headmaster to suspend you for a whole week, and I'll be makin' damn sure yer father knows about it. So you can just forget about a playin' hooky and lying to yer Pa about missing school."

David's face hardened again. "I never tell a lie, sir. Ever."

Reilly scowled at the boy; very few students stood up to the crusty old teacher. "Maybe yes. Maybe no. I'll be a speakin' again to you, MacDougall, before yer suspension starts. Brian! Toby! Come with me to the Headmaster's office. I want the old man to see the damage for himself."

At that moment, little Rose McDonald yanked on Mr. Reilly's sleeve. She wanted to say something to him in David's defense, but Reilly patently ignored her and motioned the two bullies to follow.

Grinning from ear to ear, the two McConahays strolled away, glancing over their shoulders with satisfied smirks at David. He glared at them as they left. Toby looked ridiculous trying to smile with a badly split lip and caked blood all over his ugly face.

A handful of school chums came up to him, thanking him for beating the twins and consoling him for the unfair turn of events. Sweet Rose made a point of hugging him tightly and saying just how sorry she was.

Except for Rose's attention, David didn't care about admiration or sympathy from the others. Given the same circumstances, he would do the same thing again. In his mind, his father was a very good man—the best man he knew—and his mother was as close to an angel as humanly possible. In her youth and against all social mores of the day, his dear brave mother had left her first bastard husband, the mean drunkard Andrew O'Henry, because of his ceaseless affairs and constant physical abuse. Once free, she met and married the older but infinitely more easy-going and highly respectful Jonathan MacDougall.

Yet divorce by a woman was still unthinkable and universally scorned.

At least, I wisna defending meself, but me saintly mother instead, David thought.

His father got the story twice that afternoon; first when Reilly came knocking belligerently on the front door to tell the tale he'd gotten from the McConahay twins; second when Jonathan heard the true facts from David. He looked intently at his younger son as he spoke. He had half a mind to mildly reprimand David, but then thought better of it. *Mercy and grace, mercy and grace*, he reminded himself. *The boy did it for his Ma's sake.*

Claire put her hand to her heart as she listened. Afterwards, she walked up to David and wrapped her arms around him as tightly as she could. He was almost as tall as she was now. With tears in her eyes, she held his face in her hands and kissed him on the cheek.

Chapter Three

Three different times David's life was seemingly spared as a boy. In each situation, a family member came to the rescue at the last second. Already attuned to things of the church, in young David's mind the circumstances seemed to carry the hand of the Almighty, leading him to believe God must have something special planned for his life in preserving him so.

In the first instance, David's family had been visiting second cousins of his mother, the Walkers, a couple of villages over next to the big town of Taynuilt. He was eight years old, almost nine, but already as tall and broad as a stout eleven year old. He, Robert, and Andrina were out in the field playing football against three of the four Walker children, Brian, Bran, and little Blane. Sister Briana sat on the sideline watching the game.

"Blane, you neap, you're kickin' it at the wrong goal! You're supposed to be a going the other direction. Get outta the way, lemme have it!" yelled Brian, dashing over to take the ball away from his brother, who stood glaring at him.

"I'm not a neap. You're a choob."

Racing with the ball toward the correct goal, Brian

kicked a forward pass to Bran, who called out over his shoulder, "Aye, you're really a bas, little bro, but mother's just too kind-hearted to tell ya the truth."

"You're a bas!" cried Blane, tears in his eyes, running with his head down like a miniature charging bull.

David was the first line of defense, and he rushed toward Bran to intercept. More a lucky accident than intentional, his foot grazed the edge of ball just as Bran attempted a cross-over move, bouncing the ball sharply to David's left. In his excitement at actually having a shot at the ball, David aimed a kick back down field, but instead squibbed the ball off the side of his foot, driving it forty feet further left. It bounced off the hard ground, soared into the air, landed in the middle of a rocky knoll and suddenly disappeared. Moments later, they all heard a dull thud then splash echo into the afternoon air.

"What was that?" asked Robert, coming to a stop and standing with a puzzled look, hands on hips.

"Be jibbers, I bet it went down the old well," said Brian, frowning. "Och, rotten luck, tis. That's the only ball we got."

"Sorry." David stared at his feet. "I'm sorry. Bad kick."

"Well, maybe I can get it out," he said brightly, looking up. Before any of the others could say a word, he ran over to the knoll's edge which was covered with a heavy thatch of weeds and grass, and cautiously took a step forward. The covering was so thick around and on top of the spot that he couldn't tell where the hole actually was.

From the back porch where the adults sat talking and

drinking their tea Claire suddenly looked up with a strong foreboding. She saw her youngest son running toward the stubby knoll rising in the distance like a massive grave.

"Och, Sarah, isn't that where that old well be?" She pointed frantically toward the mound.

Mrs. Walker stared at the hillock. "Aye, that be it. Now why is he a goin' over there? Dinna he know that old shaft is dangerous? Must go down a good forty feet or more 'fore there's water. Filthy stinkin' water tis, too."

With that, Claire jumped off the porch, tore off her shoes, and broke into a dead run on her bare feet straight for her son.

"Och, sweet Saint Andrew! Claire? Ya needna be a doin' that, girl!" Mrs. Walker called after the departing figure. "Alan? Alan. Alan!" she snapped at her roly-poly husband engrossed in talk with Jonathan.

"Huh? Aye, whit is it you want, woman? I'm a busy the noo."

"The youngin's be playin' 'round that nasty old well head."

He glanced up with a surprised look on his red face at the racing form of the Mrs. MacDougall and beyond at the kids at play. "Aie! Get away from there!" he yelled loudly, waving both his arms dramatically.

"Oh, dammit, Alan—'cuse me language, Jonathan—get your lazy arse up and go down there, and tell 'em to be a stayin' away from the place."

Jack King

By then Jonathan MacDougall had risen from his chair and hurried into the yard, putting his hand over his eyes to shield the slant of the mid afternoon sun, as he looked over the scene beyond.

"David. David! Och, please get away from there, me darlin'! Step away!" Her heart pounding in her ears, her throat dry, Claire sprinted the last twenty yards the fastest she'd ever ran.

Startled, David twisted around to face his mother racing toward him. As he turned, his left heel caught on the ragged edge of the hidden opening. His foot slipped into the hole, and he tumbled backwards, flailing his arms forward in windmill fashion trying to keep his balance.

Claire MacDougall reached her son and grabbed one thrashing hand in time to keep David from dropping into the deep well.

Everything had happened so fast the other children had stood and watched with wide eyes and open mouths.

Claire firmly pulled her son several yards away from the danger and wrapped her arms around him, suffocating the boy with her hugs, kisses, and tears.

Remembering the episode later, David never could decide if he would have slipped or not if his mother had not come. He only knew that he had slipped upon her approach and she was the one who came to his rescue.

The second time David's life was saved was several years later when the local gang of boys, including the two

MacDougalls, had gone to swim at Murphy's Spring, as they facetiously called the deep, dangerous, irregularly-shaped gravel pit left behind by a failed mining operation of decades ago. The early summer rains had been torrential that season and the vast old crater had filled. No one had ever been to the lowest point of the ragged bottom and determined the full depth of the middle. But it looked scary.

From countless past swimmers—fathers, uncles, older cousins, big brothers—the boys had been made to understand that underneath the shale-grey surface of the seemingly placid waters lay twisted ledges, jagged rock spires, and places below where heads could smash into unconsciousness, or arms and legs could become jammed and stuck, the erstwhile swimmer frantically struggling to dislodge their limb while precious air ran out. Four unlucky youths had drowned in the crater in the past seven years, and all the boys had been strictly forbidden to take a dip in old Murphy's, which meant every lad over the age of eight took it as a personal challenge to brave the death-pit as often as they could get away with it.

Out on the northwest side leading down into the pool was an earth and rock outcropping that made a natural diving platform. The two easygoing MacLeod brothers whom everybody liked, the four Hunter boys, fatty Ross Fraser, the always mouthy Conan Gray, little Sammie Kelly, and Robert had already all jumped in, feet first. The water directly below and to the right of David was churning with bodies: one doing a backstroke, two attempting to float but only fatty

Fraser succeeding, three doing a basic front or back crawl, the rest doing some variation of the dog paddle.

Back on the diving ledge, David wavered. There was no place to go without leaping well beyond the mass of figures. The small left hand opening among the swimmers was too close, in his opinion, to the ragged shelf wall. Peering up, Conan saw David's hesitation and grinned evilly as he yelled out, "Och, lookit the little sissy, boys! Tis afraid to come in, he be. Aye, does little Davey need his little mommy to come hold his little bitty hand? Does he want his sister to jump in for 'im?" Conan looked over his shoulder to see that there was a gap behind his group further out in the menacing middle of the pit. "Hey, MacDougall! I double-dares ya to takes a flyin' start and dive in head first into the middle." He pointed to the space beyond him.

When he heard his surname called, Robert twisted around in the water to face the speaker. He saw the boy's taunting expression and his brother on the ledge. His face whitened. "Dinna do it, David. Tis too dangerous. Conan's just a smart-mouth, he is. A big coward, too. He'd never try it himself. Wait 'til some space clears right in front, then go in feet first. Tis safer that way."

David's jaw tightened. He hated to be thought afraid of anything. Plus, he was a good athlete for his age. He mentally calculated the distance beyond the crowd of boys. He could jump that far out. Rather than do a belly-flop or feet first, he would dive headlong, too, just to prove the point to Conan.

"David, dinna do it. No!" Robert waved both arms in a stopping motion.

Ignoring his brother, David backed up on the ledge to give himself more room. He gathered his wits and concentration, momentarily paused, and then sprinted to the edge like a racer. Catching the very end of the rock, he gracefully swan-dived far out and hit the water with a near perfect entry, with almost no splash.

By now, all of the rest of the boys in the water had stopped their commotion and rough-housing to pay attention to his act of bravery. Even Conan Gray watched with a slack-jawed expression. He never thought David would actually do it.

They all held their breath.

Many seconds passed. Then more seconds. Then more time. Over a minute had expired now, but no David appeared. No form burst through the surface.

"Och, me brother. Dear Lord, help me." Robert shot a look of disgust at Conan. He quickly swam to the spot where David entered the water, took a huge breath into his lungs, and dove into the depths.

The water became darker and murkier the deeper he went. He could only see all of four or five feet in front of him. Finally reaching a rock ledge at the very bottom over thirteen feet down, he spun around several times but could see no David. Desperately, he swam out in a widening circle. His air was beginning to go, but he thought he saw something ahead.

In the inkiness, he barely made out a figure above him to the right slumped over another rocky protrusion rising almost six feet above the jagged floor. Reaching his brother, Robert grabbed him securely around the middle and kicked hard for the surface.

His free arm and legs padded and stroked as fast as he could, but his oxygen and strength were almost gone. Six more feet. Four more feet. The sunlight upon the waters above. Finally, Robert burst through, holding his brother's head aloft and pulling in ragged breaths of air. Many hands were there to help support and take him and David to the south side where the mild slope made it possible to climb up out of the pit and onto the grass.

David's face was ashen and he wasn't breathing. Roughly shoving the sputtering apologetic Conan aside, Robert began mouth-to-mouth resuscitation. He had seen his father do it once to save the life of an old fisherman who had tripped and hit his head on the side of his boat coming into shore, just as the MacDougall father and son were passing by. After that incident, Robert's father had been careful to go over the steps with him again to ensure he remembered how to do it if ever the need arose.

There was no response with Robert's first attempt. Grimly, he tried again. This time, David vomited up a great deal of water, and began breathing on his own. Robert silently thanked the Good Lord.

When David came to, he had a throbbing headache.

Probing gingerly, he found a huge bloodied lump on the side of his head.

After that experience, none of the boys went back to the old pit.

The last instance where David knew for certain his life had been saved happened three years later. He was beginning high school now, and though he wasn't yet called to be a minister, he had taken to reading and meditating on scripture in his spare time over the mid-year break. It was a hot, muggy summer afternoon. Boiling clouds approached in the distant horizon, with increasingly loud thunderclaps, and lightning arced across the sky. David was sitting underneath the shade of the massive oak tree that stood at the edge of the fallow field. The huge tree lay some twenty-five yards further from the house than the mangled, smaller, and much older oak on which a two-seater swing had long been attached.

Swing or no swing, David liked the bigger tree. The ground beneath it was soft, spongy, and covered with a nice layer of leaves and loamy soil that felt good to sit on. The large trunk was so broad and uniform it was the perfect back support. And the shade it provided, he knew from experience, was heavenly. The canopy was so thick and vast that not a single ray of sun peeked through. Whatever the summer temperature was, he could count on it feeling twenty degrees cooler underneath, especially with the way the location seemed to catch and attract every possible breeze.

So as the summer storm began to roll in, David was

content to just sit it out. The circumference of the overhanging branches was such that he could count on staying perfectly dry even in a heavy rain, unless the wind was blowing parallel to the earth itself. He had finished his self-made Bible lesson for the day and felt sleepy. *I may as well be a taking a nap right here*, he thought, peacefully, letting a sense of drowsiness overtake him.

The angry clouds with their blasts of thunder and torrents of water came closer and closer. David closed his eyes, oblivious to the potential threats around him.

Suddenly he heard his name being called in a loud feminine voice. Again he heard his name. Loud enough, the shouts popped his eyes open and got his attention. He watched as his sister hurried from the back of the house toward him. She was soaked to the bone. She seemed very upset.

"David! David, you be a getting yourself out from under that tree. Right now!" Andrina's eyes and voice were blazing as she stepped into the shadow of the hanging branches. A myriad of water droplets raced down her golden brown locks, off her nose and chin, and from the hem of her soaked dress. "Hinna you got the sense the Good Lord gave you? Sitting here, a reading scripture under a tree, of all places, with the lightening all around you? Are you a wantin' to go to heaven 'fore your time?" She put her hands on her hips and sternly looked at him.

Taken aback because his sister was the most easy-going person he knew, he sat there for a moment in disbelief.

At his delay, Andrina became really angry. She stomped her foot and shook her finger down at his surprised face. "Now you be a getting up right this second! You get up and march into the house 'fore you cause both of us to be cooked like two roasted pigs."

Shaking his head in wonder, but not wanting to further agitate his dear sweet sister, David got up and tucked the Bible inside his shirt to keep it dry. He nodded to her, and together they bolted for the house.

Not ten seconds after they reached the sanctuary of the back porch and stepped inside the door, a crackling lighting strike hit the huge tree at its tip, sending white fire along its spine, followed by a second hit to the middle of the tree, causing two major branches to explode in blazing bits and pieces. As they watched in horror, what was once a majestic towering tree soon became a raging inferno despite the pounding rain. In minutes, the destructive side of nature had destroyed what the creative side of nature had taken over a century to grow.

Turning to his sister, his eyebrows furrowed together in wonderment, David hugged Andrina tightly. Somehow she had known. Premonition, perhaps? A warning from the Lord? Lucky guess? Coincidence? Timely nagging? From a human perspective, maybe it was a combination of all of the above reasons. But David felt the hand of the Lord in it, and it made his heart even more open to the tugging of the Holy Spirit as he entered manhood.

Chapter Four

Rossalyn Elspeth McDonald and David Adam MacDougall had known each other since they were little children, playing together and taking up for one another at recess at the same aging, dirty grey-bricked school building on the northwest side of the winding little village lane where David had fought the McConahay brothers. They had grown up together and rather naturally become sweethearts at the innocent ages of seventeen and fifteen and a half, respectively. Headstrong "Bonny Rose" was David's first true love.

Everyone said Rose McDonald had matured into a pure Scottish beauty. Flirtatious, chatty and casually friendly to every man she met; Rose had half the male population in the town lusting after her. Fergus Brown, the village rake, would mutter under his breath every time he spied her, "Be-jesus, but that lass could raise a woody on a dead corpse, she could."

She had full, luscious lips—incredibly pink, angelic yet mischievous at the same time, alive with personality—that mesmerized a man into submission. Just to watch her talk was heavenly, David thought; to be with her when she was in a glad mood was divine. When angry, her wrath came out in her cat-eyes. But her happiness was shown in the varied manifestations of her mouth: rapt expressions, enchanting utterances, peals of laughter, and delightful sighs. Her light auburn hair cascaded in gorgeous tresses upon her lovely shoulders, with forelocks seductively playing cat-and-mouse with her eyes. Her figure was perfect: ample bosom, tiny waist, swaying hips, slender legs, and matchless feet and ankles.

David MacDougall had become a superb physical specimen with chiseled muscles, top to bottom. He had a handsome yet earnest expression. Most of the young girls in town were in love with him, and all of the married women secretly admired his good looks from afar. His facial features were strong and symmetrical in a way that contributed to his attractiveness while conveying his intensity of soul. He had a manly nose, square chin, full lips, penetrating bluish-gray eyes that became grayer whenever he was impassioned or angry, and curling light-brown hair that flowed over his high collar in the back and over most of his ears on the sides. His careful speech and generous intelligence revealed no trace of guile.

To the casual eye, the two young people seemed perfectly matched: David, thoughtful and deliberate in discourse, Rose, impulsive and joyfully talkative.

Only his faith could rival his feelings for Bonny Rose.

It was during Chapel the Sunday before Thanksgiving

of his freshman year at the University of Glasgow when David had finally felt the pulling—the longed-for Reason why his life had been spared the three times in his past. Campus Chaplain Ernest C. Wallace was preaching that morning. Wallace was a great bear of a man: barreled-chested, thick roof of curly dark brown hair that extended into an equally curly beard leaving only the tips of his heavy lips visible, and a fine bass voice that carried across a packed auditorium without need of amplification. Beloved by the students, he had a boisterous laugh but also a seriousness about evangelism that riveted even careless listeners with the majesty of his message. Before converting to Christianity at the age of thirty-three, he had been a prize fighter, a pugilist of some repute, and after that, a sea captain oft bound for exotic ports in India, the Far East, and South China seas.

It only seemed natural, then, that his talks were imbued with spiritual warfare and exotic missions. His sermons conveyed both the adventure and the authority of the committed Christian life. "God's authority, your adventure," he frequently said. "Never a dull moment, when you're a staying in the center of God's will. Where the Lord leads you, he always equips you."

Settling comfortably in his pew seat, David waited with rapt expectation for the Chaplain to begin his sermon.

"Our message today is a coming from two well-known texts: Matthew 28:19 and 20, and Acts 1:8. Two familiar passages of scripture, perhaps, but poorly received and woefully obeyed by modern Christians. If you brought your Bible, children, read it silently with me as I read aloud."

David chuckled as he found the first scripture and put his finger in to mark the second passage. Whenever addressing the university students from the pulpit or face-to-face, Chaplain Wallace called them "children" or "child" though some of the graduate students surely had to be close to his own age.

MacDougall glanced over with a slight frown. The two people on his right, a man and a woman, were whispering and laughing, oblivious to the fact they were in chapel. He started to say something, but then shook his head and focused instead on the scripture reading.

"'Go ye therefore, and teach all nations, baptizing them in the name of the Father, and of the Son, and of the Holy Ghost: Teaching them to observe all things whatsoever I have commanded you: and, lo, I am with you always, even unto the end of the world. Amen.' And now let us turn to the second passage. 'But ye shall receive power, after that the Holy Ghost is come upon you: and ye shall be witnesses unto me both in Jerusalem, and in all Judaea, and in Samaria, and unto the uttermost part of the earth.'"

For nearly an hour, Wallace spoke of the urgent need for missionaries to go to the great land of China and elsewhere in the mysterious Far East. Pastors, evangelists, youth leaders, medical missionaries, and dedicated lay people were required to spread the good news of the gospel, build churches, raise pastors and teachers up from among the native populace, and help take care of the hungry, sick, afflicted, and lost multitudes of those teeming lands.

"Truly, the harvest is plentiful, but the laborers be few," he trumpeted in that melodious deep voice. "God is calling now, children! Who will go? Who will answer, 'Lord, use me. Take me. Mold me. Consume me. Make me a vessel today of your mighty love.'? Come forward, I say, children, come forward and present your bodies a living sacrifice, holy, acceptable unto God, which is your reasonable service."

David had gone forward with dozens of others to the front altar, kneeled and bowed his head while trembling with excitement. "Och, dear Lord, I do! I do surrender to your call. Take all o' me. Use all o' me. I'm yours, Lord: body, mind, and spirit!"

Coming down from the pulpit, Wallace began at one end of the row of bodies, some lying prone, some kneeling, and some standing with bowed heads. He laid his hands on each one, praying for their decision and encouraging them. When David's turn came for the Chaplain to pray over him, he felt a shock of power thrill his body. He knew beyond a shadow of a doubt he had been called to be a missionary.

"Tis undeniable, Lord. Tis a bit overwhelming, too," he whispered as he continued kneeling, immersed in awe and surrender. David had just turned eighteen. In that moment, his life was changed forever. *China!* He was filled with a sense of serenity and purpose. The feeling surrounded him like a cocoon and infused his entire body.

He couldn't wait to tell his sweetheart of his decision. "Rose, Rose, you winna believe what's happened to me!" he exclaimed joyfully. Home for Christmas, he took her hand and led her to the two-seated swing hanging from the ancient gnarled oak tree that still stood behind the MacDougall place. Throughout the years, it was there they had swung, nestled together, planning for their future.

"The Lord has called me to be a missionary to the land o' China," he beamed, eager to share his good news with her. "It happened during Chapel a month ago. But tis real, Rose. I know tis. I finally found the *reason* why me life's been spared those three times. I knew the Lord had something special for me. I just dinna know it was a calling. But it is. That's what I've been waiting for, yearning for, all this time. We've talked together about the Good Lord saving me life so many times.

"Ah, Rose, it was like a voice spoke inside me ear, inside me very soul, and said, 'David, you are to go to China.'"

She turned her pretty head and merely stared at him. "Oh?" she said, then clammed up, pretending to listen to his enthusiastic talk, but all the while, locked into her own thoughts and calculations. The next time he brought the subject up, to his surprise, she responded with objections. "Really now, David. Tis all a fantasy, tis...a talkin' about such far off places and foreigners. People get killed in strange lands, you know. The wives and children, too."

She laid her warm hand gently on his muscled forearm. "Why, with all your good looks, charm and ability to speak, you could be a takin' a nice church in one o' the big cities." She put her head on his shoulder and lightly traced a line up and down his arm with her finger. "That would suit me just fine, Mr. MacDougall." She squeezed his arm for emphasis.

"Do you doot me? Darlin', I've really and truly been called. Tis like being drafted into the Queen's army, tis. I canna refuse."

Rose ceased her finger movement along his forearm as she flashed her most beguiling smile and whispered teasingly, "Saying so disna always make it so, David. Whit happens is whit truly happens." But her eyes were guarded and there was no warmth there.

When David's graduation day finally came and went, however, he persevered in his commitment and joined the United Missionary Society of Scotland. He was scheduled to be ordained that summer and sail for China in early August. He expected Rose to be by his side, despite her sharp-tongued resistance. He assumed her reticence was due to fear of the unknown and sheer nerves.

"Judas Priest, aren't there lost people in Scotland you could be a talking to?" Rose stamped her foot, glaring up at his handsome yet fervent countenance, at his pronouncement that he had followed through and signed on with the Society.

"Ah girl, there's no need to be a cursing, now, Rose," he winced at her quick anger.

"Dinna be a telling me what I can and canna do, David Adam. I'll be a cursing if I'm a mind to! All this time you paid me no attention. I've said over and over you ought to be taking a pulpit in a church in a big city."

She scowled mightily at him, her beautiful eyes mere cat-slits and the corners of her lovely mouth curled in wrath. She blurted out, "I canna marry you, David MacDougall! I dinna want to be the poor wife of a missionary living in a God-forsaken country with the foreign devils all around me."

There was a dead silence. Rose had meant to choose a better time and place, tell him in softer language. But the frustration had been building until her fury erupted. She looked at him with those gorgeous emerald-green eyes and a frown of deep discomfort on her pretty face. Whether she was right or wrong in actions or words, above all else, Rose McDonald did not like to be made uncomfortable at any time. It was not that she didn't have a conscience or feeling about others' misfortunes, but their problems were their own. Rose enjoyed the creature comforts and material things of life, and she intended to have them, come hell-fire or the King Edward of England himself.

David's brows furrowed together, his hands to his sides with palms toward her in disbelief. He had assumed her reluctance had more to do with fear than materialism. "Ah, but you canna mean what you be a saying, Rose. Tis loving me, you are, lass.

"You'll be safe enough with me around to protect you,

I expect. And we'll be having a comfortable enough life once we get there, you'll see. I promise." He put his hands gently on her shoulders and forced a smile. He had always been confident of her affection, but now he was genuinely troubled. She had never before flatly stated she wouldn't marry him because of his calling. She had argued, cajoled, threatened, pleaded, and cried more than once. But never this.

Her stern look softened a bit, and she hesitated before she spoke. "I *do* love you, David. I love you truly and dearly."

Her big eyes widened and sparkled with fresh tears. Her expression filled with pity, both for him and her, and for the hard decision she had made. Sorrowfully, Rose said, "But no matter how much I love you, I canna sacrifice meself to a life of drudgery and poverty. And it's no use pretending otherwise."

Her lips trembled and she shook her head in finality. "The saints above know I tried to make you see reason and change your mind before it's too late. But you're as stubborn as you are good-looking, and there's no help for it."

She stepped forward, took his hand in hers, and grazed his burning cheek with the briefest of kisses. "That's not me, David Adam. I canna go with you only to have to leave you... because I would. It would only be a matter of time."

He started to object, but Rose quickly put her finger to his mouth. "One year, two years, maybe three or four years at best. But I would come to me senses, and tell meself enough is enough. And I would leave you then, David, whether we had a child or no. God forbid we had children by then, but I would leave you and take our children. Or leave them with you, if you fought with me. God forbid."

At that, David let go of her hand and stared back at Rose. He'd never dreamed she was capable of such callous sentiments. Not his sweet, beautiful, bonny Rose.

"No, David, I will not go with you. It's killin' me inside, 'tis. But I have to do what's best for *me*." She breathed deeply and looked into his anguished eyes.

Numb, David shook his head slowly at the figure standing before him.

Her next and final words crushed him most of all.

"No, David, no. I'm accepting your Cousin Michael's counter-proposal of marriage, I am. I will have him as me husband and stay home in Scotland...where I belong...and be the dutiful wife of a well-to-do engineer."

He stood looking at her, utterly stunned, his body flooded with shock.

"*No*! In all that's holy in heaven, no, you canna do this unfaithful thing! Rose, you love me, you swore you did!" Upon her sudden declaration of independence, David shouted, stormed, and lost his composure (and maybe his mind) for a brief period.

She didn't budge.

Chapter Five

David knew his sly second cousin, Michael Stewart McDougall, had always fancied Rose. He also knew only Michael's fear of his brute strength and potentially lethal fists had kept his cousin from openly challenging for Rose's hand.

Until that moment, David had treated Michael's infatuation as a bit of a joke.

Less handsome and slighter of build, his cousin was nonetheless resourceful and determined. Michael lusted after Rose; and he would have her in the end. He had found secret ways to see Rose. Their contacts while private had been platonic in the beginning, but as David's insistence upon his calling continued to frustrate her, their affair became physical.

Early on, while David stayed at the University during holiday and semester breaks (too busy with his studies and too innocent to suspect treachery), the crafty Michael came home every chance he got. To keep the village tongues from wagging, he rarely met with Rose one-on-one in public.

"Stay by me side at all times, Bruce boy, when there be people around," he commanded his little brother. "I canna have the village idiots and old women a passin' news o' me time with Rosie to you-know-who." He added, "However, you can disappear—and be right quick about it!—when we're in private."

"Can I have a taste, too?" Bruce had asked with a sloppy grin the first time he was asked to go along as a foil.

"Go on with ya, you gowk!" Michael had said savagely, giving his brother a hard smack on the head. "Mind your manners 'round her, and treat her like the lady she is. I intend to win her over as me wife, not me hoor." He glared at him.

"Sorry, I am," Bruce had replied, ruefully rubbing his noggin.

"Your only job is to come along, keep your mouth shut, keep out o' the way, and keep the gossip down."

With the aid of Bruce who almost always tagged along as a public shield, Michael found every opportunity to declare his feelings for the transcendent Rossalyn McDonald.

For her part, she never directly encouraged him, but also never refused to meet with him in the presence of company. Rose was, after all, a practical young woman and liked to keep all of her options open.

"Bruce and me be a goin' to Loch Tralaig this afternoon for a picnic, and wondered if you'd like to be a joinin' us," Michael had carefully chosen his words, his brother hovering right behind him. He was home over a school break and David wasn't. *Tough luck for Davie boy, the big neap.*

Rose frowned in thought. Her last two letters to

David had been increasingly hostile on the subject of foreign missions. *David can be so thickheaded, he just canna see reason.* Her temper was up. When she was angry, she tended to make hasty decisions based on the heat of the moment.

She stood there for the longest time, her eyes fixed on an imaginary spot in the faraway distance beyond Michael's ear. Michael balled his hands into fists inside his pockets, the tension mounting as he waited for her reply.

Finally she spoke, her mind made up. "Aye, I'll be a going with you. But only as long as Bruce comes with us. After all, tis a fine, bonnie day out. Why waste it?" She smiled dazzlingly at both of them.

Michael was relieved. He had been plotting his initial approach for some time, and wasn't sure how she would respond. A part of him feared she would be offended and tell David everything. "Excellent! Me father's got a fine new buggy I've been a itchin' to try out."

And so off they went, the first of many such times together. Once they got there, no one else was in sight. Nodding and winking to Michael, Bruce grabbed his fishing tackle from the buggy and strolled off to the far side of the lake, leaving the two alone to talk.

Or whatever.

As far as Rose was concerned, the *whatever* had been a recurring problem with David from the start of their relationship. While they both wanted sex badly, he had kept a tight rein on his throbbing desire. David was a healthy red-blooded male; he had strong impulses and desires. But he remained a Christian gentleman, guarding against his lusts. He and Rose had never gone all the way. Everything else, perhaps, but never vaginal penetration. David believed the Bible clearly taught that intercourse outside marriage was not allowed. As difficult as it had been for him, he managed to keep things in check.

"No, Rose, we cannot. We must not. Yet," he stated each time. She had panted, pouted, pleaded, and persuaded. "Hoots, mon, we're to be married, anyways. David. Let's do it just the once. Just to see what it's like. *Please!* We'll soon be living together in our own hoose."

Yet he had stayed firm to his commitment.

Michael, she quickly found out, had no such reservations. She half-heartedly resisted his urgency for the first few months before giving in to him. After that, she swallowed her guilt. She met Michael privately when it was convenient and saw David officially. She still hoped against hope he would give up the idea of being a missionary. Despite her unfaithfulness, she told herself she still loved David and much preferred to marry him over Michael.

Rose relied upon the monthly calendar rhythm method to make sure she didn't get pregnant. Her infrequent times with Michael became centered on the days she couldn't conceive. Her conscience bothered her, but she stubbornly fought it off, convinced that Michael was a passing fancy. *Tis you, David, I really want. And home in Scotland is where I want you.* However, one without the other was no good.

But now David knew about her and Michael. The truth was out. The game was up. She watched the wrath quickly building in that handsome face.

"Now, don't you be a causing any bother, David Allen. Your poor cousin did nothin' wrong; twas me that made the decision."

Ignoring her protests, David rushed off in a black rage. Soon, he found Michael and Bruce at the Black Sheep pub. He saw them getting steadily drunk at a far table to the right of the bar, surrounded by town never-do-wells, idle farmers, and a few university buddies. He heard Michael boasting to everyone present about winning the lovely Rose's consent to marriage that very morning. David stood in the doorway, his heart frozen but his head hot, listening to every word, gnashing his teeth.

"Aye, lads, such a beauty to behold is the amazing Rose McDonald. You poor mutts can only *dream* about possessing a body so fine," he smirked and winked, slopping another gulp, half in his mouth, half on his soaked shirt.

The bartender, burly Hugh McHugh, only shook his head in open disgust. Being a barkeep, he heard all the news in the village, both good and bad, and had long suspected such was going on behind the younger MacDougall's back. He'd always liked David and greatly respected his father Jonathan. Many of the pub regulars through the years could afford drinks at the pub as well as keep food on the family table because of forgiven or postponed renter debt on the part of the elder MacDougall.

"And MacDougall never suspected a thing, hey?" smirked Alan Russell, a classmate who had also just graduated from the university. "Och, he always struck me as the naïve type, he did."

"I'm a finding that yarn a bit hard to choke down, meself," exclaimed Tavish Milne, the town blacksmith, whose forearm was bigger than Michael's scrawny neck. "The poor fool."

"No matter, he's none the wiser, and an idiot to boot. Tis all true and she's all mine. Aye, we'll make quite the couple, won't we, little brother?" he crowed, elbowing Bruce by his side. "The intelligent, soon-to-be-rich, engineer-husband… and the gorgeous, calculating wife, och? As I was say—"

David rushed in.

"Behind me back. All this time. *All this time!* To me face, you put on the false smile, but when me back was turned, you played the Judas!" David cried out. He couldn't stomach the sorry spectacle of Michael's disgusting boasting a moment longer.

Trembling, the MacDougall cousins stood up with uncertain legs to face their doom. People close to them began sidling away. David Adam's fighting ability was well known throughout the surrounding regions.

Blood drained from Michael's face. Holding his hands

out in a show of peace, he mumbled, "Wait a minute, cousin. Lemme explain."

David ignored his words. In a fraction of a second, his mind measured the distance, calculated the reach, and processed the best methods to damage his foes.

"Ah, you sneakin' snivelin' excuses of human beings; horse's arses you are, and a plague on the both of you!" David roared before hurling himself across the table at them.

Michael attempted a single feeble swing. Bruce leaped upon David's back, trying to slow him down.

It was no contest. Even with the inebriated Bruce riding him and Michael flinging wild blows, David still broke Michael's nose, blacked both his eyes, and loosened three front teeth. For good measure, he threw Bruce to the hard floor then twice knocked him down as he attempted to get up.

The rest of the bar crowd watched MacDougal punish the two brothers. Not unexpectedly, no one offered to step in and help the poor souls. Behind the bar, McHugh glared at the fight scene with a satisfied glint in his hard eyes. He hated cheats.

Serves 'em right, the double-crossin' bastards.

Chapter Six

Thoroughly crushed and humiliated by his beloved Rose's last-minute rejection, David attempted to speed up his ordination and his scheduled date for sailing. That evening, knowing his family would soon learn the sad story anyway, he told them everything. Jonathan had listened quietly, folding his arms and looking upon his son with eyes of deep compassion. Claire sat at the big table, hand to throat, softly tutting her dismay at the sordid tale of treachery. Robert was sailing home for the summer from America, but would not arrive in the village for five more days, at least.

"The Good Lord has got someone the better for you, He does, little brother," said Andrina, coming over to hug him from the back, throwing one arm around his taut stomach, gripping a muscled shoulder with her other hand, and squeezing both tightly. "For me part, I never trusted the pretty little vixen, from the very first. She always struck me as being the connivin' type."

The next morning, his father took him in the family buggy to the nearest large town with rail service. They rode the fifteen minute trip in unhappy silence to the station. He bought a ticket to return to the university where the

Missionary Society was headquartered only three streets over, close to campus.

When he arrived in the city, he headed for the Society office. He walked rapidly to the building, oblivious to the greetings of friends as they called out his name. Waving to the secretary and others as he came through the front door, he hurried down the long hallway. He found the elderly Executive Director in the library filing away some books and papers.

"Reverend Johnston, is there anything you can do to get me to China quicker?"

Swiveling his head toward the door, Johnson spotted the young man, and his eyes lit up with pleasure. He turned around to face his visitor. "David, me lad! Good to see you again. So you finished your senior exams in fine form, did you? Yes, yes, the Society is movin' as fast as we can." He strode forward to shake David's hand.

"Ah, you be eager to begin the Lord's work, are you?"

The older churchman smiled, but upon seeing the dark look on the young man's face, Rev. Johnston leaned forward, puzzled, and gave him a penetrating stare. Reaching out to touch David's elbow, he asked, "There wouldn't be anything a troublin' you now, would there, lad?"

"No, sir," David lied. "I just...want to be a leavin' as quickly as possible, sir." His only goal now was to join the Scottish Christ Is Lord mission in Beiping, the capital of China, and throw all his broken-hearted energies into evangelism.

"I'm afraid the scheduled date of departure is the

earliest we can get you away, lad." Rev. Johnson looked at him kindly.

"Well," David paused, not happy at the answer but reluctantly accepting nothing could be done about it, "August it is." He forced a smile and shook the churchman's hand. "Thank you, sir. I'll be ready then." He turned and walked out.

He dreaded the next few months, being back at home before leaving for good.

Then and there, he determined he would not seek a replacement for the unfaithful Rose. David realized his carnal flesh and mind were unable to discern the innermost recesses of a woman's heart to gauge whether she was the right spiritual mate. *God Himself will have to put that lady into me life, so I know, of a certainty, she is the one, just as I know I've been called to China.*

And if he had to remain single, so be it. The Lord Jesus would be his constant companion. At least *His* love was faithful and enduring.

He spent the rest of the summer grieving, learning a new sport called Basket Ball from his big brother, Robert Allen, home from Boston, and avoiding any unnecessary contact with Michael or Rose. It was a small village, and people talked. Soon it seemed everybody in the entire town and elsewhere knew of his misfortune, including his third, fourth and fifth MacDougall cousins in the surrounding villages and even those in the distant Lowland cities. The varied MacDougal clans seemed to be able to communicate long distance through thin air.

He threw himself into learning the new game and competed with Robert in the early mornings and late afternoons. When not playing, he lifted weights and ran, turning his already hard muscle into pure chiseled stone.

Finally the day of departure arrived. His whole family came to see him off.

"Och, David. It breaks me heart, it does, to lose me youngest boy, the baby o' the family. Robert Allen will be a goin' back to America. And now I'm losin' you, too. God only knows when you'll be a returnin' to us," Claire MacDougall held her son as tight as she could, weeping into his brawny chest.

His sister Andrina, the middle child, took her turn next. "Aye, David Adam, you're nothing but a baby—a big ol' teddy bear. You're only good for one thing, and that's a good punching in your fat belly." She hugged him then thumped him in his rigid six-pack stomach, laughing and crying at the same time.

He and Robert hugged each other in a rugged fashion, pounding each other on the back. They broke away and shook hands vigorously.

Then his father stepped forward. His pa he would miss most of all. His kind heart, common sense, and stout faith had been David's anchor growing up. He hoped he could live up to his father's standards.

"I know you'll do fine, son. I be proud o' you, awfully proud, for stayin' the course, becoming a minister, and servin' our Lord on the mission field. We'll be a prayin' for you. I love you, son. We all do." Jonathan reached out and clasped his son's arms firmly below the elbows as David clenched his father's arms in same way. They looked at each other for a full minute before hugging, chest to chest. His father slipped one hand free to grip the back of David's neck and pull his son in tighter. When they stepped apart, both faces glistened with tears.

"I love you, too, Father. And the same goes for the rest o' you. I'll be a missing all o' you so much."

The goodbyes done, David boarded ship. He stood by the side railing, gazing at his family's faces until they slowly turned and left for home some twenty minutes later. He continued to stare at the spot where they had been until the vessel pulled away.

A miserable week passed at sea. He tried hard to forget, but...

Rossalyn Elspeth McDonald.

Her name surged through David's mind as easily as the strong West Indies breeze now whipped though his thin cotton dress-shirt and woolen undershirt. Distracted and upset with himself for giving in to the forbidden thoughts, he tugged up his high collar and jerked his sleeves down for greater warmth.

Traveling northeast, the converted tramp steamer the

Jack King

Ayrshire was plodding its way toward the rough and ready city of Perth in Western Australia, the landing point for thousands of English convicts only a few decades ago. Having departed the northern hemisphere on the other side of Africa, the ship was positioned well below the equator. The September equinox was six weeks away; locally, it was early springtime and the weather still carried a slight chill.

Despite his steely-eyed resolve, David could not keep the bitterest-sweet memory of Rose out of his conscious thoughts, any more than he could stop the constant tugging of the fierce cool winds upon his body. Groaning miserably, he shook his head to clear his agitated mind. "God help me to forget." At times during the voyage the loneliness and loss seemed overwhelming, like a black cloud encircling his soul, almost more than he could bear.

"I've just got to become tougher; I've got to get over her somehow." He clinched his hands against the rail. Restless, unable to sleep, he'd gotten up well before daylight to prowl the silent main deck alone in his misery.

He leaned forward over the ship's railing to face the more violent gusts head on. For the longest time, he continued to stare without seeing into the heaving mass of white-capped ocean swells as the blue-green horizon began to glitter with the first yellow shafts of the rising sun.

"Rose...Rose...me darlin' Rose. How could you be a leavin' me? And for him? For *him!*" He slammed his meaty fist into the top rung of the railing. His heart ached with grief, the emotional wound still fresh and raw.

Scowling at the skyline, David shifted his position to get more comfortable against the hard railing. But still the hurtful memories lingered. He should have seen the warning signs. Mostly, he berated himself for being so naïve. Rose had vacillated back and forth during his four years at the university, hoping he would renounce his missionary calling and follow in his third uncle and second cousin's footsteps and become a prosperous respectable engineer or even a business manager, instead.

She had incessantly hammered him on that point. The remembrance of their bitter last argument still burned his soul like the Gobi Desert sun.

He replayed *her* words and *his* words in an endless loop of *what ifs*, a torturous mind game he felt powerless to stop.

"Aye, tis fine brains you be a havin' to go with a strong body," she had purred at him with hands on hips, a petulant pout playing on her sweet lips, before the discussion had spiraled into hurtful words and a revelation of betrayal. "David Adam, I've told you so many times; you ought be seeking a position with a nice-sized church. Please stay here. In Scotland. Why, any large town would suit me the fine. Or if not the church, there be other things you could do to make a good livin'. There's work and a plenty in shipbuilding and other money-paying trades in any of the bigger Lowland cities. With a university degree, you'll be a manager o' some kind."

"Ah, sweetness, me heart yearns for China," he had always calmly replied through those years when the arguments came. "The Good Lord himself has put the yearning deep in me soul to spread his Word to the lost people of Beiping, and to Beiping I am bound."

Now the tumult of the sea and the hectic winds continued unabated while he gazed into the distance, lost in his jumbled thoughts and endless loop of self-deprecation.

Chapter Seven

"Yes, Thomas, I see him, too. We'll go over and say hello to him," a female voice whispered behind him, followed by several muffled barks, a low but non-threatening growl, another yelp, and several approaching footsteps.

"Good morning, Reverend."

His unhappy reverie broken, David turned around to face the matronly Jane Chesterfield accompanied by her nine-year old grandson and their mischievous classic reddish-brown dachshund.

Mrs. Chesterfield was a widow. Her husband had been a career military man and a long-time Major in the British army when his regiment was called to the Cape Colony to quell the second Boer Rebellion. Unprepared for the guerilla tactics of the stubborn Dutch-speaking farmers, the unit had lost over two-thirds of its men including John Chesterfield due to death, injury, disease or capture on the battlefield before hostilities ended.

Mrs. Chesterfield's eldest son had followed his father's example and joined the army right out of college. Last summer, the young captain had sent his oldest son, Thomas, to live with her and attend boarding school in England. His mother was lonely and besides, he reasoned, the educational facilities were decidedly better back home. Captain Chesterfield was presently serving a three-year tour of duty in Perth and had his wife and other two children living in Australia with him.

The widow was taking her grandson to Perth to re-join his family. She had not made up her mind whether she would stay the year or sail back to England after a short visit.

MacDougall knelt down to better stroke the sleek reddish-brown coat of the dog now straining to lick his chin. "Good morning, Mrs. Chesterfield. And to you, young Thomas. And especially to *you*, Mason." He affectionately petted the ears, crown and elongated back of the squirming, prancing animal. The dog leaped, again and again, in its efforts to reach David's chin. Each time, he raised his head up at the last possible moment to avoid its darting tongue.

"*Mister* Mason. Me good Mister Mason. How have you been lately?" The dog was an exceptionally handsome and intelligent pet, in his opinion, and he liked him very much. "Master o' this ship, you be, and *everything* on it. We winna tell Captain Wotherspoon that you be the real boss o' this here vessel, will we?" He had to admit there was nothing like a good pet to forget one's troubles, at least for a while.

Finally, David stood up to converse with the humans.

"Reverend, we were out taking our normal stroll around the ship before breakfast and saw you standing there. I hope we're not disturbing you.

"Mason! Hush. Hush now," she gently rebuked the dachshund as it clamored for further attention. "Thomas, please," she looked over at the boy. The lad picked up the wiggling dog and held it firmly in his arms. Mason continued to look longingly in the direction of David.

At the age of fifty-one, Jane Chesterfield was still a nice-looking woman, albeit with a quiet, long-suffering countenance. She was a devout Church of England attendee and firm believer in God's providence.

"So, have you decided whether you'll be spending the year with your son or no?" David asked. He really wanted to get back to his sad musings, but as a newly ordained minister felt an obligation to be cordial and available to everyone on board, even if he was not of the mind for light conversation.

"Thomas here has been pestering me to stay through next summer." She sighed with a trace of sorrow. "Aye, it would have been far happier to visit them with my beloved John, but...such is life, Reverend."

She reached out to caress Mason's ears. "Yes, I do believe I will. When one gets past a certain age, it's difficult to be alone in life."

David moved his head in empathy. "I know what you mean," he said.

"Well, I guess we need to continue our walk around. The dog is getting antsy. Good to see you. Might you be coming to breakfast this morning?"

"Possibly. But thank you ever so much for asking

me." David nodded again. He waved good-bye to the pitter-pattering Mason as the party turned to leave.

He wanted to resume feeling sorry for himself, but the moment was past. David stood, looking out to sea for several minutes, when he felt a sudden nudge at his elbow. He hadn't heard anyone approach due to the noise of the sea and the thoughts in his head.

"Och, there you be, laddie!" After searching the sleeping quarters, galley, passenger dining hall, bridge, and outside decks, fore and aft, Dugan Sinclair, the ship's first mate, had finally tracked down his prey.

"Hidin' out from the ladies 'gain, are we now?"

The always jovial Mr. Sinclair stood with his thick legs wide apart and his ham-like fists on his hips. "Miss Annabelle's bin lookin' for you, she has, high and low, this good mornin'. She'll be a wantin' some gentlemanly comfort, I 'pect, after the ordeal of yesterday's storm."

"Lo, Duggie."

His black thoughts now fading out to sea for the second time that morning, David turned and forced a smile at the squat, sunburned face grinning up at him. Dugan was his favorite member of the crew. He had been born in a village near to David's own township and he showed more than a passing interest in things of the Lord. In his prevailing grief, David had felt enough of a connection to share a bit of his lovelorn plight with the older man in the first days of travel.

"Come with me now, David."

Short but stout, a winsome personality but boisterous, the First Mate was a man of many words and even more enthusiasms. To him, the sun was always shining even in the blackest nighttime.

Dugan winked mightily and twitched the young man's elbow again. "There be a bite o' nourishin' breakfast and mugs o' hot tea a waitin' in the formal mess. I wager there'll be a few lassies that wadna be disappointed to see yer ugly mug appear, too. But for the life o' me, I dinna know why."

To change the subject from women, David asked, "Did you ever find those three missing hens from the galley hold?"

The two men turned and walked together toward the central part of the ship where the smaller common mess area for the crew and the larger adjoining passenger dining room were located in the middle deck. It was not uncommon for steamers of all sizes, even tramp ships, to board live cows, sheep, chickens, or pigs for fresh meat, particularly if they had a journey of many weeks ahead of them.

Dugan laughed and slapped his massive thigh. "Ah, two were found wanderin' 'round the boiler room by the mornin' crew. And one sweet hen—God bless her!—somehow sneaked into the captain's quarters. Just sittin' on his bed, cluckin' away, she was, when the captain came back from his early spot o' tea."

"You dinna say?" David raised his eyebrows at the news.

"I do say! It has bin an outstandin' mornin', it has.

Ha! I'd give up me first born, just to see the 'pression on old Wother's face when he seen that chicken scratchin' on his precious bed." Captain Ian Wotherspoon was known to be a fastidious person when it came to his eating and sleeping arrangements. Only the finest china setting and the most expensive linen sheets and French-made blankets would suffice.

Dugan clapped his friend on his back and exclaimed with teasing delight, "Ah, a spot o' hot tea, and even hotter ladies, be a waitin' for you, laddie!"

David merely shook his head and shrugged at the shorter man. There was no denying that First Mate Sinclair loved to joke and harass. The two men made their way to the mess hall.

Chapter Eight

The *Ayrshire* was a larger-sized, three-island style tramp steamer displaying raised structures at bow, amidships, and stern. She was powered by the coal stored in her several bins. She also had a large auxiliary bunker built to supplement her long distance capacity. For enhanced stability, her engines had been installed in the center section along with most crew and traveler accommodations. Built in spring 1900, she was practically new, with still-bright paint, little rust, a manageable number of small cockroaches, and few rats. The decks were all wooden, stained a luxurious color, above the bridge deck and on the after deck house. The forecastle house and bridge house bulkheads were also of wood.

As far as tramp streamers went, the ship was first class compared to her common working brethren. "Aye, she be a real beauty for her type o' vessel. Sassy, she is. A gen-u-ine sea lady," boasted Dugan to him. Dugan and the second mate, Findlay Kincaid, stood talking with David one morning.

"We gets compliments on her, we do, whenever we dock," interjected Findlay, watching with the others as some large fish broke the waters several hundred yards out into the churning ocean surface. The winds had been gradually building since early day.

"One o' me uncles is in the shipbuilding business. But I know very little 'bout sailing vessels meself. I can tell she be a nice looking ship, though."

The ship had electricity throughout supplied by two powerful generators of the latest model, which meant she had lighting available over her length and breadth, and even large-scale refrigeration for perishable foods in her modernized and expanded kitchen.

Originally intended as a premier ship of burden, the *Ayrshire* was now semi-converted; within the first year of the ship's construction, almost half of her original cargo space had been transformed into passenger cabins and other necessary amenities by the owning partners. The retro-fitted vessel could accommodate up to one hundred and nine paying customers in addition to the ship's hands. It had sufficient remaining storage for a generous haul of goods: dry or wet; legal or otherwise, including white, gray and black-market articles.

"Be-jesus, a while back, we had one wealthy Dutch bugger try to bribe the Capt to run a cache o' arms from the Congo to the Boers in South Africa, we did." The first mate wiped his brow and the side of his face with the back of his hand as a spray of water crashed over the railing, dousing them with a fine mist. "Remember that, Fin? I'm right glad ol' Wotherspoon's got some backbone and turned that one down. Dinna matter how much money. We might've been caught and clapped into irons for treason. There was a *war* goin' on, for Christ's sake."

"But you do handle some cargo that's a bit dicey, now n' then, Duggie?" David asked.

"Aye, mate. I'm not at liberty to be a tellin' all the black market goods we get in here. I wadna want to shock yer tender minister ears." He laughed heartily, and punched the young man in the shoulder.

David discovered the ship had a rich assortment of other travelers. As one way to relieve his boredom, he began keeping track whenever he noticed a new face. He eventually counted eighty-seven passengers on this trip, plus a crew of eighteen men and one boy. In all, there was a captain, first mate, second mate, boatswain, chief engineer, assistant engineer, signal operator, fireman, chief cook, assistant cook, steward, five sailors who stoked the engine with coal, two general seamen, and a seaman's apprentice.

Among the crew were seven Scots, three Irish, two Welsh, one South African, one English, one Pole, one Somali, and one Zanzibari, and two members whose ancestry was so clouded that, as Duggie told David one morning after breakfast, "The poor lads dinna even know who their real ma or pa was. Both mutts they be. Orphaned as little tykes and raised by strangers. All they knows is, they're mostly white blood, but what kind o' mix, they hinna got a clue."

"Well, they're all human beings, Duggie. All deservin' o' God's grace," David replied.

Duggie chuckled and elbowed David in the side. "Methinks some o' them deserve to be tossed overboard, laddie." As the first mate explained, there were fierce rivalries on board between deck and engine departments, and between the bridge crew and the rest of the sailors.

The ship was now a full day past the Cape of Africa, where turbulent storms had halted the vessel's progress for one night and part of the next day. Many of the oldest and youngest passengers, and not a few of the women, had gotten seasickness for the first time this voyage with the violent rocking of the ship. David himself had to fight hard to keep his meals down during the worst of the storms.

Sailing from the southwest of Scotland, the *Ayrshire* had made scheduled ports of call in Wales, France, Morocco, and Congo/West Africa, thereby avoiding the heavier shipping traffic in the busy Mediterranean and through the Suez Canal. Her stay at Cape of Good Hope had been hurried due to rough seas. There, the vessel had filled its regular bins as well as its auxiliary storage with surplus coal for the continuation on to Perth. The ship would replenish its stores again at Perth.

The scheduled stopover at Cape L'Agullas was aborted altogether because of the increasingly difficult weather. Off the coast of South Africa, David watched as a bull's eye squall developed unexpectedly.

"Fasten her down," the captain bellowed to the crew as they pulled away from the angry shoreline into the crashing waves.

At each port where she was able to dock, though, the ship continued to take on more goods and people.

While the *Ayrshire* was a floating testament to the richness of variety of the human race, the majority of female passengers were of European descent including several English, Scottish, Irish, Welsh and French; their ages ranged from young teen to grandmother. These ladies comprised an unofficial but competitive clique of admirers of David.

Annabelle Dougherty had set sail with the ship in Scotland, a member of the first group of passengers, along with David. A recent widow in her mid-thirties, Annabelle was not only childless, unusual for the times, but quite youthful for her age. She was easily stimulated by male company and, in return, had an equally stimulating effect on most men she met. To her amazement and challenge, the handsome MacDougall remained prim and proper in her presence; a perfect gentleman in fact.

"Och, what's wrong with the stud?" she complained to a friend, after deliberately bumping into the young reverend several times, plying her feminine wiles, and getting nothing but innocent conversation in return.

"I'm a fine hot-blooded woman," she said, watching him walk away after one polite but brief meeting. She wiggled her hips suggestively as if to reassure herself she still had ample appeal. "Hell's bells! I get most men all worked up n' slobberin' for me. Can he not get his tally whacker up?"

However, David was so good-looking his coolness

only inspired her to greater heights of feminine tricks. It was she who tasked the first mate with searching for him that morning.

The lovely, red-headed Marguerite Rousseau came aboard in France; never married at the age of twenty-seven, intelligent, sensual, headstrong, and unaffected by the stuffy Victorianism of her distant English kin. She was descended from landed nobility, and groomed from infancy to view the control of men she desired as her birthright. Mlle. Rousseau assumed natural claim to David Adam MacDougall as soon as she laid her hazel-gold eyes on him.

"Oo la la! Maybe zis voyage will not be so boring after all," she whispered with wicked delight, viewing David's form on the far side of the deck as she came up the gangplank.

The willowy Emma Watson Jones just turned twenty and was part of the original contingent. English to her core; quiet, unpretentious and intellectual—she possessed innate beauty both within and without. She also displayed more than a passing interest in religion, which inherently gave her a leg-up on her rivals for the attention of the newly minted Minister MacDougall.

"Tell me more, Reverend, about the meaning of the Eucharist," she had asked, upon finding out he was ordained.

Finally, there was the Madam O'Mallory, a voluptuous, boisterous, forty four year old widow with a zest for life which two previous husbands could not keep pace with. Margaret, or Margie O'Mallory was a force of nature, quite unlike anything the ship's captain, or the crew, or David, had ever met. She was irrepressible yet delightful at the same time. It was difficult not to like the woman; her personality was so overwhelmingly pleasant.

"Aye, there's nothin' like an extra soft bed and an extra hard man," she had said, meeting David for the first time and thumping his chest. He had startled a bit at the suddenness of her impulsive action, but had remained cordial and polite, as was his norm.

Even the faithfully married Duggie had cottoned to the Madam; their personalities were so much alike. Besides, he had always liked meaty women. His own wife had serious padding in all the right places, as far as he was concerned.

Other ladies aboard such as the good Mrs. Chesterfield vied for scraps of David's attention. But the Gang of Four, as Dugan waggishly called them, were the main warriors in this Amazonian game of conquest.

Chapter Nine

But we return to the present. The formal dining hall was filled with the early morning crowd when David and the first mate entered the room. The Madam held court at one of the long tables, regaling a dozen passengers plus a few off-duty crew members, all gathered around listening with big grins and sipping their mugs of hot coffee or tea.

"...Then he asks the wifie, 'Maggie, could you be a sewin' on a wee button that's come off o' me fly? I canna fasten me pants.' 'Oh Angus, I got me hands in the dishpan. You go up the stairs and see if Mrs. McKenzie could be a helpin' you with it.' About five minutes later, the wifie hears a terrible crash, a bang, a bunch o' cursin', and the sound o' a big body a fallin' doon the stairs. Well sir, in comes Angus back through the door with a blackened eye and a bloody nose. The wifie looks at him, she does, and says, 'Me God! What in hell's name happened to you? Did you ask her like I told you?' 'Aye.' says Angus. 'I asked 'er to sew on the wee button and she did. Everything was a goin' fine, but about the time she bent doon to bite off the wee thread, Mr. McKenzie walks in.'"

The whole table exploded in laughter. Madam

O'Mallory gave a loud guffaw, and slapped her ample thigh in appreciation of her own joke.

Her breakfast finished, the bookish Emma sat reading a novel, undisturbed by the surrounding din. Her table was shared by two middle-aged married couples and several older passengers, including Mrs. Chesterfield and her grandson. Leashed to the leg of Thomas's chair, the ever-eager Mason stood alert to intruders of his space and succulent food scraps, all the while barking his displeasure at the noise coming from the Madam's table.

The thirteen male passengers from Morocco, the Congo, and South Africa occupied a third table by themselves.

As usual, the sultry Mlle. Rousseau was still sleeping in her quarters; she didn't take her strong black coffee until late morning.

But Annabelle Dougherty, who had strategically positioned herself at the table closest the entry, stood up at once upon seeing the reverend and the first mate enter. Clapping her hands, she exclaimed, "You *found* the rascal at last!" She motioned to the empty places on either side of her chair.

"David, come join me." Annabelle patted the seat cushion of the chair to her left. "And you, too, Master Sinclair. You'll be takin' the seat on the other side o' the table from me, you will! I know how you love yer coffee."

David blushed, but did as he was told.

"Tea, sirs?"

"Yes, thank you," replied David.

"Aye, I'll take me coffee, Blaine."

The steward hastened to fill David's cup with a teabag and hot water. He put a pot of fresh coffee on the table for the first mate. There was fried bacon, fresh eggs from the remaining hens, buttered toast and jam, and heavy cream for the tea or coffee.

Annabelle laid her hand on David's right thigh under the table as he sat down. She gave it a naughty squeeze. Immediately, he slid his napkin onto his lap and took the opportunity to nudge her exploring hand off his leg. He saw the first mate watching them closely; worldly-wise Duggie missed very little. David swallowed hard and pretended nothing had happened.

Dugan gestured at the far serving dish, and David reached to pick it up. There was quiet clanking of silverware and platters of food passed around as the first mate and the reverend filled their plates. It was the second breakfast that day for Dugan, who was known for his prodigious appetite. After his early morning melancholy, David found he was hungry. Impatient, Annabelle watched the men eating for a few minutes before resuming her onslaught.

She smiled sweetly at David. Reaching over and squeezing his massive forearm, she cooed, "It's a *big* comfort, it is, to have such strong manly lads as you two 'round when there be *violent* storms outside. David, you are a lifesaver, you are, helpin' me put me things back in the suitcase."

Mouth full with a big bite of scrambled egg and toast, he could only bobble his head in response.

She sighed dramatically. "Whit, with the tossin' o' the ship with the waves, I think it musta fallen off the rack and broken open. I dinna know *how* it happened, otherwise. But you were *so good* to come to me room and help a poor damsel in distress."

Annabelle batted her heavy eyelashes for effect.

"Were you able to get a good night's sleep after the storm blew over," David ventured, changing the subject.

"Aye, thanks to you and yer chivalry, I..."

Annabelle was not to keep the reverend to herself for long. Hearing David's voice from across the room, Margie O'Mallory jerked her head up. The Madam excused herself from her attentive audience and made a bee-line for the other table. Interrupting her rival, she dove right into the conversation.

"Ah! Mr. MacDougall. You made it. I see yer hungry for some *real* female company this fine mornin'."

She glared pointedly at Annabelle, who stuck her tongue out. Carefully positioned across from David so he would get an eyeful, Madam O'Mallory put one hand on curvaceous hip, the other hand on Dugan's shoulder, and leaned over most provocatively, allowing her massive bosom to strain her over-worked blouse-top.

At the mammoth sight displayed beside him, First Mate Dugan's eyes bulged out as much as the Madam's cleavage. "Uph-h-h!" He dribbled some hot coffee down his front and squawked in embarrassment.

David hastily put his hand to his forehead, partially covering his eyes, "Aye, a good morning to you, too, Madam O'Mallory."

He politely motioned her to sit down, before she fell down, in the chair next to the first mate, facing him. "So, how did you fare during the past storm, Madam?" It seemed he was becoming an expert on both sea storms and changing the subject.

"Ah, I was wantin' a stout drink the night 'fore last, I was."

She laughed a deep belly laugh. "O' course, havin' a supple...hard...young...body," she emphasized each word and paused between for effect before winking at the reverend, "a lyin' next to me in bed, a keepin' me safe n' warm durin' the high winds, wad have bin *much* better than strong drink.

"Dinna you think so, Dugan?" She turned to the first mate with an innocent look on her handsome face.

"Huh! What?"

"I asked you if havin' a companion wad have bin a comfort to a vulnerable single lady such as me-self," she purred at him, "durin' a time o' sech tribulation and danger as the recent storm."

"Och that! Ah, I—" he glanced at David's reddening face, "wadna know, Madam. I mean, me bein' a happily married man and all, I dinna really think 'bout sech things, you see. But well, others who be *unattached* may think 'bout sech things, I suppose."

Annabelle cut in. "Come now, Madam O'Mallory. The truth be out, there's no room in yer bed for two people since you take up so much space yerself. A fat milk cow wadna be as huge."

The battle joined and the Madam swelled, if possible, to even greater girth. "And there be *some* ladies aboard this here ship who dinna have 'nough flesh on their bones to possess *real* womanly curves and female beauty. *Some* carry too much flesh in all the *wrong* places."

"How *dare* you, you overgrown heifer!"

Madam O'Mallory stared daggers at her foe, who returned the favor. The Madam pressed her advantage. "Healthy boys, red-blooded men that is, likes to see solid hips and a gener's top on their women, they do, something they can hold on to," she gloated.

Her eyebrows knitted together in an expression of feigned pity. "Och aye, havin' a haggard-lookin' puss with cheap make-up a splotched and a sprayed all over it canna hide the plainness beneath, I'm afraid."

Annabelle hissed, but her furious retort was cut short by the languid approach of Emma Jones.

"David, am I interrupting anything?" A cool voice interjected.

Chapter Ten

Both the first mate and the reverend appeared immensely relieved by Emma's timely arrival. Able to fully defend himself against any physical foe, David was unequipped to handle feminine attack, whether friendly or otherwise. During the brief escalation of words, Dugan clutched his coffee mug until his fingers were white as bone. He breathed out his relief. His own wife and three portly daughters were as jovial and peaceable as he, and he had no practical experience with warring women.

"Miss Jones. How very nice to see you this morning. You'll not be interrupting anything o' grave importance. The good ladies were, ah, just discussing…ah, the recent turbulent weather, I do believe."

"I thought some more on what you said the other day about the Lord's Supper being a metaphysical representation of the New Covenant as contained in the New Testament potion of scripture. Would you be so kind as to expound further on what that really means in terms of it being an Ordinance versus a Sacrament of the church?"

Her face locked in thoughtful pose; she gave only the

briefest of nods to the other ladies then turned her undivided attention to David. The unexpected mention of such a serious religious subject was music to the reverend's ears, but Emma's topic caught the other two women off-guard. Miss Dougherty looked bewildered. Madam O'Mallory's jaw dropped.

Not only was Emma's slender build the exact opposite of the embellished hour-glass appeal of Annabelle and the Madam, her intelligence and desire for learning put her in a totally different category of competitor. For the moment the two adversaries were at a loss for both words and action.

"May I sit down?" she asked, pointing to the open space at David's left.

"Oh, most certainly, please do," he said.

As Emma gracefully walked around the table and settled into her chair, the Madam leaned back into a stiff proper carriage. Continuing to expose her plunging cleavage to the men would never do in the face of such refined enemy conduct. Annabelle, too, sat straight up; her expression confused.

"So, explain to me again what it was you were trying to tell me about the Lord's Supper," she said, placing her unfinished book on the table.

David quickly finished the last of his eggs and toast, and took a sip of tea, before beginning.

"Aye." He cleared his throat. "Well, first, you must understand there be considerable disagreement among various Christian denominations. Some hold the Lord's Supper is a holy sacrament equal to, say, a baptism or a marriage ceremony. They feel it's a channel o' real imparted grace to the, ah, participant. The physical elements o' the wine and bread transform, or become, the actual blood and body o' Jesus at the moment of communion. That is, at the instant they be consumed by the person. The Roman Catholics and Eastern Orthodoxy call this transubstantiation."

"I follow what you're saying."

He paused for a second to see if she had any comments or questions. He then continued, "Other denominations, particularly most o' the reformed or Protestant belief, hold that Jesus is spiritually, but not bodily, present in the elements. The Lord's Supper tis a special ordinance: A time for Christians to reflect and remember our dear Lord's sacrifice, a time for us to be a renewing our commitment as true believers."

He looked expectantly at her. "Does that help?"

"Yes, quite," she said, her hazel eyes fixed on his handsome face. "Oh, steward," she called out across the room. "Would you be so kind as to bring me a cup of tea? Thank you so much."

By now, the other ladies were noticeably irritated, but did not know how to regain control of the situation. Dugan took the opportunity to reach across the table and pile his plate with a second helping of everything.

"Tell me more, David, about your recent appointment to China. It sounds like a fascinating assignment to a most intriguing and exotic locale."

She smiled and put her soft hand on top of his. Like most English girls, her skin was very pale; it was obvious to him she wore gloves most of the time to protect against the sun.

"You must be very excited."

He didn't pull his hand away. "Aye, I am right eager to get started. Truth to speak, I've been looking forward to this since me freshman year in university. The Lord called me to be a missionary in China when I was just a lad o' eighteen."

He smiled warmly at her. Emma's interest seemed genuine.

"The United Missionary Society o' Scotland ordained me only three weeks ago. They have a number o' efforts throughout the country o' China and the Far East. In northern China, their biggest work is the Christ Is Lord mission church in the capital city o' Beiping. Before the recent outbreak of native hostilities, the so-called Boxer Rebellion, the church had a congregation o' over a thousand dear Chinese people. Alas, in the three years since the late conflict, its attendance has dropped dramatically."

The steward finally made it to their table with a large pot of tea and another carafe of fresh hot coffee. He also brought a clean teacup for the lady.

Emma and Dugan thanked the man.

Watching the steward leave, David sighed, "At last count, down to four hundred and twenty-six members, actually." Turning his gaze back to Emma, David had a determined expression. "But the Society and the local pastor are hopeful with the Good Lord's blessing above, that the time is ripe to rebuild. We *will* grow the church bigger than ever."

"I know you will do wonders." She squeezed his big hand.

"Harrumph-h-h!" The Madam cleared her throat loudly. "Harrumph!"

Startled a bit, the other four persons looked at Margie O'Mallory.

"The Lord's Supper be a fine thing, a holy observance, I'm sure. *If* we were all in a church. In me own humble way, I can observe all the niceties and be as good a Christian, I'm sure, as the next soul. But debatin' topics o' religion winna help us much if we get attacked by the pirates."

They stared quizzically at the Madam. She surveyed the group with a smug manner. At last, she had stopped the skinny English prissy from dominating David and the conversation.

"The captain says we be in real danger o' pirates the deeper we gets into the South Seas. Only yesterday, he was a sayin' to me that in the last two months some five ships have bin boarded, looted, and rich-lookin' passengers taken captive for ransom. Women and children have bin captured. Worse done than that, too. Just the other side o' Australia and a wee bit closer in to the China coast, this happened, this did."

She paused for effect.

"The captain told me hisself he's got a cabinet o' three rifles all locked up tight in his private room. He was a tellin' me that him, the second mate, the first engineer, and one other sailor called MacFarlane be the only ones on this entire vessel that's bin in the military, bin in combat, knows how to shoot and fight. The captain kept his old army revolver. Half the crew has knives. But whit use is four guns and a handful o' pocket knives 'gainst twelve or fifteen or even more blood-thirsty bandits? All armed to the teeth, all killers?"

She looked around the table. "Now, 'fore we was interrupted by Miss...whit's yer name, girl?"

"Excuse *me*?"

"I asked yer name, little sweetie."

"Miss Emma Watson Jones." She frowned at the Madam's tone of voice.

"Well, 'fore we was interrupted by the Missie Jones here, we was all talkin' 'bout the great storm o' two days ago. Now, we has an even bigger problem than a few puffs o' wind. Whit's the plan o' action, Duggie? Whit does the captain and crew got up their sleeve if we be stopped?"

First Mate Dugan pushed his plate away. It was not quite empty, but his enormous appetite was suddenly gone. The third helpings he had envisioned were lost forever. He gaped at the staring Madam and gathered his thoughts for a few seconds before answering.

"Well Madam." He folded his arms across his barrel chest and assumed what he thought was an air of confidence. "Bein' a good-sized vessel with tall sides, and a fast-movin' steamship at that, it's highly unlikely that we'll be stopped, let 'lone boarded, by any sech pirates."

He elaborated further. "You see, only one o' the five ships in question was close to the size and speed o' the *Ayrshire*. The captain o' that ship foolishly allowed some pirates to come 'board disguised as payin' passengers at the port o' Jakarta. So when the pirate boat approached 'long side with the rest o' the scurvy bunch, the officers and crew was in disarray from fightin' off the devils already on the vessel."

He vigorously shook his head. "No, ladies and David, too, it's highly unlikely any pirate vessel can overtake our ship or outwit our captain. He's a seasoned veteran with long years o' experience in dealin' with challengin' situations and dangerous conditions."

With that, Dugan labored to his feet and stretched. He had spent too long socializing. Duty called. He needed to begin his work day.

David excused himself as well, "Thank you all, ladies, for the pleasure of your company."

"Ah, David!" Dugan exclaimed before they left the mess hall together. "You must remember to come by the captain's quarters at noon. Old Wother told me he does enjoy the competition whilst he's havin' his meal. You're invited to dine with him in his cabin, and the two o' you can finish up your game o' chess."

The first mate beamed at the younger man. "The captain says you be a right smart player. I'll give you half a pound, laddie, if you can beat the old codger. Payable at our next port o' call."

Chapter Eleven

Another day and a half passed. The *Ayrshire* drew steadily closer to its next port of call at Perth. Only three years earlier, Western Australia and its five sister Crown Colonies had finally formed a united federation and joined the British Commonwealth of Nations. The King of England, Edward VII, was now their monarch and head of state as he was for MacDougall's native Scotland plus England, Ireland, and the other countries of the British Dominion.

To help keep his mind off his misery, David took to jogging the perimeter of the top deck as part of his daily routine. He varied the time when he ran his twenty circuits, so as to prevent unwanted encounters with any lady admirers.

As the young man swept around the rear of the ship working on his sixth lap, Dugan stepped out onto the aft bridge above and spotted him below. The first mate called down to him, "Ah! David, me man."

"Och. 'Lo, Duggie." MacDougall stopped his run for the moment and glanced up.

"Dinna see you at breakfast. You doin' all right, are you?"

"I'll be fine."

His somber mood was in stark contrast to the beautiful day. There wasn't a cloud in the gorgeous pastel-blue sky. The bright sun was mostly eclipsed by Dugan's head as David stood there, but intense rays still filtered around the man's crown. The reverend grimaced and shielded his eyes as he looked up.

"Still dealin' with all the hurt inside me. Still working through…everything. Been keeping to meself a little bit. Doin' more praying and soul-searching, I have."

He saw the concern on the first mate's face and immediately made a conscious effort to sound more positive. "But thank the Good Lord, tis a lovely day, though, Duggie. Appreciate you asking, I do."

"Aye, Rev, tis a right gorgeous afternoon."

Dugan patted his ample middle in a mood of great contentment. Of course, the man was always happy, it seemed, which is why David was attracted to his company. "The weather's bin as mild as a baby lamb." Indeed, no further squalls or bad weather intervened to slow the ship's speed, which ranged between nineteen to slightly more than twenty-one knots per hour in the placid seas.

"Aye, well, I need to be a movin' along, Duggie. I'll catch up with you later if you have time to be a stoppin' by the passengers' mess hall for your second dinner." The reverend smiled, waved goodbye, and resumed his pace.

David's heart was badly broken. Of that, there was no doubt. And it would remain bleeding and fragile for the foreseeable future. Physical pain had limited effect on him;

God had blessed him with a body that was durable and tough. But emotional pain he found much harder to deal with.

He knew he had to rise above the despair and get on with living. As a Christian, he also knew he had to forgive Rose, and that was something he continued to pray about. It was a struggle. He couldn't even imagine doing to another person what she had done, especially someone he had long loved. Loyalty was a deep and natural part of his being.

Outwardly, he was incredibly tough, a physical beast. Inwardly, well, that was a different story.

David had placed his romantic inclinations into the hands of the Lord, and therefore avoided the formal dining area as much as possible. *Hoots, mon, I canna deal with all these females constantly fightin' for me attention. Och, I just want to be left alone in peace.*

He began taking his meals secretly with the crew in the smaller mess hall or having his lunches and dinners with the captain while playing numerous games of chess. Sometimes, he skipped breakfast altogether.

More and more, David spent his hours reading scripture and praying in his cabin, or exercising. In addition to jogging daily, he sometimes snuck into the passenger cargo room and lifted suitably heavy containers, packages, and chests that he found stored inside. Out of sheer boredom, he'd also fallen into the habit of playing whatever games were underway at meal time with the crewmen at hand: Checkers, chess (in which he was very good), dominoes, and darts, among other contests.

However, a new mistress was emerging; one that had the power to replace his sad remembrances of Rosie with glad anticipation.

Of growing interest to many sailors and some officers was an exciting new sport David had learned from his big brother, Robert Allen MacDougall, and was now teaching the eager men of the *Ayrshire*. The crew shoved their two dining tables into one corner and tacked up two large fruit baskets, with the bottoms tore out, at either wall of the mess hall. Chalk stripes were drawn for the free throw lines. Any equal number of the men could play, from four to six to eight to ten, as long as each team had the same amount of players.

Three years older, Robert had gone to seminary, been ordained as a minister, and left Scotland for America in 1901, gaining work as an associate with the Boston Chapter of the Young Men's Christian Association, or YMCA. There, Robert, taller by two inches and but fifteen pounds skinnier than David Adam, discovered the novel game of Basket Ball.

First created by James Naismith in 1891 as a winter-time indoor diversion for physical education students at the YMCA International Training School in nearby Springfield, Massachusetts, the game unexpectedly spread to YMCAs around the world, which in turn evangelized the sport to other denominations and missionaries. Basket Ball was introduced to the Chinese people in 1896 by YMCA outposts in that country, in Shanghai, and many other southern cities.

By the turn of the century, the game was evolving.

In the summers of 1902 and 1903, Robert had returned home on sabbaticals and taught his brother everything he knew about the rules of the fledgling sport. Of course, being creative and energetic, they made up rules on the fly that made good sense to them.

The brothers had found a good spot for a Basket Ball court on the west side of their house. A smooth, flat playing surface had been created over a sixty-year period due to the constant wear of the horse-drawn buggy and its predecessor. The same parking space and path had been used by great-grandfather MacDougall, grandfather, and now their father.

The brothers nailed a basket onto the sloping roof of the house where it measured ten feet above the ground. Across the way, they fastened a second basket into the trunk of a large elm tree, again measuring ten feet from the ground.

"Lookie here, David. You can be a holdin' the ball out.

"Like this," Robert straightened and extended his right arm to the side at a forty-five degree angle above his shoulder with the ball in his upward facing palm, "and you fling your arm toward the basket. Like this," he arched a hook shot at the tacked up apple bucket. The round football hit the front of the rim and bounced away.

"Well, anyways, you get the drift o' it. Toss it back. Let me do it again."

"I'm a thinking I be likin' this sport better than the football," exclaimed David after playing and experimenting with Basket Ball for nearly three weeks with his brother.

Jack King

Day after day, the two played in the warm afternoons and early evenings. Often friends joined in, but sometimes it was just the brothers. Athletic and competitive, especially when playing against Robert, David quickly mastered the basics. In no time he improvised fresh ideas about how to move with the ball, how to beat your opponent, and how to score.

Although *dribbling* did not become an official part of the game until 1909, Robert and David discovered for themselves the value of dribbling the ball to move it forward. In their contests, they allowed the technique of either continually tossing the ball in the air and catching it oneself, or of dribbling the ball—bouncing the ball from your hand off the court back into your hand, as you ran toward your basket to score a goal.

Using their imagination and athleticism, the MacDougall brothers experimented and practiced with techniques that were advanced for their time. They strove to outdo one another in exotic forms of scoring such as the *two-handed set shot*, the *hooking shot*, and the *underhanded shot* for free throws, as well as innovative passing methods like the *bounce pass*, the two-handed *chest pass*, the two-handed or one-handed *overhead pass*, and the *passing while dribbling* method.

David became as much an evangelist for the new sport of Basket Ball as he was for Christianity. And he now gladly shared his enthusiasm with the crewmen of the *Ayrshire*.

A group crowded around David at the other end of

the small mess hall as he explained some of the rules: "The ball can be thrown or batted to a teammate or oneself in any direction with one or both hands.

"A player can continually throw the ball in the air to himself and repeatedly catch it as he runs toward his goal.

"However, a player canna run with the ball held stationary or be kickin' it like a football.

"The ball can only be held in, or between, the hands.

"A player canna slam his shoulder into, or be a holdin', strikin', pushin', or trippin' an opponent; to do so is a foul.

"A player canna be a strikin' the ball with his fist like a volleyball; to do so is a foul.

"In the event o' a foul, the opposing team gets a 'free throw' attempt, worth one point if made.

"In the event of three consecutive fouls, the opposing team gets awarded a 'bucket,' worth two points.

"Each made bucket is worth two points.

"A bucket is made when the ball is thrown or batted from a player's hands or from the grounds into the basket.

"The time o' play is two fifteen-minute halves, with five minutes rest in between.

"The team with the most points at the end o' the game is declared the winner."

Chapter Twelve

The two men stood inside the command bridge; one listening with a dry but amused expression, one talking animatedly.

"Captain Wotherspoon, I assure you this new game o' Basket Ball be a perfect sport, tis, for men servin' on ships o' larger size like the *Ayrshire*, where there be space enough to play."

David's brawny countenance shone with missionary zeal.

"Really, sir, tis far better than sittin' on one's arse—I mean, backside—and a playin' tiddlywinks or dominoes. It gets the heart rate up, improves digestion, prevents sleeplessness, increases energy, builds camaraderie, and helps the men learn how to work together as a team. Tis the best form of exercise we could be a teachin' them, sir. Tis the latest trend, I assure you. People all over the world are a playin' it!"

He paused for breath, and continued, "What do you say, sir?"

The meticulous iron-rod figure studied the face of the enthusiastic young man in front of him. Captain Wotherspoon truly liked the reverend. For one thing, he was an exceptional chess player; it took all Ian's concentration and experience to best David. He was forthright, honorable, and caring. The ship's officers had nothing but good things to say about him; a first rate passenger.

Wotherspoon considered the matter for a full minute before speaking. He had been an officer at sea for many years. Life on a ship was tedious and repetitive. The captain knew too much inactivity off duty led to fatigue on duty. The men became lazy and lacked focus and careful attention to their tasks at hand. He understood that rampant boredom was the cause of much of the surliness and fighting among the crew.

Finally, he replied. "Reverend, if a majority of the men, other officers included, vote to reserve part of their dining space to use as a playing area, you may proceed. I have but two stipulations: any man found playing during his watch hours, or caught fighting while playing or watching, will be expelled from the game and further punished as their officer sees fit."

"Done already!" David exclaimed. "We already did a ballot at lunch, and fourteen men including the first mate and first engineer voted to use the back half o' the room for a court. And yes sir, I already laid down the *law*, I did, about absolutely, positively, *no* playing during hours and *no* fighting whatsoever."

Ian's eyes widened with mild surprise.

"Aye? Well, then. I see."

He shook his head. "Well, then, ah, in that case." He glanced at David's broad smiling face. "Did anyone ever tell you that you would make a fine preacher or even an honest politician one day?"

The captain half-heartedly returned the younger man's smile and patted him on his burly shoulder.

Within the hour, David and the participating crew had their first official game of Basket Ball. It was 6:36 in the evening and the dinner meal was finishing up. Dugan walked over and switched on the extra set of ceiling lights inside the small mess hall. The men opened the external door as wide as possible to catch some of the cool breeze swirling in from the side deck.

Several fellows who played some version of football had stowed the round-shaped association footballs as part of their personal effects. These they brought to David. "This one here looks to be in the best shape," David said, choosing the newest of the lot for the Basket Ball game. He bounced it on the floor and tossed it up several times, testing the amount of air.

David had told the men since their playing space was a bit cramped—less than half the length and width of a regulation court—they would play with four players on a team and not five.

In all, two sailors, one seaman, Assistant Engineer Nevin Ferguson, Second Mate Finlay Kincaid, the fireman, Seaman's Apprentice Andrew Young, and MacDougall comprised the initial set of participants. Meanwhile, Dugan, the chief engineer, the boatswain, and two other crew members sat at the crammed tables to watch the activities from the sideline.

David quickly sorted the players. "All right, me lads. We want to make it fair, we do." Looking around, he said, "Ah, let's have meself, Nevin, Finlay, and the boy, Andrew, on the one team."

He put the two sailors, the seaman, and the fireman on the opposing squad. One man he didn't know. "And what be your name, sir?" he asked, reaching out to shake the man's hand.

"Abdi Karim."

"'Tis good to meet you, Abdi. Let's have you, and Sweeney there—that's correct, right?—and Roy and Hugh on the other team."

David elected to guard Roy, who appeared to be the best athlete on the opposing side. At six-feet three, Nevin was assigned to Abdi, the tallest opponent at over six-feet four; Andrew took the youngest; and Finlay was assigned to the remaining man.

To save time, David allowed the other team to go first. David called out, "Remember, lads, you canna use your hands to grab or hold or strike your opponent. You must crouch down and move your feet like you do in football. Keep your body between your opponent and their basket at all times."

The other team inbounded the ball, made a second pass, and then attempted a long throw down court. With lightning quick reflexes, David intercepted the lobbed pass from the fireman to the seaman, and raced to the other end, throwing the ball up and catching it as he ran. As he got closer, he took two dribbles and rifled a sharp bounce pass to the somewhat surprised Nevin, waiting under the basket.

"Toss it up, Nevin! Put it up!"

The lanky engineer turned his shoulders inward and heaved the lightweight ball upward with one hand placed by his ear like a shot-put. He aimed for the top of the fruit basket. The ball bounced hard off the wall a good ten inches above the basket, hit the right edge of the bucket, caromed straight up in the air, landed on the front edge and barely missed going in, but instead fell to the floor.

Before the seaman could even react, David sped forward, picked it up and scored using a two-handed set shot that banked off the wall behind the basket.

"Think of billiards and angles, Nevin! Shoot more softly, too."

The reverend clapped his hands loudly to get attention. "That goes for everyone! You can use the wall behind the basket to bank the shot in for everything except straight-on side shots. Trust me, lads. Me brother and I experimented, measured, and practiced all types of trajectory until we were blue in the face."

He handed the ball to the other team, and said, "Aye, tis much easier than trying to aim the ball over the front of the rim."

His team hurried down to the other end. While they

waited for their opponent, David called out instructions on how to play good defense.

"Crouch down low, men. Always keep your knees bent and your heads up. You want to be moving side to side, cutting your man off from the bucket, using angles. That's it, Andrew. Put both hands out, one to the side and one in front o' you, switching according to which direction your man is going, like this.

"Watch the ball. Be ready to block a shot or deflect a pass or steal the ball. Face your man at all times, with your body between him and the bucket. Try to stay an arm's length or closer to your man. Think fast. Move quick. Be helpin' your teammates defend."

The eight men played two games, each thirty-five minutes long including the five minute recess in between halves. David's team won the first game, fourteen to two, with him scoring six of the seven baskets. The second game was much closer, twelve to eight, as the other team began to make better use of their passes and positioning by the basket.

Nobody knew how to shoot the ball as well as David. Both teams had many passes stolen. Both teams threw up many shots, with few going in. No free throws were awarded or fouls accessed since there was no official referee.

The night air turned a bit chilly as the evening progressed, but the players sweated on the make-shift indoor court. By halftime of the second game, every player had stripped their shirts off to cool down.

"Yow, tis a bit warm in here, innit?" said Nevin, wiping beads of perspiration from his brow, and still breathing mightily. He was the old man on the court.

But they were all enthusiastic; ready for a third and final game. The spectators were having almost as good a time. The first mate began to make bets for which other players besides David would score in the third game.

"I got me money on you, young Andy, don't be a lettin' me down, now," he called out. Duggie appointed himself the designated time-keeper, letting the teams know when five minutes was left in each half and also when the full fifteen minutes was over.

After the second game, the men took a mutually agreed break of ten minutes to catch their breath and drink something cold. After a few hasty gulps of water, David used this time to coach his novice teammates. As always, he was serious about winning.

Motioning them over, David picked up the ball and gathered his players at half court. He said, "Aye, lads, we have 'bout five minutes left. Spread out in a big circle now." In succession, he demonstrated how to throw a sharp bounce pass, a precision chest pass, and a high lob pass. The four men took turns practicing good passing techniques to each other.

Then the last game started.

Chapter Thirteen

David received the ball in-bounds from the other end. Forgoing the self-pass technique, he instead dribbled twelve times (a record best), weaving between opponents, all the way to the free throw line, before lobbing an arcing pass to Nevin. The assistant engineer waited until two defenders hastened toward him while he held the ball, then he hurled a crisp bounce pass to Finlay in the corner. The second mate let his man rush at him before relaying the ball to Andrew at the wing position left of the free-throw line.

"Go 'head, shoot it!" David shouted.

Young Andy threw a shot that hit the front rim of the bucket and bounced awkwardly up in the air in the direction of the foul line. Darting in, David blocked out the nearest defender from the ball, leaped high, and tapped the sphere with his outstretched fingertips to Nevin. The big man smoothly pivoted around his surprised opponent and used both hands to bank a nice-sounding shot that cleanly went in.

Two to nothing, and David's team had scored first.

"Way to go, laddies!" In celebration, he smacked Nevin's open palm with his own, then did the same with Finlay and Andrew.

It was clear that David's teammates, as well as the other players, were beginning to catch on to the subtleties of this amazing new game. They thought it was rollicking good fun.

His team streaked down court to get ready on defense.

By the third game, the other team demonstrated marked improvement, too. Roy was becoming adept at using the self-pass tactic to quickly advance the ball. Almost as fast as David, he showed a devious talent for using his teammates' bodies as screens to get open. He also had a nasty tendency for throwing his elbows around to clear space, smacking David in the jaw several times before the reverend adjusted his defensive style.

"That'll teach you to be a backin' off," Roy growled.

After the last love tap, David glared at the man. But then he caught himself. Rather than losing his temper or getting frustrated, he brought his arm up in a defensive boxing posture facing Roy's closest side to block further blows, be they intentional or otherwise.

Och, got to be a takin' it easy, I do. I'm a minister now. I canna be assuming Roy's deliberately playing me dirty. The man may just be nervous. Or he may have a bit o' a jerking motion going on. Remember the captain's rules: No fighting.

Nevin, meanwhile, had his hands full guarding the angular Abdi, who made two nice hooking shots, one from six feet and one from eleven feet out, each arching softly into the top of the basket. The last shot had everyone gaping in amazement.

The swooshing effect of a cleanly made bucket, no

matter which team made it, sounded like sweet music to David's ears. *'Tis like nothing else in the whole world.*

At half-time, he pulled his players off to the side to discuss something in secret with them. "Now Nevin, when you got to the other end, I want you to . . ." he lowered his voice and continued speaking. Watching, the other team saw David talking animatedly and heads bobbing up and down at whatever was being said.

Both teams were hitting more of their shot attempts now. The score was eighteen to sixteen, with less than three minutes left in the second half. The competition was fierce, but clean. All of the men were drenched in sweat. The older players were breathing heavy with the exertion. But every one of them was having more enjoyment than they had yet experienced on the trip.

"So zis is where you 'ave been 'iding out from me, Monsieur David. You naughty, naughty man, you!"

A throaty feminine voice sang out from near the tables. As David's head jerked around at the sound of his name, crafty Roy took advantage of the momentary distraction. Before David could recover, he swept around him to receive a pass in the lane from Hugh, and nimbly shoveled the ball over the top of the rim.

David glanced at Mlle. Rousseau with a stricken look on his face. The score was now tied.

Marguerite stared hungrily at David's gleaming, muscled, hairy chest. "Finish your little game quickly, Monsieur. We have zings to talk about."

She watched with unrestrained fascination as he turned back into the fray. Her hedonistic eyes found this new game much to her liking. In her mind, it exhibited all of the males in the most alluring and sensual manner possible.

With the contest even, David went into hyper-competitive mode. He thought now was the time for his team to attempt to execute that set play he had devised and discussed at the end of the first half.

He and Nevin passed the ball back and forth to advance all the way down the court. Then Nevin held the ball head high, out in front of him, positioning himself at the free-throw line, facing out from the bucket. First Andrew, next Finlay, in rapid succession, crossed over from their high wing to low wing positions, using Nevin's body to screen their men out. Nevin tossed the ball in the corner to Finlay, who had gotten more separation from his man than young Andy did from his opponent. Then David, working in front, feigned a dash on one side of Nevin then cut back around the other side, causing Roy to slam into the big man.

Unguarded now, David sprinted to the basket with Nevin trailing along. Finlay threw a quick bounce pass to David, who took one step and laid the ball up with his right hand against the center section of the wall just above the basket. The ball hit the wall and fell into the bucket.

"Time's over, laddies!" Duggie called out to announce the end of the game.

David's team had won, twenty to eighteen.

Chapter Fourteen

avid shook hands with teammates and opponents alike before heading toward the table where his undershirt and dress shirt had been folded.

"You play zis game *very well*, Monsieur David. What is eet called?" Marguerite boldly stepped out to intercept him coming off the court. As he stopped, she reached out to touch and pat away some of the beads of sweat entangled on his chest still heaving with exertion.

"Tis called...please dinna do that. I mean, I'd rather you didna..." his voice trailed off, apologetically.

He felt ill-mannered, correcting her like that. From early childhood on, he didn't like, and avoided whenever he could, confrontation with the opposite sex. On his very first day of school, at noontime, he had mistakenly sat in an older girl's spot in the dingy break room where most students ate their pitiful lunches.

"Go on, ye little brat. That's me place yer sittin' in." Fifth grader Molly Gordon, who looked more like a boy than girl with her red hair close-cropped and wearing one of her father's old battered flat caps, had smacked his face resoundingly. His cheek bright red, young David simply got up, embarrassed. He tried yet another desk, and was again rejected. Finally, he found an unclaimed spot in the far corner, next to pretty Rosie McDonald. All this he did without saying a word in irritation or self-defense.

While he could fight the toughest of men, he was uncomfortable being inhospitable or disagreeable with females of all ages. However, he was even more uneasy having the impulsive French woman touch and rub him with his shirt off. David was not a prude; he was just respectful of himself and other people, particularly ladies.

"Let me wipe down and get me shirt on, Miss Rousseau. Then we can talk more at ease." He took one step forward, but then stopped. "And, tis called Basket Ball, miss," he added.

As he hurried to the table where his clothes lay, he turned his head and called out over his shoulder, "I'm glad you came to watch the game, I am. Very kind o' you. I'll be interested to know what you think about it."

Using his undershirt as a towel, David wiped his wet frame. He stood for a minute letting his body further cool down, then slipped the dress shirt on and turned to face the waiting Marguerite.

Arms folded and toes tapping, she eyed David with undisguised amusement. "You know, Monsieur David, zat most French men I know would be puffed up like zee rooster if a really good-looking woman, like moi, admired zere bare chest.

"Are you embarrassed by your physique and

appearance? Non?" She smiled like a cunning cat about to catch and consume a helpless canary.

"You know I am very attracted to you, oui? And I'm sure you find me *most* attractive, oui? I cannot imagine otherwise, Monsieur. I have no competition among zee pitiful group of women on zis ship."

She reached out and felt his chest beneath his shirt, startling David.

"You are so unlike French men. Zey are so vain about zere bodies. Monsieur David, maybe zat's what I like about you. So natural, you are. Like a big, handsome, unspoiled boy."

Marguerite tilted back her head to one side and openly examined him.

"So, tell me more about zis game zat you were playing just now."

Glad that her hand was next to her body and not his, for the moment, David proceeded to explain the game of Basket Ball. The more he talked, the more excited he became. She listened with feigned interest for five minutes. Suddenly, in mid-sentence, Marguerite put one hand on her hip and waved her other forefinger in his face to stop him.

Frowning slightly now, she put both hands on her hips.

"I'm not sure I really like zis new game of, what you call eet, Basket Balling? I zeenk, perhaps, you like eet better than the ladies, non? Maybe, eet is more competition to me than all zee women 'ere put together."

Patting his chest one last time for effect, she nodded her head, and said, "Let me zeenk about zis question." Moving her hand up, she gently patted and stroked the side of his face, leaving him blushing furiously.

She smiled broadly at the effect. "I will see you later, Monsieur David. Stay away from zee other women, hey? But maybe you want to stay away from zis Basket Balling, too."

As she strode away, her shapely hips swayed like a pendulum beneath her long loose French skirt, riveting every man's eyes to the sight. David watched her walking for a few seconds before shaking his head free.

That was the last thing he needed to do: get involved with any female where the circumstance didn't have his Lord's stamp of approval.

No! Be strong, he reminded himself.

Of all the women on board, Mlle. Rousseau was the most dangerous. She had a more refined level of craftiness, intelligence, determination, and resourcefulness than any other lady. David was a full red-blooded male and he certainly had the requisite impulses and desires. But he had always been a gentleman and had always guarded against his lusts. Even with Rose. Seeing as how she had broken off the engagement, he was doubly glad he had kept his virginity.

In retrospect, he often thought perhaps that was one reason Rose had left him. She wanted sexual fulfillment; he was willing to wait until after their vows. At any rate, he was certain he wanted a Godly woman for his wife, if and when the Lord brought her across his path. The over-sexed Mlle. Rousseau did not fit that description.

In the meantime, David would remain constant for the Lord.

That means playing a whole lot more Basket Ball. He grinned to himself.

So it did. Like magic, word of this exciting new game spread to other men on the ship. Passengers and seamen alike turned up the next evening, first to witness, then to participate in the sport. From that day on, the other half of the small mess hall filled at 6:30 with men and older boys queued and waiting their turn to play Basket Ball. The atmosphere was electric.

As could be expected, many of the women began to crowd in around the tables to watch the men. Both sexes began to look forward to these after-dinner contests as a fresh way to relieve some of the monotony of ship life. Almost all the children on board gathered to watch the action, too. There were only so many games of pinochle, backgammon, cards, and dominos one could play, so many books, old newspapers and magazines that one could digest, so much stale conversation and old gossip one could stomach.

To the uninitiated, the sport seemed fast, furious, and exciting.

Meanwhile, the ship was approaching its next destination. With luck and fair weather the *Ayrshire* would reach Perth in four more days. It would unload cargo and a few passengers and take on more supplies, goods, and new people. There the ship would also refill its many coal bins for the difficult last leg of the outbound journey. It would travel around the north-western coast of Australia, below southern Indonesia past Timika in western Papua now called New Guinea, through the treacherous Maluku islands, and around the Luzon tip of the Philippines into the exotic city harbor of Hong Kong.

After docking in Hong Kong, the *Ayrshire* would follow the eastern coastline of China, stopping next at Shanghai, and then arriving at its final port of Tianjin, some seventy miles from inland Beiping.

After he got to know the character of the young man, Captain Wotherspoon had asked David, as the only ordained minister on ship, "Lad, would you like to take charge of the Sunday morning worship service? Take over for me, hey? You attended the first one, so you know it's held in the main dining hall at ten-thirty sharp."

"Aye, captain, I'd like that very much," David smiled broadly at the prospect. "I'd be most honored." He grasped Ian's outstretched hand and shook it vigorously.

Wotherspoon's eyes twinkled at MacDougall's enthusiasm.

"Reverend, you do realize that while your topics will be articulated for those of the Christian faith, we have passengers of other religions aboard this ship: Muslim, Hindu, Buddhism, and the like. Understand that on a vessel with paying customers, everyone is welcome to attend. It's possible a few other persuasions may show up. So you must take care to make your sermons as accommodating as possible without losing sight of the central message, hey? No heavy-handedness, shall we say?"

To that, the reverend agreed. David's heart was inclusive because the gospel was inclusive. All men were invited. All men were equal in the sight of God.

He was excited as he prepared. This was a chance to do a little bit of what he had been called to do.

Bless the Lord, I finally get to evangelize! His sermon experience had been limited to nervous performances in front of the stern-looking United Missionary Society review board the two months preceding the trip.

The next Sunday David finally got his opportunity to preach before a live audience.

Chapter Fifteen

By ten-thirty that morning, seventy-one of the eighty-seven passengers plus eleven members of the crew, all off-duty, had crowded into the big dining room. There were not enough chairs for everyone, so nine men surrendered their places to the young girls and older women. Word had spread that the handsome and likeable young reverend was to be preaching the service, and attendance swelled to nearly triple that of the previous Sunday.

The Gang of Four came, all dressed in their most expensive church finery and sat at the closest ends of the lengthy tables facing the front open area.

"Och aye, a *fine* lookin' man o' God you be," the Madam called out just as the service was starting.

At the next table, Annabelle sat preening and shifting her profile to present the most attractive contour to David's view. Emma had brought her Bible, and looked at the reverend with quiet anticipation and a bit of a smile, too. Marguerite, a non-practicing Catholic, made a calculated late appearance at 10:47 to completely upstage the others. She marched in and stood waiting impatiently up front until finally, an overweight middle-aged male passenger sheepishly gave up his excellent first-row seat to her.

"Zank you, monsieur. I do appreciate it," she gave him a bored smile as the heavyset man pulled himself up and nearly tripped over his own feet, causing her to have to back up to avoid being knocked down. Her smile this time was hard-set, and her eyes flashed at the poor man.

"Forgive me. Tis sorry I be, Madam," he mumbled, shuffling off around the corner.

A squat wooden liquor bar had been requisitioned as a makeshift pulpit. Standing beside it, David witnessed the man stumbling away, and watched the various manipulations and facial expressions of the four women with an air of tolerant bemusement.

He stepped behind the podium. There was a still in the room. Every eye was on him.

David waited another minute, letting the anticipation build and savoring the excitement within himself. Finally, he lifted up his hands. "Please stand. Let us open with prayer. After which, Captain Wotherspoon will lead us in some songs o' faith."

Chairs scraped back as everyone stood.

"Oh Lord, we be a thanking you for your goodness and mercy. For the multiple blessings you bestow on us each and every day. Open our hearts to your awesome and ever-living Word. Keep us in perfect safety as we each o' us travel to our own destination, both on this trip and in life itself. Tis in your glorious and holy name we pray. Amen."

He peered over at Wotherspoon to see if his choice of language met Ian's approval. The captain nodded ever so slightly. David stepped back to let Wotherspoon briskly lead the assembly in three well known hymns.

Scattered here and there on the tables were a dozen well-beaten hymnals, but few used them. Most of the people, whether rough-hewed or cultured, poor or middle-class, were religious to some degree and knew the words from childhood. It was a different time and place; although the Victorian Era with its veneer of strict public morality and social restraint had officially ended, replaced by the Edwardian Era with its greater emphasis on wealth and power, the outward appearance of religiosity was still important.

Wotherspoon had a fine natural baritone singing voice of which he was justly proud. To his left, a quartet of ladies including sweet-natured Mrs. Chesterfield formed a small but fervent choir.

David stood behind the captain singing the old songs with all his might. Of all church activities, he especially enjoyed high-spirited praise and worship. From an early age he and his brother had been predisposed toward things of God. Their father Jonathan was an example of a good man who influenced his sons and daughter.

David belted out the last hymn, "What a friend we have in Jesus...All our sins and griefs to bear...And what a privilege to carry...Everything to God in prayer."

The final chorus ended. The captain and ladies stepped backward to their small row of seats set to the back left of the pulpit. Mrs. Chesterfield gave David a warm encouraging smile before she turned away.

Somehow the familiar verses still touched his heart. David wiped the corners of his eyes. Clearing his throat loudly to cover up his softness, David looked up at the crowd.

"Today's message is on the Great Commission. That awesome command o' our Lord to carry His gospel o' love and divine forgiveness to all those who be willing to hear His story. If you have your Bible with you, please turn with me to Matthew 28:18-20 and Acts 1:8."

He waited several seconds for people to find the text. "Now please follow along silently as I read out loud: '*All authority has been given to me in heaven and on earth. Go therefore and make disciples of all the nations, baptizing them in the name of the Father and of the Son and of the Holy Spirit, teaching them to observe all things that I have commanded you; and lo, I am with you always, even to the end of the age.*' Now let us go to Acts: '*But you shall receive power when the Holy Spirit has come upon you; and you shall be witnesses to me in Jerusalem, and in all Judea and Samaria, and to the end of the earth.*'"

He paused to let the words sink in and the Holy Spirit open hearts.

"The Great Commission is one o' the most important passages o' scripture in the entire Bible. Tis Jesus' last words o' instruction to His disciples before He left earth and be His last words to His disciples today. Tis an urgent command to all who be in the Lord's army. Tis a Christian's call to action, the bugle sounding forth to charge, toward the host o' the lost and dying world before us.

"If you be a true Christian believer, meaning, you've personally accepted Jesus' sacrifice on the cross as payment for your own sins, you've acknowledged His Lordship over your life, and you've committed everything you have or ever will be to Him, then the Great Commission applies to *you*.

"Let's be takin' each verse piece by piece, and see exactly what the Lord is a saying to us. *'All authority has been given to me,'* tells us that Jesus, as the only begotten Son o' God and as part of the Triune Godhead, has all authority in heaven and earth. Authority to be a establishing, growing and nurturing the Kingdom o' God in our world. The scripture implies that because He has power, all believing Christians have power. Brethren, you might rightly ask, we also have been given power, but to do what? Is it the power to be self-centered and amass earthly treasures only to consume them on our own persons and loved ones? Is it the power to be unfeeling, unloving, and unkind to those around us in clear and dire need? Is it the power to retreat into our own private sanctuary o' life, unfettered and untouched by the multiple troubles o' humanity?"

He pounded the countertop of the liquor bar, sending forth a dull booming echo from inside the thick wooden walls of the heavy cabinet.

"No brethren, a thousand times *no*! But let's be seeing exactly what the Lord has in mind for those o' us who be soldiers in his glorious army. He commands us, '*Go therefore and make disciples of all the nations*'. Now a disciple is one who learns at the feet o' a master, and then goes forth to speak and teach what he or she has learned as they know the truth to be. That means whatever we, as fellow Christians, have gained from our Lord and Savior, whether it be forgiveness, or love, or restoration, or healing, or virtue, or humility, or obedience, or circumspection, or freedoms, we are to go forth and share our personal testimony o' salvation and eternal life in this world and in the world to come, to every human being we can, with the help o' the Holy Spirit."

As the spirited sermon continued, many of the women present were moved to emotion and a delicately whispered "Amen" could be heard at times. Some of the men, particularly those who had begun playing Basket Ball with David, clapped their hands or pounded their friends on the back whenever he made an especially stirring comment.

Almost all the players came, even non-Christians, to support their new coach. Three of the leading ladies—the Madam, Annabelle, and Emma—made a show of dabbing away tears from their eyes at opportune moments with their dainty silk hankies.

Marguerite, however, sat watching the handsome reverend with a detached, almost clinical, eye; imagining him in a partial state of disrobement in a much more private setting.

Her catlike stare was disconcerting to David. More than once, as their eyes met, he had to shift his gaze to others in the listening audience.

"Finally, brethren, being as we are to spread the good word o' the gospel to Jerusalem, Judea, Samaria, and the uttermost ends o' the earth, it behooves us to tell others what Jesus has done for us. First, we are to do so at home to our family and relatives, our closest friends, and our associates. Then, we do so to people we know or meet from further away. And lastly, we are to willingly share the good news with people and strangers from afar."

He looked out over the crowded room and surveyed the upturned faces with a piercing expression.

"God's call, His glorious call, is for all true Christians to share their faith with all sincerity and hopefulness to all they be a meetin'. Whosoever the Lord causes to cross your path in life, you have the obligation and the great honor to tell them about your wonderful Lord and Savior."

He raised his hands, motioning the ship's packed congregation to stand up.

"As most of you know, I be bound for the distant city of Beiping, China. Tis a calling I received me freshman year at the university."

He paused for effect.

"The calling is as real to me as the air I breathe, the food I eat, the sun I feel, the sights I see. God is so real. His words are so real. His plan and purpose for your life is so real.

Reach out to him. Reach out, and he will meet you more than halfway, I assure you."

He bowed his head and said, "Let us pray."

Chapter Sixteen

After the service, the captain took David aside and spoke to him in the main bridge. A staid and highly liberal Church of England adherent, Ian Wotherspoon was uncomfortable with outright evangelism and muscular fundamentalism. To cover his own discomfort, he again took the tack of reminding David that people of non-Christian faiths might be attending.

"Reverend, you may want to, ah, *tone down* your intensity in future sermons, hey? We want a nice soothing service without too much emotionalism. Nice effort for a first try. Maybe a wee too heavy it was, in spots. But, all things considered, a good job."

"Aye, I'll try to do a little bit better, sir," David said with a wry expression.

Wotherspoon didn't bring up specific examples, thereby relieving David of making specific commitments. On the other hand, he could not but speak the plain gospel. It was embedded in the very core of his being.

It seemed that David's forceful sermon and its demonstration of genuine godliness only brought out greater lust in the Big Four. "Sech a studly man o' the cloth. I'd like to be a takin' him on a Sunday picnic in the woods, jest the two o' us," exclaimed the Madam.

The presence of such a delectably innocent morsel only ignited their competition to new heights.

Except for David's jogs, late afternoon Basket Ball games, and Sunday morning services, he made himself scarcer than ever; spending more time in prayer alone in his room, or sneaking off to the baggage storage compartment to weight-lift heavy boxes and cartons for hours on end.

With the end of his trip and Beiping nearing, he sought the Lord's guidance and direction with all his might. "Heavenly Father, just give me strength to hold out, avoid temptations, and continue doin' the right thing."

All of his meals were taken with the captain or in the crew's mess, where every mother's son of them had sworn an oath to keep their harried Basket Ball coach's frequent dining there a secret.

One more day remained before the *Ayrshire* reached Australia.

The Madam would be debarking in Perth. She had a "professional partner" left over from her rollicking past who lived just outside the city, one who would be setting up the redoubtable Madam O'Mallory in a co-venture of pleasurable means servicing eligible male companions.

Annabelle Dougherty was also leaving the ship in Perth. Having reverted to her maiden name and eager for a fresh start after the death of her husband, the vivacious Miss Dougherty had a female cousin who owned a prosperous laundry and dry-cleaning establishment. Business was booming in the rapidly growing city and the cousin wanted to open another shop run entirely by Annabelle. As her cousin gleefully noted, Perth was also booming with good-looking British soldiers as well as an abundance of young West Australian men.

"Ooh, I'm a lookin' forward to a takin' real special care o' me best customers, Gladis. Personal attention is whit they need," Annabelle had written her cousin beforehand. Handsome young men were exactly what the prime of Miss Annabelle Dougherty was seeking.

Marguerite Rousseau would be staying with the vessel until it reached the eastern central coast of the Philippines across from Manila. There, the sultry Mlle. Rousseau would take a rowboat escort to shore to meet her oldest brother, Philippe. He supervised a large farming plantation in the southwest region of colonial French Indochina, or South Vietnam. Together, brother and sister would travel with some of his armed workers across the Philippines and board the company vessel on the Manila side to sail to Vietnam.

Alone among the Gang of Four, only the elegant and intelligent Miss Emma Watson Jones planned to stay on board the *Ayrshire* until its final port destination of Tianjin. Having graduated a year early from a prestigious women's university in London, she had just turned twenty-one. Her family's funds were short, and so she chose to do a cheap version of Le Grande Tour. Instead of touring continental Europe and Russia for the entire summer as many of her well-to-do friends were doing, she was traveling by tramp steamer to that mystical and ancient capital of the east, Beiping, and back again, after a three-week stay in the city with English acquaintances.

Much to David's relief, half of the Gang of Four would be gone in another day's time.

When the ship docked safely at her quay in the Perth harbor, David made sure to say a fond good-bye to Jane Chesterfield, Thomas, and especially Mason the dog. Mrs. Chesterfield had been the staunchest supporter of his enthusiastic Sunday morning messages.

"Reverend, you've been an encouragement to me and my grandson on this voyage. I really, truly enjoyed your sermons. You have a real gift of plainly speaking the scriptures and the truth. Don't ever lose your focus on the Master."

"Believe me, Mrs. Chesterfield, I won't. I can't. Tis belonging to the Lord Jesus, I am. I'm his for life."

He knelt down to pet Mason's gleaming dark red coat for the last time.

"Mister Mason, now you take care o' your mistress and Thomas, you hear? Watch over them and don't let any bad folk come near."

Mason lay down and rolled over on his side in great contentment, letting David stroke his smooth silky coat and pat his thick chest.

Jack King

"Such a smart dog, such a good dog you are." The reverend wove his thick fingers gently around the sides of the animal's face and ears, petted the length of the back, and then massaged the top of Mason's head.

"Aye, you be a wonderful companion. Say! That could be your nickname: Wonder Dog." He looked up at the boy with a grin. "What do you think about Mason, the Wonder Dog?'

Thomas laughed and shrugged his shoulders. "He's only a wonder when it's time to eat."

David laughed, too.

"Och, well, you fine folk must be a going."

He stood up and shook hands with Thomas and held Mrs. Chesterfield's warm hand in his for a second. "God's blessings be on you and your family."

Jane held his hand. Impulsively, she gave the young reverend a tight hug. "I'll be praying much for you in your China ministry, David."

"Thank you, Mrs. Chesterfield." He waved and watched them walk away onto the adjoining wharf, a trace of sadness on his thoughtful countenance.

After Perth, the days passed in quiet fashion. The *Ayrshire* rounded the corner of Western Australia. She kept in sight of the long northern coast of the continent, staying just beyond its treacherous shore waters, changing riptides, and submerged reef lines. Three hundred years of slipshod or unlucky sailors had left the hulks of dozens of rotting wrecks littered closer in to land. The tropical cyclone season ended in early May, but the local sea weather could still be volatile. Captain Wotherspoon was a cautious pilot.

Marguerite sometimes saw David during, or spoke to him before and after, the daily afternoon games. Emma saw him at Sunday worship services, during her infrequent morning walks, or at random times when he was in between activities and going to his next destination.

Mlle. Rousseau had given up her strong pursuit of him.

She didn't like being ignored, or worse, minimized, or worse still, kindly patronized. She decided David was just an odd duck. She admitted to herself that he was handsome, muscled, and intelligent, but he was also entirely too apathetic toward sex for her indulgent tastes.

She liked her men to fall madly and passionately in love with her. It was exquisite to torment those she had little interest in. And even more exquisite to conquer those she was strongly attracted to.

She had heard, of course, about his failed engagement. "But she quit you, oui? Eet is better zis way. Obviously, she was no longer in zee love with you. Foolish girl."

Truthfully, no matter her words, Marguerite had little patience for such childish emotions as broken hearts and tender feelings. To her, sex was a synonym for *war*, and love was another word for *game*. You played. And you won if you could.

At the ripe young age of twenty-seven, she exhibited the strong appetites and casual cynicism of her noble female ancestors; past generations of courtesans and royal wives who had learned to play the jaded sexual politics of the French court with flair and finesse.

Meanwhile, Emma continued her polite and sincere queries about matters of religion before or after church services. Only her enigmatic smile carried a trace of mischievousness that piqued David's interest. She was a refined young woman, but he sensed a hint of playfulness beneath the surface. He thought there was a liveliness within her just waiting to be released.

Besides sleeping and eating, David spent the remainder of his time exercising, playing ball, praying, reading the Bible, or preparing his weekly sermons. Except for the rabid collection of afternoon Basket Ball players, who viewed the sport as the highlight of the otherwise dull journey, the faithful Duggie and the captain were his only consistent companions.

Eager to avoid the remaining two members of the Gang of Four, David steered clear of the main dining hall.

Chapter Seventeen

The next several weeks were mostly uneventful except for the ordinary trials of ocean-bound life. Old Miss Hays was just going to bed one night when a huge rat the size of a young kitten darted across her floor, stopping to nibble a crumb of food that had been caught and then fallen out of her petticoat. It stood on its hind legs, holding the particle with its front feet, eating and boldly looking up at her with its shiny rodent eyes.

"Help! Help me! There's a monster in my room."

The old lady stumbled to the door, keeping her eyes fastened on the massive rat. She opened the door and fled into the hallway, still screaming, causing a great commotion. People spilled out of their cabins to see what the devil was going on.

"I'll get it for ya, ma'am."

Having gone to bed early from playing too much Basket Ball that afternoon, and still half asleep, Bert Miller went in and chased the varmint out the door by stomping his feet and waving his hands. He searched around the cabin for something to use as a weapon but saw nothing except an umbrella in the corner. He dashed back into the hallway.

Amidst yells and screams and swat attempts up and down the faintly lit corridor, the big rodent managed to escape uncaught and unharmed.

A large contingent of fearless, large brown ship rats had scurried aboard at the last port, creating havoc among squeamish female and elderly passengers, but delighting the few children on board and making more work for the two general seamen and the young sailor's apprentice. It took the vessel's four resident cats, numerous rat-traps, and unrelenting attempts by the three humans to eventually kill or catch all of the unsavory invaders.

Coal and food supplies were replenished in Perth. A total of fourteen passengers left the vessel. Six new passengers came on ship, including a young energetic Australian missionary student named Ralph who was bound for a year's tour at a burgeoning Methodist outreach in Beiping. Also added were replacement chickens and pigs as well as one hot-tempered black & white goat that attacked anyone who dared to approach him with its hard head and harder horns.

Naturally, some enterprising hens escaped and by sheer mad luck found their way into the captain's personal quarters; strutting, fouling, and pecking away to their hearts' content before he came back to his cabin that early afternoon. For the next several nights, crew and passengers alike feasted on plump chicken for lunch and dinner. The humorless Wotherspoon was never a forgiving man.

An hour or so after the evening's last Basket Ball game was over, Dugan found David leaning by the forward bow, alone and cooling himself in the gentle night air.

"Ach, aye. There you be, laddo," Duggie flashed his ever-present smile, nudging David in the back as he walked up. The two of them looked out to the darkening sea, the long jagged coastline of Australia bending off into the distant horizon on their right. A half-moon shone feebly through the drifting clouds above, casting intermittent yellow highlights on the tips of the dancing greenish-blue waves.

Finally, the first mate spoke what he came to say. "You know that our dear sweet Capt be not entirely happy with yer choice o' words in yer Sunday mornin' talks."

"Aye, I know. He's scolded me a time or two already."

"Capt says you be a little too evangelical for his tastes, a little too...what's the word noo?" He scratched his head, trying to remember. "Och aye, tis too *fundamental*, Capt said. He likes his religion watered down like his whiskey, he does."

David answered, "I can only speak what I feel inside and know to be the truth. I dinna mean to offend anybody, but scripture makes it plain that the gospel be a sword. It wounds some and heals others, as their own choice may be.

"Ian can certainly remove me as a speaker, if he so wishes," David added.

"Och, no need for you to be thinkin' all that," said

Dugan, appalled. "The captain never said such a thing. Why the crew and passengers would be rebelling, they would, if he tried to stop you preachin'. He just wants you to be toning it down a wee bit, lad, that's all."

"Aye, well. What happens, happens."

Deep in thought now, David exhaled softly. He ran both hands through his thick mane of light-brown hair, and rubbed the heavy evening stubble on his chin. "How much longer tis, until we get to Hong Kong, did you say?"

"Ah, laddie, we should be gettin' there in 'bout five or six more days, if the weather holds nicely."

Duggie looked at his friend's jutted profile. "We'll be portin' for half a day. If you'd like to go ashore and see the sights a bit, well, I'd be honored to have you 'long. Hong Kong be a jeweled queen o' the east, she is."

David broke away from his mild brooding and smiled warmly.

"Aye, that's sounds like a plan, Duggie. Thanks for asking; you've been a good friend, you have. I'll be glad to join you. You know me brother works for the YMCA organization in the fine city o' Boston in America. He said a YMCA office was opened in Hong Kong just three years ago. I would like to see their operation for meself, I would."

In four days' time, the *Ayrshire* reached the eastern coast of the Philippines, directly across from the capital of Manila on the other side of the central island. As pre-arranged, the ship dropped anchor close in and lowered down one of its lifeboats with three persons inside. Two sailors rowed the formidable Marguerite Rousseau to shore where she would join up with her brother and his party to travel back to his plantation in south IndoChina. The sailors returned with the rowboat back to the *Ayrshire*.

The quick-witted and sharp-tongued Mlle. Rousseau couldn't resist giving the reluctant reverend a parting public shot before leaving the vessel. With a fair number of people standing around watching her departure, she called out, "If you ever learn 'ow to make zee use of your body, which is actually very nice and very meaty...." She patted his muscular chest a couple of times before he could pull away. "Or if you learn 'ow to use your 'andsome 'ead for somezing constructive besides zee blushing and talking zee excuses," now she lightly traced both sides of his rapidly reddening face with her lithe fingers. "Maybe someday, just maybe, you will become a real man, hey?

"Au revoir, my pretty little boy," she said, leaning forward and kissing him most passionately on both blazing cheeks.

"Be *bad*, now, hey? Life is much too brief to be lived in such a boring fashion. C'est la vérité."

With that, the mesmerizing Marguerite departed, leaving many of the males present looking slack-jawed and glassy-eyed in her provocative exit.

As she glided away, David shook his head vigorously as if clearing his ears of water. Just then, Emma stepped out of the gathering of onlookers and approached him from behind.

"Reverend?"

He turned toward her. The corners of Emma's ruby lips and dainty eyebrows were tightened slightly in a sweet yet totally rehearsed expression of sympathy.

"I'm so sorry. That must have been quite embarrassing for you."

"Aye. That it was, just a mite."

"She has a great deal of, ah, experience, shall one say, in the ways of the world. And noble ancestors, too, I've been told. But for all that, I'm afraid she's still not a proper lady, wouldn't you agree?"

David rolled his eyes, but said nothing. They stood looking at each other for a full minute. Emma desperately tried to think of some authentic sounding task or request she could make of him, but for once, her clever mind failed her.

Finally, David answered, "Well, I must be a going. I have some things I ought be attending to. It's nice to see you again, miss. I look forward to your presence at the next Sunday service, and whenever else we happen to meet. Tis always a pleasure."

She blurted out, "Reverend, do you play chess, by any chance?" Having conferred with Captain Wotherspoon, she knew he did and that he played it well.

David hesitated. "I be a bit o' a piker. Not much more than a rank amateur," he fibbed, with a trace of guilt.

"I'm not very good myself. But I would love to play a few games after breakfast. If you're willing, that is."

Emma batted her lush dark eyelashes. She, too, could hide the fact that she was a gifted player.

Innocently, she studied his face.

I'm trapped like a rat. Just like the big brown ones the cats and the sailors be killing off.

David knew he had no chivalrous way of escaping. Ruefully, he agreed to play a few games with her the very next morning.

As Emma turned to leave with a satisfied expression on her face, David could only cluck his tongue in defeat.

On the bright side, three down, one to go, he encouraged himself.

The following morning, in an attempt to maintain their respective deceits, the two expert players engaged in a tortured version of suicide chess, each determined to prove he or she was the weaker opponent. The game took twice as long as normal because each person was fixated on giving away but not taking pieces, a mind-numbing situation that required an even higher degree of calculation of possible opponent moves and counter strategies. Finally, after an agonizing period of well over an hour, the contest ended in a draw. Two kings, one bishop, one knight, and three pitiful pawns were all that was left, with no way to get a new queen or force a checkmate.

Emma brushed back a dangling lock of light brown

hair from her lovely face and leaned back in her chair. "I must confess, David."

He glanced up from the board as he had made the final move. She gave him an impish grin.

"I'm not really quite as bad as I intimated." She folded her arms and shot him a rueful glance.

He smiled back.

"Aye, I could tell right off. Even a less than average player should have backed me into a corner with all the pieces I gave up. But you gave away as good as you took. It takes real skill, that."

"Yes, and you're not nearly the incompetent you claim, either," she said accusingly.

They looked at each other realizing the jig was up, and broke out laughing. The next game was played with normal verve and strategy. It took all of David's skills to finally defeat her. She was quite good, and very clever at setting traps for him to fall into.

Emma winked at him and laughed again. "In the words of the great recently departed Miss Rousseau: En garde, Monsieur. Let's play again!"

Part II

Mountain Rats and August Moon

Chapter Eighteen

In another day, the ship steamed into the scenic, breathtaking, mountain-encased harbor of exotic Hong Kong. The mile long view of city lights blazed and twinkled in the early morning mist. For once, David was thrilled to be going ashore. This was part of the celebrated country of China. His newly adopted land and people. His calling.

Dugan stood by his side as he watched the approaching city from the side railing. "Tis beautiful, Duggie. Like a huge sparkling jewel, tis."

Yes, he would get to see the country and witness some of the culture, complexities, and contradictions of life there. *Maybe I'll get to speak to some Chinese locals.*

And then there was the recently opened YMCA with its emphasis on sports, fitness, and leisure activities to entice and strengthen attendees as well as spread the glorious message of the Christian gospel. Perhaps they had heard of the magnificent new game of Basket Ball and already played it there. *If not, I can teach them everything I know.*

He was as excited as a Scottish terrier puppy straining on its leash to be free. China at last!

He had researched the history. He knew that all of Hong Kong, the main island and the adjacent Kowloon peninsula, was a British crown colony. The British also had a 99-year lease on the New Territories surrounding Kowloon including the islands of Lantau, Lamma, Tsing Yi, Kau Sai Chau, Tung Lung, Po Toi, and others, thanks to the Second Convention of Peking signed between the Qing Dynasty of China and the United Kingdom just six years prior.

"Did you know the Chinese call this region Xianggang, Dug?"

"No, dinna know that particular fact, reverend."

David called it a little bit of heaven. When he and Duggie went into the city, he simply had to experience the real China for himself.

"Dugan, I want to be seeing the west side first, before we go to the YMCA." The west side of the island was where the natives lived and worked.

Hearing the Cantonese language and observing the sea of humanity, mostly Chinese men, some in European-style business suits, but most in traditional clothes, flowing in and out and around the shops, market streets and tea houses filled David with excitement. The few petite women he saw in their native dress seemed colorful and alluring to his naïve Scottish eyes.

"Say, let's take a ride on a rickshaw," he enthused, "just to say we did it."

"I be game, laddie, but what about doin' one o' these

here sedan chairs," the first mate replied. He watched two sinewy coolies, one young and one much older, their long, sweaty black queues trailing down their backs, striding rapidly by in step-cadence carrying one of the ornate enclosed litters.

"Too fancy, I think. Let's be a sticking to the rickshaws."

In Hong Kong, the sedan chair was used only by tai-pans, big shots, persons of great status, particularly wealthy Brits living in elite Victoria Peak on the highest, most scenic section of the island bordering the sea on its western half, otherwise known as Mount Austin. David felt as a minister he shouldn't be ostentatious.

Flagging down a couple of passing empty carts, he and Duggie climbed in their rickshaws. Soon they were traveling at a herky-jerky pace along the winding avenue, a continuous parade of exotic sights and sounds filling their senses. Paying the coolies, they entered an elegant-looking tea house. There they did the entire yum cha experience—sampling white, yellow and green hot teas as well as a variety of tasty dim sum dishes.

"Oh me, Duggie, try one o' these bun thingies with the pork inside." The waiter had called it *cha siu bao*. "Ach aye, tis good but spicy. Whew!"

David fanned his mouth and took a sip of his scolding tea, burning the tip of his tongue and lips and bringing tears to his eyes. *Tis well I be a strong Christian. I near cursed like a blue-blooded sailor there. Dear Lord, forgive me.*

Afterwards, they entered a few shops, witnessed the

merchants hawking their silk, jade, and other valuable goods to customers, both foreign and Chinese.

"It is very good. You like? I measure you." One particularly aggressive shop-keeper pressured the men to buy European-type shirts he claimed were made of the highest quality silk.

David waved him off graciously.

"Ah, we're not really in the market, good sir." To placate him, David felt the sleeves of one shirt, "Aye, it does seem like good material. But thankee, sir, no."

The man continued to press them until they got outside the door into the street.

The day was sunny, mildly breezy, and warm for the time of year. Relaxed and sated from their dining, the reverend and the first mate rode a larger double-seated rickshaw past the middle of the city, but then decided to take some exercise. They walked the remaining 15 blocks to the European YMCA located on the upper floor of the Alexandra Building on the British side of the island.

Passing now through the southeastern portion of the island, they wondered at the great affluence surrounding them. In the distance, they could make out the oval outlines and stadiums of a race course. A bit closer in, but still faraway, there were parade grounds and military barracks, the mid-morning sun glinting off the dull gray walls. To their right and well beyond, they noticed cricket pitches and polo fields with lush green grass, nestled like a park among grand Victorian mansions. Everywhere they turned, they saw opulence: stately courtrooms, grand hotels, post offices, tony shops, massive government buildings, imposing museums, and large libraries. It was the height of Great Britain's colonial might and nowhere was elegance spelled out in such abundance as the rich entrepôt that was Hong Kong.

Inside the foyer of the new YMCA facility and offices, David introduced himself and his companion, shaking hands all around with the Y Director, John Roberts, and his young zealous assistant, Edward Henry.

"Me name is David Adam MacDougall, licensed with the United Missionary Society o' Scotland and bound for the Lord's work in Beiping. And this here is Mr. Dugan Sinclair, the venerable first mate on the good ship *Ayrshire*."

"And how long will you be staying in our fair city, Reverend MacDougall?" asked Mr. Roberts.

Duggie pointed to his watch and mouthed the words, "One hour more."

"Ah, we have about an hour before we must be heading back to the ship, sir."

David got an enthusiastic summary of the various programs. He exclaimed, "I'm right impressed, sir."

"Yes, well, jolly good then, Reverend. We also have a Chinese-specific YMCA on the Kowloon mainland with a Cantonese-speaking staff."

In both of their Y's, the Director explained, classes and sessions were available on everything from self-improvement, personal health and fitness, and general life training as well as Christian religious teaching. Exercises and physical activities included boxing, gymnastics, weigh-training, volleyball, rugby, soccer. They even had a class on the uniquely American sport of baseball.

David inquired about their knowledge of Basket Ball. He was pleased to discover they'd heard somewhat about it from other Y's. He lobbied for them to add Basket Ball to their program, eagerly telling them everything he knew and everything he had experimented with regarding the sport, not stopping until Dugan tugged on his sleeve many minutes later.

"So sorry, kind sirs, but we must be a hurryin' 'long. A good day to you, Mr. Roberts, and to you, too, Mr. Henry."

He looked at the reverend with mild exasperation. "Come *on*, David, we maunna be late. Wotherspoon'll throw a hissy."

"Dinna forget about using the backboard and angles in the shooting. Well, good bye, then," David stuck out his hand to shake that of his hosts, but the first mate was already pulling him away.

Frantically flagging rides in the street in front of the building, they rode them all the way in. Arriving at the wharf, they bounded out of their rickshaws, threw money at the coolies, and sprinted down the dock. David was in the lead and Duggie wheezed for breath well behind him.

They made it back twenty-seven minutes past the

one o'clock deadline. People on deck watched them dash in. Several of the boys and girls laughed and cheered. David's Basket Ball mates applauded enthusiastically. A few booed at them in good fun.

One observer, however, was not amused.

"If this was a railroad instead of a ship, you two gentleman would have been left behind," deadpanned the captain. Arms folded, he pointedly stared at Dugan's sweaty face and David's flushed countenance, as they hustled up the gangplank onto the deck.

"Mr. Sinclair, I want to remind you that you are, in fact, a commissioned *officer* of this vessel, as ludicrous as that may seem to me at times. And Mr. MacDougall, you are a *chaplain* on the *Ayrshire*, is that correct? In the future, please set suitable examples for the other crew and passengers, won't you?"

"Aye, captain."

"Yes, sir."

They stood stiffly at attention, like two guilty schoolboys, while Wotherspoon continued to berate them. In the background, they could see almost all of the crew that played Basket Ball watching, hooting under their breath, and slapping their thighs at the hilarious sight of the two being dressed down.

Finally, the captain turned his back to them and strode off, parting the crowd of onlookers, his icy glare silencing all of the watching crewmen as he passed by.

David and Dugan glanced at each other with relieved expressions—the tongue-lashing was over. The corners of their mouths twitched as they struggled not to break into laughter.

Controlling himself, David raised his eyebrows and shrugged, "Well, at least I got to be a tellin' 'em about the Basket Ball, Duggie."

Chapter Nineteen

Forty-seven of the ship's dwindling band of passengers stayed behind in Hong Kong when the *Ayrshire* sailed away. The city was a major port of call for both Europeans and Easterners. Only seven new travelers came aboard and to David's delight, four were oriental. But despite his repeated attempts to make conversation, all four rebuffed him and kept to themselves.

Upon boarding, two of the Asian strangers quickly disappeared. The other two men brought on a long, narrow wooden trunk with carrying handles on either end. Asked what was inside, they eyed each other.

One replied, "Tools. For garden."

"Aye, but all baggage that's not personal items or clothin' to be worn on the trip must be stored in the cargo area," the second mate explained.

"It's the captain's orders," he added. "Sirs."

He didn't usually address Asians as such unless they were rich and of the upper class; he mentally congratulated himself on how un-bigoted he was being.

"*No*. You no take. For garden."

Defiantly, the two men picked up the ends of the chest, glared at Second Mate Finlay Kincaid and dared him to get it from them. "For garden!" they repeated.

"Say, where'd yer friends go off to?" Finlay craned his neck, looking around for the other two Asians, but couldn't spot them anywhere on deck.

Perplexed, Finlay scratched his head. He'd never had this particular problem before.

"Well, I can't allow you to be doin' that, sirs. We'll be a keepin' it nice and safe in the storage room. It's plenty secure there, trust me." Smiling in what he hoped was a reassuring look the second mate reached out for a handle, only to have the closest Chinese man shove him away.

"Ah now, there's no call to be actin' that a way. *Sirs!*"

Frowning now, he stepped back and snapped his fingers at a group of four sailors standing by and surveying the scene. They came up behind the two Asians.

David had seen the commotion and wondered what the fuss was about. He looked across at Dugan and nodded. The two stepped up and joined Finlay on either side.

Surrounded by seven bigger men, including the strapping David MacDougall standing right in front of them, the two Asians backed down. They flung the trunk handles against the ends in frustration and scowled at the two sailors assigned to carry it to storage.

"Where take? We follow," one said.

"Aye, but you must be a leavin' it there for safekeepin'

'til you be ready to depart ship for your final port. Sirs." Finlay frowned at them.

The four men left for the cargo room, led by the aroused second mate.

David observed the two Asians leaving. For the life of him, he couldn't understand why they would react that way. *Most peculiar. Very strange indeed. Perhaps their trunk be filled with jade or other such jewels o' the East. Aye, but for their precious garden, o' course.*

Bemused, he got on with the rest of his day. *Och, well. More Basket Ball tonight after dinner.*

He rubbed his hands in anticipation.

The four Asian men mostly stayed out of sight except for meals, for which they came late to eat every time and huddled by themselves with their plates of food always at an empty corner of the most vacant table.

With Emma the sole remaining member of the Gang of Four, David now felt free to take his meals again in the main dining hall. He tried to approach the oriental men whenever he spied them eating at an empty table, only to be either ignored or waved away.

David saw them just once outside the dining room; he was walking the upper deck enjoying the evening breeze and cooling down after that night's Basket Ball games. He didn't call out to them, but stood by and studied the scene, undetected by the men. To him, the Asians appeared anxious; even nervous.

Tis like they be expecting something important to happen.

He noticed their view was fixed on the massive shoreline barely visible in the thickening sea mist off to the left. Flickering lights were just beginning to come into view on the approaching landfall. In the dense fog and deepening night, the wavering iridescent colors seemed ghoulish and threatening.

Earlier that day, after breakfast, the captain had informed David that about three hours or so after dusk, the *Ayrshire* would be passing close to Shanghai, that bustling, sprawling, chaotic port located on the east tip of the Yangtze River Delta, halfway along China's great eastern coast. Since there were no passengers slated to debark there, and the ship's supplies had just been replenished in Hong Kong, "We won't be stopping," he'd told David, "but sailing on."

David looked at the four clustered men for a minute more and then shook his head. Strange as their aloof behavior seemed it was no business of his, he decided.

He turned on his heel and headed to the storage room. He believed in mixing muscle and strength-building workouts with exercise that aided the heart and lungs. So a quick weight-lifting session was in order before bedtime.

After finding out in the first week of the voyage that the agreeable young MacDougall was a minister, and that he, oddly enough, liked to lift heavy things for exercise, Finlay Kincaid had given David the extra third key to the storage bay, with the first mate's tacit approval. Finlay and Duggie had the other two keys. Old Wotherspoon was kept in the dark. But within a day or two, all of the other crew members learned through gossip that the reverend kept a key and why.

David looked down the hall both ways to make sure he wasn't seen. He unlocked the door and hurried inside. He closed the door and turned the iron dead-bolt. Flipping on the switch for the one overhead light, he saw the elongated trunk that had caused so much commotion.

"Och me. There's the piece o' luggage all the fuss was about. The mysterious jade garden tools." He laughed.

Curious, he carefully lifted up one end.

"Well, I'll be. Tis not heavy at all. Tis the right size and proportion as a barbell, too."

He picked the case up. Kneeling down with his back straight, he expertly balanced the trunk flat on both hands, stood up and began doing military press reps, in blocks of twelve each. After twenty minutes of vigorous lifting, a large brown rat, perhaps the last surviving one, scurried across the floor not six inches from his feet.

"Uhmmm!"

Startled by the rat, David jerked just as he had the trunk fully lifted over his head. Before he could catch it, he lost his hand balance on the right side and the narrow crate crashed to the hard steel floor and burst open.

"What in St. Paul's name? What deviltry be this?"

David stared at the wreckage. Four carbine rifles, one with its stock now partially cracked, lay in the ruins of the wooden case. Boxes of ammunition lay among the guns, two boxes smashed and the shiny metal bullets scattered everywhere.

Click. Click. Click. His brain whirled.

Duggie's booming voice flooded his memory, *'The captain o' that ship foolishly allowed some pirates to come 'board disguised as payin' passengers...the pirate boat approached 'long side with the rest o' the scurvy bunch'.*

David raced to the door, unlocked it and relocked it behind him.

They must not get the guns. They'll be a taking the main bridge first. The captain!

He sprinted down the hall to the steel stairway leading four levels up to the top bridge deck, his body bathed in sweat but his mind ice-cold with battle fury. In a twinkling, David had switched into warrior mode. A minister of God he may be, but he would still fight to the death to keep the other passengers and crew out of harm's way.

Me life means nothing, but oh Lord, the dear women and children.

Chapter Twenty

As was his custom, First Mate Sinclair had just finished his evening inspection of the ship and was strolling back from the aft bridge to the mid-ship staircase to get to his sleeping quarters below on the third deck. Amused by the scene, Dugan watched the young reverend hurdling up from the middle rung of the metal steps onto the deck in front of him.

"David! Saints above, I dinna expect to see you clamberin' up and down the stairs tonight after all yer Basket Ball and yer weight-liftin', too," His brassy voice carried in the still night air.

"Hush now. Quiet, mon." David's face was taut with combat intensity.

"Aye, what's up, laddie?" Dugan whispered, his big eyes opened even wider in query.

The reply was equally whispered. "Just now, in the cargo room, I was a liftin' the trunk o' the Asian men and accidently dropped it."

"So?"

He pulled the first mate closer in.

"So Duggie, there be four rifles with ammunition in that truck." He nodded his head for emphasis. Holding up the key, he said, "I locked the storage door."

Dugan Sinclair stared for only a second. He instantly understood.

"The captain! We needs find him. He's got the only key to the cabinet in his room where the ship's guns be. You go locate him. I'll be roundin' up Kincaid, the chief engineer, and a passel o' stout lads. I've got a spare key to the captain's quarters. If you can't find him, we'll have to bust the cabinet open."

Dugan grabbed David's shirt to keep him a moment longer.

"Gimme yer key to the storage room. I keep mine locked up in the chest by me bed. I'll have a lad round up the bastards' four rifles and ammo outta the storage bay."

"Right. Here you go," David tossed him the key.

"David?" Dugan said.

"Aye?"

"I dinna hear or see anything suspicious on my rounds. I dinna think the other cut-throats be aboard yet. But in this pea soup, it's hard to see more 'n fifteen or twenty feet out in any direction. I suppose they could get their rowboats close 'nough without makin' too much noise, by not talkin' and a bein' careful with the oars."

He ran his stubby fingers through his thinning hair, thinking fast.

"Reverend, we'll meet you on the first deck outside the chow halls in fifteen minutes. We can spread out to the four corners o' the ship to sound the alarm if we hear or see them approachin'. We'll give a shout-out as a warning."

His normally happy face tightened into a grimace.

"One more thing. I'll get six other lads to be a lookin' for the four scurvies already on board. They canna have rifles on 'em; maybe a brace o' pistols but more likely knives. But *hell*—sorry 'bout that, reverend—we've got bigger knives amongst our boys, we do."

They parted ways.

David sprinted to the main bridge, slowing down when he heard the mixed sounds of scuffling feet, soft whimpering, and harsh oriental cursing coming from inside the room. Peering warily into the port window on the partially open door, he saw one pirate clutching Captain Wotherspoon's arm tightly from behind and holding a knife to his throat. There were two thin red lines on the captain's neck where the blood was already dripping down.

A second pirate paced and gestured angrily in front of Ian's frozen figure, thrusting his knife over and over, each time narrowly missing the captain's frightened face and eyes, first on one side then the other. A third man had Emma trapped in the corner with a knife at her breast.

Three against one, and I have no weapon except surprise. It would have to do, David reasoned.

Suddenly, the pacing man stepped over to Emma's

quivering body, motioned the other pirate aside, and cut the top button from her dress. Ignoring her pitiful moans, he turned and leered toward the captain and spat further invectives at him.

It was obvious what the pirate's intention was. David didn't need to speak his language to know. He or they all would molest Emma in front of the captain and possibly kill her first if Ian didn't do whatever it was the pirate demanded.

He'd seen enough.

Moving with lightning speed, he squeezed through the narrow opening and charged before anyone knew he was there. David hit the lead pirate in front of Emma with a brutal tackle, driving his rock-hard shoulder and two hundred twenty-four pound mass into the smaller man's vulnerable kidney area and slamming both their bodies into the second man, who hit the wall and fell unconscious. David leapt to his feet and smashed his right fist flush into the nose of the first pirate as he attempted to get up. He heard a satisfying crunch. A hard left jab to the side of the man's jaw crumpled him to the floor for good.

David retrieved one knife and handed it to Emma. "If either one o' them so much as moves, don't be a scared to defend yourself."

He picked up the remaining knife and turned to the third pirate.

"Now, the odds be even. Now, we'll be playing for

real." His face tightened into a hard knot as he stared at the man. The wrath of the Lord had settled upon him.

To David, Ian's neck looked to be superficially cut a third time. The Asian brandished the blade so close to his captive's skin that David thought perhaps it was not intentional but from sheer shock at his own sudden appearance.

No matter. He intended to save both Emma and the captain without further harm.

"You stay away. I kill. I *kill* him! I kill all you!"

The man slowly backed away, keeping his knife tight at Ian's throat and forcing Ian to step back, too. David could see the captain's left arm was pinned awkwardly behind his back.

Undeterred and calm, David gently tossed his weapon a few inches into the air and lightly caught it flat by the blade end. He held it as if he intended to throw it at his target, much like an American Indian. He brought the knife behind his head with his arm cocked and ready to release. He brought his left arm out straight for balance.

"I used to play games with me brother when I was younger, I did."

He glared at the pirate as he advanced closer.

"We tossed knives at knotholes in trees, crows on the ground, snakes, small varmints, tops o' big flowers off in the grass, whatever we could find to aim at. Got pretty good at it, too. Very good, actually."

David's voice was casual, but his body was taut and ready for action.

He walked in a carefully measured stride toward the scared and jabbering pirate, who by now had his own blade taut and ready to cut the captain's jugular.

Before the Asian could act, David's knife flew. It sank deep in the man's exposed right thigh peering out from behind Ian's trembling right leg.

"Ai-e-e-e-e!"

Involuntarily, the pirate bent forward in pain, pushing the captain's body away. His knife hand jerked outwards and downwards in the direction of the wound, while his other hand momentarily let go of the captain's wrist. For several seconds, Wotherspoon didn't realize he was free.

"Captain!" David shouted. "Move. *Now, mon!*"

Ian snapped out of his paralysis. He stumbled forward until he reached David, grabbing his outstretched hand to steady himself.

Seeing his captive was now free, the injured pirate stared white-faced for a moment, but then regained his composure. Reaching down, he jerked David's knife out of his leg. He screamed in pain and dropped the bloody blade on the deck. He extended his own knife in a mock show of ferocity, stabbing the air repeatedly in David's direction, but hobbling backwards until he felt the wall behind him.

"Others coming. You see. No hope for you. No hope. We kill all in revenge!" he shouted. Beads of sweat trickled down his panicked face. The main bridge room had one door, on the same side as the stairwell leading to the lower decks, behind David. There was no escape for him.

David glanced at Emma in the corner hovering over the motionless forms of the other two Asians. They were still out cold, David noticed with grim satisfaction.

"Emma?"

"Yes?" she replied with a shaky voice.

"Pick up the spare knife off the floor and walk over here."

She did so and stayed close by his side.

"All right then," he nodded at her. "Listen, both o' you. There's not much time."

He gripped Wotherspoon's shoulder tightly, preventing Ian from moving to his other side and thereby keeping both the pirate and the captain in his line of vision.

In a strong steady voice he issued commands. "Captain, take Miss Jones' knife. Kindly escort her to the safety o' her cabin. Then go to your own quarters fast as you can. Doctor up, bandage, whatever needs be, to stop your bleeding. You might find your gun case smashed open. If it be so, that's good. It means Duggie and some boys are already patrolling the deck on the lookout for the pirate ship. You ought be joining them."

He let go of the captain's shoulder and nodded twice.

"But first, send a couple o' men to tie up these three and lock them in the brig. I'll join the party as soon as our guests o' honor here be tucked away."

A muted gunshot reverberated in the thick night air somewhere outside, followed by the sounds of several rifle shots closer in.

"Hurry now, captain. I'll watch our friends here 'til your men show up."

Emma put her still trembling hand upon his tensed forearm.

"You saved me from...you saved my life and my honor. How can I ever thank you enough?" she said. Tears streamed down her awe-stricken face. Shock was beginning to set in; the trembling in her hand spread over her entire body.

Without taking his eyes off the muttering pirate, David softly said, "Tis only what any gentleman worth his salt would do. Getting you out o' harm's way so you can make it to Beiping in one piece is reward a plenty, miss."

He jerked his head toward the partially open door. "Be off with the two o' you now."

Wotherspoon steadied himself. He took Emma by the arm and guided her gently out of the room.

In control of the situation, David stood, watchful and alert, as the agitated Asian continued to hurl horrible curses and dire threats in Cantonese and broken English at him.

"Well, laddie, we can be a doing this the easy way. Or the hard way. You can drop the knife...kick it toward me...and sit down against the wall." David pantomimed each action to make each point perfectly clear, pausing in between for effect.

"That," he raised his eyebrows, "or I can put this knife

into your other leg. Or perhaps an even more sensitive part o' your body."

Once again, he lightly tossed his knife into the air and easily caught it by the blade-end, posturing as if to make a second deadly throw.

Even with the pirate's limited grasp of the English language, David knew the man realized exactly what he meant.

He advanced closer to the pirate and expertly tossed his knife up one more time and caught it in a position ready to throw.

"Aye, man. Tis your choice."

Chapter Twenty-One

Meanwhile, on the leeward, or coastal, side of the main deck below the fore and aft bridge structures, Dugan and his men met together just in time.

"Lads, gather 'round to hear me," the first mate whispered as quietly as he could manage in his big brass voice. "Stay down when you head out," he motioned at them.

"As you're lookin' for 'em, use the side rails to be a hidin' yer faces. Don't be a bobbin' yer head up like a big turkey, 'pecially you, Collin. If you see 'em, make a noise like a bird to the man nearest. He's to do the same to the next man, and so forth down the line, 'til everybody knows they've been spotted. That's there the signal for every mother's son o' you to hurry over to the side they're coming at us."

He held them a bit longer.

"'Nother thing. They'll be a fightin' like devils to get on this ship. Act sharp. Shoot straight. Innocent lives depend on it. Ours, too. We dinna want any more o' these slant-eyed varmints on board, if we can help it."

Bending low, they moved out around the perimeter of the *Ayrshire*. Each man squatted at his station to stay out of sight. Peering through the thick rungs of railing, two sailors saw without being seen. Their pre-arranged alert gathered everyone together at the point of attack, catching the pirates off guard in the four huge rowboats that appeared like shadowy ghosts out of the darkness. Each boat was swarming with Chinese cutthroats.

The odds favored the attackers who had thirteen repeater carbines, three pistols, many knives, and a warrior's sword, versus the defenders who had savaged the three usable carbines from storage plus the four ancient single-loading rifles from the captain's quarters. However, the element of surprise and having the higher ground enabled the first mate and his stout sailors to strike first and wound five of the invaders.

The *Ayrshire* crew kept up a constant volley on the four boats, raising their heads just enough to aim and shoot, then ducking for cover again.

"Dugan, they're a comin' over!"

"Push 'em back, lads! We maunna let them get on board!"

They saw hooked ropes hurled toward the ship out of the thick fog, catching and holding on the top railing bar.

The fighting turned vicious. The attackers had not expected any opposition and were enraged. Duggie's men shot three more pirates as they came scrambling up. The sailors rushed forward to grapple, in hand-to-hand combat with the Chinese who made it over the side. Many of the attackers had wicked-looking knives in their mouths as they climbed aboard. Two had their pistols cocked and ready.

Bewildered at the unexpected defense, some of the pirates remaining in the boats had returned fire without any clear targets while others had hurled their grappling hooks in a panic.

The battle was over in fifteen minutes.

The pirates had counted on their four comrades already onboard to have completed their part of the plan. Fierce fighting was not their forte; ambushing an unsuspecting vessel was their game.

So the skirmish, though desperate and deadly, was brief. The men had beaten off the boarding pirates before the captain and David could even arrive with reinforcements.

One of the defenders was killed as he stood up to take aim, one sailor was stabbed in the shoulder and another hit in the arm, but all things considered, the crew and passengers of the *Ayrshire* were lucky indeed. David's strange habit of weight-lifting items of cargo turned out to be a genuine blessing. His discovery had given the alert and saved many lives.

"Aye, take that, ya bloody brown bastards!"

Duff and Lorne, good friends and mates of the two wounded sailors continued shooting at the departing figures until the boats were swallowed up in the inky blackness of night.

"Aeiiii!" "Wángbādàn!" "Argghhh!" "Gǔnkāi, guǐlǎo!"

"Si fut lo!" By the retreating sounds of cries and curses, it seemed Duff and Lorne had added yet more wounded or killed foes to their tally.

The ship was now twenty-three hours away from the end port call of Tianjin. Wotherspoon asked David to join him for breakfast in his quarters the next morning. David arrived, unsure of what the captain had in mind. He had prepared himself for a sharp rebuke over his unauthorized access to and use of the storage room.

Each man was uncomfortable as they sat at either end of the handsome hand-carved oak reading desk that doubled as the dining table for in-room meals.

The men focused on their eating; solemnly munching their marmalade-spread toast, replenishing their plates with more fried eggs from the huge-iron skillet, and refilling their cups with the steaming potent Ceylonese black tea Wotherspoon was so addicted to.

Ian methodically poured heavy cream into his cup, measured two and a half spoons of raw India brown cane sugar, called jaggery, and stirred thoughtfully before finally breaking the silence. A man of rigid bearing, military pride, and proper etiquette, the captain found it extremely hard to express emotion.

He coughed meaningfully and looked up.

"At the very least, I owe you my ship, the lives of many of my crew, and the welfare of every legitimate passenger on this vessel."

The last was a bitter reference to the legally paid but nefarious presence of the four Asians. He should have been more suspicious. He blamed only himself. Upon hearing the report of the men's belligerent behavior upon boarding, he should have investigated more thoroughly. It was entirely his fault; he couldn't expect Dugan nor any other member of the crew to ascertain such things.

No, he knew it was his omission, his lack of decisive leadership that almost proved their undoing. And only providence and chance saved them all.

"Miss Jones, also, I'm sure, will continue to express her great appreciation. One shudders to think what might have happened if you hadn't turned up when you did, Reverend. My own life means nothing, of course." His face reddened.

"But when I think about the loss of my ship, the deaths and abuses to my officers and crew, the unspeakable acts they would have visited upon the opposite sex and other helpless passengers. Well . . ." Ian reached up and rubbed the red lines curving around his neck.

Embarrassed, he coughed again and stared at the calm pastel colors of a painting hanging on the opposite wall behind and above David's head; a picture he liked very much of the South Pacific Ocean at sunset.

Turned his eyes back to David, he finally and simply said, "Thank you."

"Ah, captain, there be no need to say any—" David began, but Ian cut him off.

"We all thank you. You did a timely and heroic deed, lad: A man of most decisive action, impressive fighting ability, and real courage. In some ways, you remind me of Anthony C. Booth. When I was young and newly enlisted, posted to South Africa, he was a sergeant in the late Zulu wars. He saved my life not once but twice at the Battle of Intombe. He was fearless and cool-headed under fire. A brave man; a natural in battle.

"He won the Victoria Cross," Ian added.

"Sir, the only cross I be wanting to gain is the cross o' Christ."

"Oh, yes. Of course. That brings me to my second point of conversation. In light of how you courageously put your life on the line to save others, I take back my, shall we say, criticism of how you preach. Any minister who can do what you did has the right to speak their religious convictions freely, I think."

David sat up straighter, surprised but pleased at the captain's words.

"I'm much obliged, sir. Very touched, I be. You're a man of, ahhh, strong convictions, and I'm sure twas difficult for you to be allowing that."

They finished the meal, both a bit awkward; one unable to give gratitude, the other unable to receive it.

Wotherspoon rarely smiled in humor, but he came as close as he ever did with his next statement. Pouring yet another cup of tea, he said, "However, now that I know you have that extra key to the cargo bay, I'm afraid I'm going to have to ask you to give it back."

David grinned in spite of himself. He reached into his pocket and slid the offending key across the table top.

"Considering how your deceit wound up saving the ship, I'm grateful, mind you, that you, my first mate, and my second mate conspired to put one over on me."

The captain's mouth struggled to turn both corners up. In the end, it appeared half smirk, half frown, but it was best he could do.

Chapter Twenty Two

Hearing there were other serious chess players on the ship, Ralph Harrison, the young missionary who boarded at Perth, became excited.

"That's ace! Romping good. I was a champion of sorts during my Uni days." Together, he and Emma badgered the captain and David to play a four-person, double-elimination tournament promptly one hour after lunch and to continue the competition that night, if needed, after the Basket Ball games were finished.

A stickler for protocol and circumspection, Ian Wotherspoon uncharacteristically capitulated to their combined zeal. Humbled by how very near he came to losing both his ship and his person, having bonded on some unspoken level with Miss Jones through their shared life and death experience, knowing they had less than a day to Tianjin—he decided it was a small concession to make.

David suspected Emma had engineered the whole thing. But she desired his company and he couldn't refuse as a gentleman. Whether inspired by the dangers of the night before or not, Emma played liked a person glad to be alive and well.

Jack King

She defeated Harrison and even tough Wotherspoon with surprising ease, and bested David in the championship game.

"Oh, what a wonderful match this was, David," Emma clapped her hands and beamed at him. "Well played on both sides; a truly amazing contest. But when you moved your King to F3 and your rook to E4, I thought I was done for.

"Ahhhh," she sat back to savor the moment and eyed him mischievously, "but it's awfully sweet to win, you know. Even sweeter to just be *alive*," she added, smiling a brilliant smile. Emma swept a lock from her happy face and tucked it behind her ear.

It was almost half past eleven when the four went to bed, nearly two hours past normal retirement time.

Earlier that evening, to David's intense delight, before the Basket Ball games began, the men had gathered around him to present two brand new soccer balls such as what they used for playing Basket Ball: One for him to use, and one as a keepsake. The second mate had secretly purchased them in Hong Kong. The latter had the inked signatures of every player crammed all over the top and bottom halves. Around the middle of the sphere was a written message, which Finlay solemnly read out loud:

"Rev. M., best coach & watchman
Fr the Basket Ball addicts of Ayr."

"Not only did you teach us 'bout a crackin' good sport, and how to play it. But I'm o' the mind you also saved the whole darn ship and a good many lives by soundin' the alert on those murderin' skunks. So, it's our own skins we be a thankin' you for, as well as learnin' us the spankin' game o' Basket Ball."

He looked around at the crowded boisterous faces.

"I'm a thinkin' that every Mother's son here feels much the same way." Heads nodded up and down.

The second mate handed the gifts to MacDougall and kept his right arm extended out. David balanced both footballs in the crook of his left arm and shook the offered hand with his right.

Despite his resolve, David became misty-eyed. His voice was husky as he replied, "No, twas the good Lord above that saved all our lives. He it was that put the very thought into me mind, to even be doing a late night workout before retiring to bed. Me natural habit, as Finlay well knows, is to work out with the weigh-liftin' in the mid-morning or afternoon."

Overcome with the feeling of camaraderie and bond of teamship, he stared down at his feet in an effort to contain his emotion. He dabbed his eyes before continuing.

David raised his head and breathed in deep as he surveyed the assembled men with great affection. They had become his Basket Ball mates, his friends, and outside of daily prayer his main outlet for relieving stress.

"No, men, in this case, I was but a simple messenger, at best. I can be taking no credit. Anyone o' you would have done the same or better, I'm sure."

Regaining his composure, he grinned, "But when you talk about the excellent sport o' Basket Ball, aye, *that* I can be a taking all the credit, which I humbly do, and hope that none o' you loggerheads forget it, nor stop playing in the months to come."

"Aye!"

"Hear, hear!"

"Och, aye!"

"Never, laddie!"

"No way, mate!"

"Well then. Aye, that's settled." David rubbed his hands together, "Well, let's be a playing!"

The men eagerly paired off into teams of five to start the first game. Since this was to be David's last chance to play Basket Ball on ship, the goodwill and competition among everyone was the usually spirited.

It was hard clean sport at its best.

Chapter Twenty Three

After the heart-pounding events of the previous evening, the *Ayrshire* pulled into the ancient Chinese port of Tianjin without further incident shortly after midnight. She docked unnoticed off the main quay, ready for her bulk of passengers and crew to debark the next morning.

David, Emma, and Ralph were among a company of nine traveling on to Beiping, some eighty miles over rough and hilly terrain.

"Hey mates, let me try to talk to them. That one old man there seems to be a leader of some sort."

Ralph, who had learned a few basic words in Chinese from a college professor who studied Mandarin, attempted to barter using his tiny vocabulary and sign language. In the end, between their limited Chinese and the guides' limited English, the group was able to communicate well enough to rent three large ox-carts with the owners as escorts to carry them and their belongings to the great city.

David had read that only a few thousand miles of train track existed in all of China. None was laid yet between the port Tianjin and the capital city. And so they had to travel by foot.

It was the last day of August. The weather was hot, muggy with the breeze from the sea, and overcast but otherwise fair, with no storm clouds in sight. They would have to camp that night beside the rocky winding road and complete their journey late the following day.

David took the precaution of asking Wotherspoon if he could take a couple of the carbines along with ammunition from the splintered remains of the pirates' trunk in the cargo bay.

"Captain, I've been forewarned by several o' the crew that the mountain regions to the north, northwest, and west o' the city o' Beiping be teeming with bandits like those that attacked the ship. Travelers between Tianjin and the capital city are not safe either. I don't care about me own life, understand, but there will be three ladies traveling with us. We men must be able to protect them, at all costs. Praise God, the rascals were not armed with guns the other night in the bridge room. Else all three o' us would have be dead and Miss Jones ravaged as well, but for the tender mercies o' the Lord."

Ian gravely considered the matter.

True, the weapons were the property of the vessel as confiscated goods. But then, he owed his ship and likely his life to the brave young man standing in front of him. After a pause, he replied, "Reverend, why don't you take the three undamaged rifles and most of the cartridges for your needs. I'll keep the gun with the broken stock to add to the ship's store."

"Agreed! Much obliged. Thankee, Captain." They shook hands.

Unknown to Wotherspoon, David also kept three of the confiscated pirates' knives. He was very good with a knife; better even than with a gun, at which he was proficient. He knew if fighting became close quarters, a rifle was useless except perhaps as a makeshift club.

By twenty past ten in the morning, the party left the outskirts of the bustling port city for the dusty road: A collection of twelve people plus six ill-tempered oxen. There were two animals to each cart, pulling large wagons filled to the brim with more valuables and personal items of wealth than the accompanying wizened, bow-legged Chinese men together with all their children and all their closest relatives could ever hope to own in several lifetimes.

The three ladies crowded onto the weathered seating of the leading ox-cart so that they could gossip and pass the long miles ahead with some companionship.

David strode ahead of everyone, a loaded carbine cradled in his left arm and a knife tucked in his belt. Behind him, the Chinese men plodded alongside their beasts. They used walking sticks to strike the oxen on their massive haunches whenever they veered off the path or reared their heads in agitation.

The young missionary Ralph hurried to catch up to David, brushing away the swarms of summer gnats with a continuous Aussie Salute as he strode forward. He kept his carbine barrel tilted skyward and it bounced across his shoulder as he walked. David had also provided him with a knife.

"G' Day, Reverend."

A lazy smile crossed his boyish face, as he waved away more gnats. "A bit of a blue with the bushrangers the other night, hey?"

David gave him a friendly smile back. That was one trait he appreciated in the people of Australia. As a rule, they tended to be more easygoing, unruffled, and cooler-headed in the midst of danger than many men he knew.

"Aye, twas a tad touch n' go, but the Good Lord saw us through."

Just then, a flock of birds rose nosily from a thick grove of gnarled trees off to the left of the approaching curve in the road. They both stopped. David stared at the spot, his right hand now rested in the trigger guard and the barrel pointed at the trees. Ralph brought his gun into position and aimed toward the spot as well.

They walked past the thicket but saw or heard nothing suspicious. MacDougall relaxed. *A fine Australian I'd be making*, he thought ruefully.

Glancing over at the young man, he said, "Aye, you were asking me the other day and I told you where I'll be a working, which missionary group, when I become a Christian, and where was I when I got me calling.

"How about yourself, Mr. Harrison? Tell me your story."

"Well, to begin with, my family is fairly well off

compared to many of my countrymen. It's both a blessing and a curse. We've got one of the larger jumbuck herding—excuse me, that's sheep—ranches in all of Western Oz."

He saw the quizzical look on David's face. "Oz, that's Australian for the Western part of the country."

He laughed heartedly.

"We Aussies have a weird sense of humor and our own twisted version of the King's English. Any ways, it's a third-generation ranch."

He looked at David. "My two older brothers have been slated since birth to eventually divide the property between them, and take over once my dad retires for good. The rest of us will get a share of the profits each year. Assuming, of course, they don't run it into the ground."

Ralph exhaled heavily and shook his head. "Yow, but my two youngest brothers, God bless 'em, are total bludgers."

He glanced back at David and laughed again.

"*That's* Australian for layabouts. What I mean is, all they do is get rotten drunk, trash things, and do the naughty all the time. One nearly got killed by a jealous husband over an affair. And the youngest has already gotten two poor single girls in the family way. Both times my father had to pay for, well, you know," he blushed.

David didn't reply, but encouraged him to continue with an understanding look.

"Except for my granddad on my mother's side, none of my family is religious. But from the time I was a little boy, I always had an aching, I guess you could call it, in my heart—deep inside. Like there was something missing. I always wanted to know more about the Creator. So I started going with granddad Sunday mornings to the Methodist church in Mingenew, which is the nearest town to our ranch. I became a Christian at the age of fourteen, and shortly after, knew I was supposed to be a minister. Or something.

"Because he had the money, once I finished high school, it was no problem for dad to pay for Bible school and seminary training in Perth. He was glad to do it. Figured it was cheaper in the long run, and a lot less embarrassment, than posting bails and paying off damages. You know, having at least one son who was religious rather than a rake."

Ralph sighed, and shifted the burden of his rifle to the other shoulder, a look of urgent responsibility etched upon his youthful face.

"I hope someday to persuade the rest of my family of the love of Jesus. Someday."

He turned toward David, a sudden grin on his lanky, sun-burnt face. "My assignment is to join the pastoral staff at the Wesley Methodist mission in south Beiping. Help them grow. Add members. I'll be like a roving evangelist for them in the city. I'm very excited about the opportunity."

"That's wonderful, lad," David acknowledged the tale with an encouraging nod. He looked back over his shoulder to see how the rest of the group was faring. He saw the three ladies on the front cart sharing two umbrellas to block the mounting sun. They were getting along famously, to gauge by the giggles and laughter. He couldn't help wondering how much of it was at the men's expense.

The Englishman, Edward Simpler, he noticed with satisfaction, was trailing the caravan and keeping a sharp lookout with his carbine at the ready.

Edward was a former soldier. He was the sole passenger to join the ship's crew in the recent battle. David felt he could trust him to stay alert. The other three gentlemen were strolling along close to the second ox-cart, unconcerned about the dangers of highway travel in northern China.

David gritted his teeth. All of those men, he knew, had been asleep when the pirates had attacked the *Ayrshire*, and the next morning when they heard, had thought it wonderful sport and jolly good excitement.

He just hoped they didn't suffer any more such 'excitement' between here and Beiping. A band of cut-throat bandits twice their numbers and armed to the teeth would find the group easy prey. The Chinese guides, he feared, were likely to bolt and run at the first sign of trouble, leaving them with three guns and knives to defend against who knew how many robbers and how many weapons. The three gentlemen would probably be worthless in an actual fight.

He gripped the stock of his carbine a little harder.

"Lord, be a keepin' watch over us," he prayed under his breath, renewing his vigilant watch of the road and terrain ahead.

Chapter Twenty Four

Past noon, the group found a comfortable grassy area underneath the intertwined majestic branches of some ancient Chinese lacebark elm trees.

They stopped for a quick lunch. David and the ladies shared their food with the three Chinese men, who liked the cheeses and hard-crust French bread loafs. The Asians especially loved a rather large strawberry jam tart that Emma saved out of her lunch basket just for them. She tore it into three equal pieces and gave one to each man, who wolfed it down.

"Xie xie ni," said the oldest Asian. *"Xie xie,"* said another, nodding his head up and down in appreciation. Emma nodded and smiled in response.

At that, one of the Englishmen popped opened a tin with a great flourish. "Here, old chaps. Have a bite of *bully beef.* It's on me. Yum, yum. Eat up." He made vigorous chewing motions and sounds, and offered some to the Chinese, who didn't understand what he said except "Eat", but did comprehend his silly sign language.

The man winked at the other two Englishmen sitting

with him. He exclaimed to the watching Chinese, "This is what all red-blooded British soldiers eat. Gobble, gobble, now."

He was grinning like a Cheshire cat. David frowned at the joke. He thought the Chinese would not like the salty, tasteless, formless meat product.

Having sampled and enjoyed the cheese and bread and tart and a bit of cold baked chicken, the Orientals readily agreed to try this, too. Their mouths scrunched, however, into intense grimaces, and they immediately spit out the dark brown goo in deep disgust onto the ground in front of them. Bully beef was the British military equivalent of the American soldier's corned beef. The Asian men didn't like it any more than the average Tommy or Doughboy did.

The three Englishmen all howled with amusement, while the rest of the party looked on with disapproval. Emma scowled at them. David thought that no good would come of humiliating their guides.

Before journey's end, our very lives could be depending on the reactions o' these Chinese men. Bad behavior only breeds more bad behavior in return.

But David said nothing.

The group picked up plates, utensils and food leftovers. Their journey resumed.

They traveled through nightfall, the luminous full August moon shadowing everything in its soft buttery light. The Chinese guides picked a small hilly wooded ravine with a natural opening in the middle of the standing trees as a suitable sleeping spot. This lay off to the right of the road a hundred yards or so.

"Aye, Ralph, Edward. Come here."

David signaled to them as soon as the caravan halted by the copse of contorted and stunted timber. Compared to the taller, thicker, well-tended green forests of England, this seemed like an oversized thicket to him.

"Let's be taking a walk, lads, to, ah, inspect the grounds." He nodded toward the woods.

David led the two men in a broad circle beginning close to the rugged highway and around the proposed campsite. He noticed the location was sheltered from the direct view of any nighttime wanderers on the road. But that also meant it was possible for anyone to approach their camp without being seen themselves. From the west, north, and east, the denseness of the scrub woods, the pockets of undergrowth, and the small ridges and gullies all provided visual protection for any bandits who might be in the area. Only to the south could they see past the rise of their own ravine into the woods and beyond.

"Gentlemen, the three o' us ought, perhaps, to stand watch tonight; maybe four hours on, four hours off. Something like that. Two men on guard at all times." He looked at his companions.

"Most assuredly."

"No worries, mate. After all, we've got to protect the women folk."

"Tis agreed, then. Ralph, you and I can be a taking the first watch and let Edward sleep first. You can wake him up in four hours to relieve you."

"I say, old chap, you're not planning to catch some shut-eye yourself?" Edward asked.

"No need, I slept like a baby last night, what, with all the excitement o' the past two days and all the hard Basket Ball playing? Hoots, man. I was out like a log as soon as me head hit the pillow last night.

"I'll be fine. Now, let's go see what kind o' mischief the good ladies have gotten up to in our brief absence. We'll set the watch shortly." The three men laughed.

Back at the site, the women had all voted for a campfire. They didn't need it for cooking. Dinner would be more cold chicken, cheese and bread. But a bonfire was a romantic idea, the evening was turning a bit chilly, and they thought a crackling blaze would be a comforting sight to fall asleep to.

David had his doubts, as did Edward and Ralph. A big fire would be noticeable from far away, and make it even more difficult to see into the contrasting darkness of the surrounding woods and brush for enemies.

David hesitated before speaking. He didn't want to offend the women, but on the other hand..."Och, ladies, I'm a thinking it may not be such a good thing to do. We all know there could be bandits close by, and, well, it might not be wise to call attention to where we be."

He raised his eyebrows. Edward and Ralph both nodded in agreement.

"Oh, come now. Don't be such a drag, old sport," blurted the Englishman who had baited the Chinese at lunch. "After all, it's nighttime. We're roughing it in the wilds of China. We could use a spot of light, hey, to see what we're doing. I'd like to read some more of Kipling myself before I'm off to bed. After all, my good man, it's for the ladies," he added. "Buck up."

The other two Englishmen took his side.

Outnumbered, David conceded. But now he was determined more than ever to keep a vigilant post until morning.

Despite their tendency to mask their feelings, the inscrutable Chinese stared in disbelief as they watched the Englishmen and the women gather kindling, small limbs, and chunks of wood. Their eyes darted nervously from one another to the still-harnessed ox-carts tethered to stout saplings on the west side of the forested ravine and to the impenetrable blackness of the surrounding trees and thickets.

If the bandits came, they would sacrifice the Yangguizi, the foreign devils, and perhaps even the Nu Laowai, the female foreigners, animals, and wagons to save their own skins.

The three Chinese men took their tattered bedrolls and made pallets at the southern-most edge of the ravine clearing, far from the roaring campfire and away from where any attack would likely come. When dinner was served, they refused to join the crowd around the blaze and instead ate their dried fish, two-day old buns, and a mouthful of peanuts.

Emma had to carry to them what she had demanded and parceled out as their portion of chicken, French bread, and cheese.

The insolent Englishman called out after her, "Now sweetheart, you don't want to waste any more of our excellent English food on them Chinamen, do you?"

She let out a deep breath of frustration and kept walking. David could only shake his head at the stupidity and prejudice of some of his fellow human beings.

This time only one of the old Chinese men acknowledged her thoughtfulness. Taking the food from her, he solemnly said *"Xie xie ni,"* and nodded respectfully. As she walked away, his dark brown eyes remained solicitous and his eyebrows knitted together in concern.

Watching her slim figure return to the others by the fire, he whispered gently, *"Bǎozhòng, xiǎo tian shir."* Take care little angel.

Chapter Twenty Five

At midnight, Simpler woke young Harrison to take his post at the north edge of the small clearing. Over on the west rim closer to the road, David sat staring into the scrub forest. He leaned against the trunk of the widest tree he could find, blocking the flickering light of the dying embers of the campfire. His sharp eyes had adjusted to the darkness. Above, the soft glow of the sinking full moon cast a silver sheen over everything, enabling him to spy deeper into the gloom toward the nearby path.

He believed any attack would come from that direction.

Suddenly, David heard faint rustling off to his right, then a muffled crack, as if a man or beast had stepped upon a dead branch buried under leaves.

They came furtively from the northwest, hurrying now after the accidental alarm, all armed, stooped low among the stunted trees, weaving in and out of the shadows to avoid detection. Through the milky darkness, David's keen vision counted eight men. Sinister black figures rushing forward intent on mischief and murder.

Dear Lord, forgive me for shedding blood.

But he aimed at the closest spectral shape and resolutely squeezed the trigger. He had to kill to save innocent lives.

The shot slammed into the side of the man's head, just above his ear. Brain tissue and bone fragments burst from the skull along with the half-spent bullet which, by chance, barreled into the fleshy part of the throat of an unlucky comrade coming up close on the opposite side. The velocity of the slug was still enough to give the second bandit a mortal injury, piercing the neck through his throbbing jugular vein.

In a heartbeat, the first man pitched lifeless to the ground as the lethal shot connected. The second man jerked to his left, dropping his gun in shock, and reflexively grabbing his throat. Blood gushed from the massive wound. Words garbled as his vocal cords flooded. In death-agony, he fell, then twisted and rolled convulsively on the forest debris damp with evening dew.

David quickly aimed and shot at another foe, hitting him full in the face above the cheekbone as the man turned toward the flash of gunfire.

The unexpected sound of rifle shots and the sight of three of their own men falling down put the rest of the bandits into a panicked rage. They were the ones being attacked! Their element of surprise was lost.

The air filled with cursing.

In the near darkness, they could see the blaze from David's second shot and immediately opened fire in his direction. David ducked behind his tree as two murderous volleys struck its thick trunk on the opposite side chest-high. More bullets thudded into the ground just past the tree.

Then another rifle rang out on David's far right.

At hearing the shots, young Ralph had stirred awake at his post. He had just been falling asleep and come to ashamed and groggy. Rubbing sleep from his eyes, he gaped at the host of bandits off in the distance.

"David! Mr. Simpler!" he yelled out in fright before raising his gun.

"They're here! The bushrangers are here! The Chinese!"

Behind him, he heard shouts of dismay and fear in English and Mandarin coming from the campsite. The noise of battle had aroused the sleepers.

Ralph's panicked first shot barely wounded his hastily selected target. His gun burst alerted the bandits they had another foe. Vicious return fire erupted from several rifles, peppering the grass near him and scaring Ralph so that his next shot was wild.

Unlike David and Edward, he had chosen ground that provided more ease than safeguard. He had moved from Edward's original hidden spot to a more comfortable location. He knelt exposed in the middle of a grassy half-circle of small saplings that offered little protection.

"Umph-h-h! Dear Jesus."

Bullets tore into his right leg and left shoulder. Ralph managed to get off one more round before he collapsed in pain, striking an onrushing bandit in the foot.

Suddenly, a gray figure emerged out of the flickering firelight of the camp into the circle of saplings.

"I'm here, Ralph."

Edward Simpler reached Harrison's fallen form. He kneeled down, simultaneously raising his weapon to blast away the hobbling Chinese man bearing down on them with his gun. Edward's bullet hit the bandit in the chest, causing the man's shot to go wide.

Two more bandits ran at them, one from either side. Ralph struggled to get his gun up to shoot before he fell back, overcome from loss of blood. Edward heard a blast. He felt a hot searing sensation in his gut. He only had time to fire an answering round into one foe before the other was on top of them. Instinctively Edward swerved his knelt body to the left, causing the other's shot to miss. At the same time, he swung his gun across his body like a club with all his might into the second robber's rifle as he fired again. The barrel-to-barrel blow knocked the aim off just enough, causing the bullet to merely graze the outside of his bicep.

Taken aback at Edward's tactic, the Chinese man stood, surprised, for a split-second before launching himself at his enemy.

"Aeiiiii! I cut heart out, foreign devil."

Quick as a cat, the bandit threw down his gun, jerked aside the barrel of Edward's rifle, and pulled out a wicked looking ten-inch knife.

"Not tonight, you bloody bastard," Edward Simpler cursed.

He'd seen tough combat in the British army. He'd killed men before in hand-to-hand battle. Though middle-aged and injured, he was still a hardened, experienced adversary. But he was in a deadly race against time and he knew it. Shrugging off the increasing effects of shock upon his body, he fought savagely, steeling his mind against the growing pain and numbness.

"You vicious, murdering chink. I'll make damned sure you've killed your last innocent victim."

Edward's breath came in rugged pulls now. With the man so close in, he pitched his own rifle down. Leaping up, he grabbed the wrist holding the knife with both hands.

The two men grappled for several moments before Simpler slammed one knee hard into the crotch of the thrashing Chinese, bending the man over in agony and thrusting his face forward. Edward had been a skilled boxer in his youth. A powerful left jab, then a second, then a right cross rocked the outstretched chin of his foe.

The man was dazed and his mouth bloodied, but he stubbornly held on to his weapon. He began slashing wildly to keep Edward at bay until he could clear his head.

The two men circled one another warily now, looking for openings.

Both the younger slimmer Oriental and the aging thickset Englishman were wheezing for air in their life-and-death struggle. Edward dodged a knife slash, and lunging forward he regained his grip on the man's wrist. He held the razor-sharp knife with his right hand, and with his left Edward twisted the thumb of the weapon-wielding hand back upon itself until the bone snapped.

There was loud shriek.

The man fell to his knees. The knife dropped. Stooping to retrieve it, Edward took one look at the tortured face of his foe before driving the knife deep into the heart of the bandit.

"You've killed your last innocent Englishman, you yellow swine."

Then Edward, his strength spent, toppled next to the dying man and the injured Ralph. He didn't know if he was dying as well. He could do no more.

Meanwhile, one bandit kept David pinned down behind his sheltering tree with a furious barrage of bullets. Of the eight bandits, five were dead or dying, one was severely injured, one had a mere flesh wound, and the one firing on David was unhurt.

The bandit with the slight gash raced out of the forest into the camp, intent on revenge, harming whoever got in his way. Rage consumed his being. All he knew was that many of his comrades had been surprised and killed.

Murder and more was in the Asian's heart, and David was unable to stop him.

The bandit quickly shot two of the Englishmen in the back as they attempted to flee. He missed the third man. Two of the Chinese guides had long since fled south down the road toward the city. But the old man who had been most cordial to Emma over dinner hung back, lurking behind a twisted old tree-scrub on the south bush-line to see what would happen to the young woman.

The three women huddled together on the far side of the spent campfire, holding each other and watching the approaching Asian with naked fear. Emma prayed with desperation, "Lord Jesus, succor us in our hour of need. Send down your guardian angels to protect us. Heavenly Father, I beseech you."

Normally, the bandits would take alive the most promising hostages, rich-looking Western businessmen and especially any white women and children. These they would be able to exchange for money from their associates in Beiping or in the mountains who had contacts with missionaries, government officials, friends, relatives, or others who would pay for the person's freedom.

Rarely could they sell unwanted Western girls or children as human property to associates. Not many natives wanted the foreign dogs even as sex or labor slaves. The bandits killed the few European victims they couldn't ransom. But they found a ready market for any Chinese captives they got. These they sold, their own countrymen, as slaves to rich Chinese.

This bandit, however, was not interested in captives or ransom.

With most of his gang dead, he only wanted vengeance.

Money alone, no matter how much, could not appease the horrible hatred the Chinese man held in his heart. These foreign devils must suffer and die.

The bandit surveyed the three women as they gripped each other and backed up as he advanced. He decided the oldest one was expendable. He smiled cruelly.

"Chòu bai biǎozi," he hissed and laughed. The bandit raised his rifle and shot her in the face as she screamed her last.

The other two appeared more inviting. His lust began to rise. Holding the gun on both of them, he walked forward, stooped down, and pulled the belt off the fresh corpse.

"Kòutóu!"

When they didn't move, he shouted in English, "Down! Down!"

Keeping the gun on them, he made the lesser attractive one lay on the ground as he roughly tied her feet together tightly with the cinched belt. He would have her later.

Now there was only the one—the prettiest and youngest one. The one he intended to have his way with, over and over, until he tired of her and decided to end her miserable life.

He wanted no trouble with the girl. In a blur, the bandit swung his rifle butt into Emma's frightened face and knocked her unconscious. He didn't need her as a partner; just her naked unmoving body would do. As the Asian man laid his rifle down and concentrated on removing and ripping the bodice, skirt, and undergarments off the motionless form, he didn't hear the faintest of footsteps behind.

Before he knew it, an angry trembling voice lashed out in condemnation.

The bandit spun around in surprise and stooped for his weapon.

It was missing! Instead he saw an aged Chinese man pointing the rifle at his midsection and jabbing its long barrel at him like a bayonet.

The bandit sneered, drawing his knife. He doubted the lǎo tóur knew how to use such a sophisticated weapon. He licked his lips, hesitating for a moment. He studied the old man's face trying to gauge whether he would really shoot or not. Then yelling a battle cry, he charged at the wizened figure.

A sudden rifle crack rent the night air. And another.

The bandit's eyes widened with shock as he stumbled forward onto his knees. Unbelieving, he gazed down at his silk top-shirt and saw two red dots become two seas of blood that stained his heaving front. He rubbed his hands over his chest and brought them up to his face, staring at the crimson droplets falling off his fingers.

The bandit looked up at the old one. He moaned once and keeled over, stone-dead.

Chapter Twenty Six

The old man dropped the rifle like it was hot coals burning his hand. He had never killed anyone in his long life. Yet he couldn't just hide and watch helplessly while that vicious *shān shǔ*, that mountain rat, molested and murdered the young girl.

Time stood still for the elderly man as he stared at the fallen foe. A full minute passed. He heard sporadic shooting off in the distance. He heard the tied up white woman moving around to the side of him. But he kept his dark eyes fastened on the unmoving figure on the ground. The bandit could be playing possum, he feared.

Blinking furiously and sticking out his tongue to the side of his open mouth, he finally faltered forward a few steps.

"Xiǎoxīn," he muttered to himself. Gingerly, he prodded the prone body with his foot, once, twice, and then kicked hard several times. The bandit was really dead.

"Please, kind sir. We must help Emma. Please."

He looked up.

The other English woman who had been tied up was loose now, pleading and motioning him to Miss Jones' side.

Jack King

Already, she had rearranged the bit of clothing that had been torn or removed, putting her own coat around the still form so that Emma was decently covered.

Together, they lifted her up into a sitting position. As they did so, every aged line in the old man's countenance deepened with compassion. Tears glistened at painful memories of long ago. When he was middle-aged, he had a beautiful young daughter much like this one. She was about to be married, but was stolen by a band of evil robbers in the employ of a local warlord. He never saw or heard news of her again.

He wouldn't let it happen a second time!

"Xiao tian shir," he repeated, tenderly moving away the long flowing locks with his free hand from the front of her pale face.

The other woman looked across at the old Oriental and simply said, "Thank you for saving our lives." It was the first time on the trip she had spoken to any of the Chinese guides. The man didn't understand many of the English words, but he knew the meaning, just the same.

"Bùyòngxiè," he replied, nodding his hoary head.

Slowly, Emma gained consciousness.

Off in the woods, three more shots echoed in the cool night air; two reports followed by one answering blast. Then silence.

David came into the edge of camp, carrying the curled figure of Edward in his arms. As David approached, they could see the front of Simpler's shirt was stained scarlet, his face was ghostly white, and around his mouth little bubbles frothed.

David knelt on one knee and laid him carefully on the dry ground next to the dying fire.

"He's been hit," he explained. "'Tis below the lung and heart, thank God. Hopefully, it missed his stomach to the left, but I'm no doctor. He's lost a lot o' blood, he has."

Rushing away again, he called out over his shoulder, "Ralph's been shot, too. I'll be back."

Five minutes later, David reappeared with Ralph in tow, bracing the injured man up under his good right shoulder while he hopped forward as best he could on his uninjured left leg. David's arm was wrapped around the young man's trunk, and Ralph's right arm was looped around David's neck.

Ralph, too, had lost blood, though not as much as Edward. He was disoriented and in shock. It had taken some coaxing to bring him around and get him into a standing position so he could hobble with David's help into camp.

David eased Ralph into a sitting position beside Edward next to the fire. Ralph groaned as his wounded leg made contact with the ground.

"Shot in the left arm; shoulder, that is, and in the right thigh. Both bullets went through without hitting bone, it seems. 'Cept for his bleeding, Ralphie's actually in fair shape."

He looked down at Simpler's still form. The man was

tough as nails; he hadn't moaned or cried out once with his injury. "Aye, tis Edward I be most worried about."

He bowed his head to pray earnestly. "Dear Lord Jesus, right now, I be asking you to supernaturally touch Edward's wound. Ralph's, too. You are the great physician. By your stripes, the Word says, we are healed. Cause the bleeding to slow and stop. Protect them from any infection. Ease the pain. Cause healing to begin and help us to get them safely to human doctors. In your holy name, we be a praying. Amen."

Abruptly, he walked off to investigate the rest of the camp grounds and the south woods. He found the bodies of the two Englishmen near the back of the clearing, but no sign of the third man, or of the two Chinese guides. All of the bandits were dead and accounted for.

"What I want is fresh clean cloth, long strips, lots o' it, for bandaging up the wounds o' Edward and Ralph," he muttered to himself.

He looked over at the unhurt English woman. She could help him search. He raised his chin at her and then nodded in the direction of the ox-carts.

She immediately understood. Leaving Emma to the care of the old man, she joined David.

He knew they needed medicine, too, if he could find any in the group's belongings. Plus alcohol, even liquor, to help fight infection and germs.

David feared there could be more roving bands in the area. He knew they best get moving. There was no time nor tools to bury the three victims. As much as he hated leaving such a dreadful scene without ceremony or committal for the dead, he could only take the bodies on to Beiping, and trust the Chinese authorities or associates of the deceased would claim them and provide a decent service.

Reaching the ox-carts still tied to their trees on the western edge, the English lady and David began rummaging with great haste through the belongings on each wagon. They were lucky to find several laundered and starched white shirts in one suitcase and two bottles of premium Scotch whiskey in another.

"Aye, very good."

One travel case yielded a pack of aspirin tablets, plus a container tin of prescription pain-killer. "Ahhh, even better."

Most helpful of all, another piece of luggage had a small ornate decanter filled with medicinal elixir made from powdered heroin.

Rushing back to the center of the camp with their treasures, David beckoned to the English lady. "I'm sorry ma'am, but I never caught your name."

"It's Samantha Agnes Johnston. Miss Johnston," she smiled tremulously at him. "You're the reverend. David, is that right? Emma has talked about you quite a bit since we started. Non-stop, actually. I feel I know you quite well." She smiled again and looked at him slyly.

David blushed. He could only imagine what had been said about him.

They both glanced over at Miss Jones at the mention of her name. They saw Emma was now sitting up by herself, but massaging her temples as if she had a horrible headache.

"Miss Johnston, could you please be a taking the shirts and ripping long strips, however you can. Try to make 'em extra long."

He looked anxiously up at the sky and into the woods. "We ought make haste. I want to leave here as quickly as possible."

Reaching down, he pulled out the confiscated pirate's blade stuck in his belt. "Here's me knife if you need it."

She took it and measured and cut a lengthy piece of cloth. "Like this?"

"Aye. That's perfect. Make the rest o' them just like that."

The elderly Chinese guide comprehended immediately what they were doing. He went over to them, but first patted Emma on her shoulder and shook his head up and down, as if to ask if she would be okay with him leaving her side.

He knew only a few English words. "Help you?"

Joining the others, he made a tearing motion with his hands. "Help."

"Aye, glad we be for you to assist us, me good fellow," David gave the old man an encouraging smile. As the Chinese man and Miss Johnston worked making bandages, he hurried to the still form of Edward, whose eyes were open but whose face was pasty and drawn.

"Here, Edward, here. Take one o' these pills."

David gently cradled up Simpler's head to make it easier for him to swallow. "Take a swig." MacDougall raised an opened bottle of Scotch to the man's lips and poured a small amount of the fiery liquor into his mouth.

"Now drink this. You'll feel better. It'll help numb the pain."

He gave the injured man a sip of the potent elixir with heroin in it. Tenderly, he lifted Edward's dirty and bloody shirt up over his head. David cleaned the gunshot entrance wound, staunched the flow, and wiped away the blood using a small cloth soaked in the whiskey.

"Reverend?"

Miss Johnston and the old man had several long strips ready. She held up a handful for him to see. David tied the pieces together end-to-end to form one very long bandage.

"Help me here," he motioned with his head at Edward's still form. Together, they lifted him into a sitting position. She steadied his body from behind, while David wound the bandage firmly around several times, binding up Simpler's injury securely from front to back, and covering everything with a clean pressed dress shirt found in the luggage search.

David took his time. Replacing the bloody shirt with a fresh one, binding and dressing the wound, all called for arm-lifting and body-shifting. They had to be careful not to further rend his injury. Edward had already lost much blood.

With Samantha's aid, he cleansed and bandaged up Ralph's injuries, too.

As he finished, David sighed heavily. With injured people to care for, the remainder of the journey to Beiping would be even more difficult.

David glanced up and saw the elderly Asian squatting and gently patting Emma on her back. The old man, he noticed, kept his personal drinking water in an old animal pouch, a pig's stomach that had been long since cleansed and tied off at the bottom. He had taken one of the spare cloth pieces and poured some water on it for Emma to use as a wet compress against the purplish bruise on her throbbing head.

David looked on tenderly. He understood.

The Oriental had risked his own life to save Emma. It was obvious the Chinese man felt protective toward her. David could see there was a bond of some sort between the old one and the young English woman.

David walked over to Ralph, who was now more alert and sitting up. He asked him how to say a phrase in Mandarin. Walking back, David shook two aspirins into the palm of one hand, took the whiskey bottle in his other. He walked over to the Chinese man, and pantomimed eating and drinking.

"Nǚháizǐ yǐn." He repeated slowly to make sure his pronunciation was clear, *"Nǚ-hái-zǐ...yǐn."*

The old Chinese man nodded. *"Chàng re,"* he answered.

David let the Chinese man give Emma the two tablets washed down by sip of Scotch to ease her pounding headache.

Running his hands through his hair, frowning a bit, David took stock of their situation. "Dear Lord, we've got three injured people on our hands."

One, he thought, was critical and life-threatening, one was serious but not grave, and one mild. He looked up at the purpling sky. It was less than two hours to full daybreak. Getting Edward and Ralph professional medical care was imperative, as was getting away from the danger of further attacks. That meant the party needed to reach the safety of Beiping as fast as possible.

He crammed all of the luggage and possessions into two carts, discarding unnecessary items, leaving one ox-cart free for Edward and Ralph to lie down. David took clothing from the deceased persons' belongings to make a pallet on the hard wagon floor for the two injured men. With David's arm around him again, Ralph was able to hobble over to the cart.

"Hate to be such a wussie, mate," he said, stifling a moan as David helped boost him over the side, spilling him onto the makeshift bedding.

Edward he had to pick up and carry. When he climbed into the front seat, his foot slipped a bit, rocking Simpler and causing a brief groan, the only utterance of pain he had heard from the man all morning. "Och, Edward, so vera sorry."

More carefully now, David eased up into the seat then stepped over into the back bed and lay Simpler down with the utmost gentleness.

He had already decided he would manage their cart,

leading the procession. Emma would ride on the second cart, with Samantha walking beside and controlling that wagon's ox. The Chinese man would drive the trailing ox-cart, his wagon, as before.

The corpses of the two Englishmen and the woman he lashed down, unceremoniously, atop the jumble of luggage and cargo in the last cart driven by the old man. There, the stiff bodies bounced an inch in the air with every big bump in the road. MacDougall hated the gruesome sight but there was no help for it. Having decided against makeshift graves at the campsite, he had no other way to transport the deceased to Beiping where, hopefully, their business, family, or other contacts would claim ownership and make arrangements for decent Christian burial or return home.

Before they left, he collected all the weapons—rifles, pistols, and knives—along with any stray ammunition he could find in the field of battle next to the eight fallen bandits. He also gathered up Edward and Ralph's rifles. All of these things he piled into at the end of the cart bed below the two injured men. He made sure his own rifle was full of ammunition, and he let the Chinese man keep the robber's gun since it had a full chamber.

"Listen up, everyone. If we be attacked again, everyone is to gather by me wagon. Miss Jones and Miss Johnston, you ladies ought climb inside, if that happens. The bed of guns and knives winna be the most comfortable, but there's still a bit o' room at the foot where you can sit, get down low, and take cover. You can be handing down bullets to me and the old man or even other weapons if we run out of ammunition."

With the morning sun just beginning to drive the shadows away from the dark mass of twisted trees, thick scrub, and tangled groundcover to the east, the weary frightened party set out on the road again.

David fervently prayed under his breath, "Heavenly Father, I'm a askin' that our road ahead be clear of any more trouble 'long the way. And, above all, give us good speed."

Part III

The Christ is Lord

Chapter Twenty Seven

David's band met few travelers on the lonely highway that day. None were going their direction northward to the capital, and just two small groups were making their way southeast to Tianjin. There were no more bandits either. David wondered if news of their battle had somehow become known.

Thank you, Lord. Edward seems to be holding steady, he does. Thank you for keepin' us safe.

David looked back at the little caravan. He noticed the old Chinese man walking close by the side of the cart with Emma in it, and he smiled for the first time that day.

David stopped the convoy often to give Simpler and Harrison more swallows of the elixir of heroin. The face of the older man still seemed deathly gray to him.

It was mid-afternoon when they finally approached the bustling outskirts of the great city, Beiping. As they drew nearer, they saw in the distance on either side of the winding highway an increasing number of dusty, unpromising rural villages. Each village was surrounded by its own brood of humble farms, most worked by tenants held in slavery to the local warlord, but some owned and operated by the same bloodline family for countless generations.

David had studied the history of the city in preparation for his missionary assignment. Beiping, he knew, was also called Peking by some Westerners. It was a historical metropolis, China's ancient and current capital, constructed with a series of concentric walls encircling the city outward from the emperor's opulent palace continuous in all directions. He had learned that much of the current city had been built during the powerful Ming dynasty.

Traveling further in they saw lavish buildings, ornate temples, magnificent stone walls, and huge gates throughout the city. The entry gates were originally intended to create awe among the common people and demonstrate the power and affluence of the emperor. The city's very design was to maintain the royal ruler's Mandate of Heaven while providing layers of protection against external enemies; an elaborate scheme of fortifications, surrounding, in turn, the mystical Palace, the Imperial city, the inner city, and the outer city.

They came through a myriad of heavy gates with archways, watchtowers, barbican towers, sluice gates, and enemy sighting battlements. David noticed some guard turrets had moat protection like the medieval European castles he'd seen pictures of in grade school books. He looked up in awe at the partial ruins of the massive towers and gates as they went deeper into the city.

They passed through teeming neighborhoods, markets, local businesses, and hordes of Chinese residents. In the center of the metropolis was a largely intact wall of imposing grey stone and brick that protected the inner city with its massive Tiananmen Square and other wonderful things. The Tiananmen Gate separated the inner city from the Imperial zone and Forbidden City to the north. Qianmen, also called Zhengyangmen, guarded the entrance to the Square from the south. The Great Qing Gate, later called the Gate of China, was located in the very heart of the great Square.

A significant portion of Tiananmen was filled with a labyrinth of shops and alleyways. At the time, large gardens and parks also sat adjacent to the Forbidden City, affording a veritable Eden of peacefulness and tranquility where the rich and elite among the Chinese came to relax.

Once within the walls of the outer city, David guided the caravan through the crowded noisy streets. His destination was a satellite office of the Missionary Society. Before he left Scotland, he had procured a detailed and useful map of streets in the city given to him by a Society minister, Spencer Mulhanney, who just returned from three years assignment in Beiping. The man had been a civil engineer before converting to Christianity and becoming a missionary, and he was meticulous to a fault. The map was his creation.

"David, you just stick to this, and you canna go wrong, lad. See here, it has the street names labeled both in Mandarin and English, me boy. I've also handwritten *precise directions* on how to get to the outer Society office traveling from the main south gate entrance."

David followed the map's instructions precisely. He had no margin of error for getting lost; knowing Edward's life might depend on prompt arrival. An hour or two extra might be too late.

Journeying further into Beiping toward the oldest portion of the city, the party began to see, sandwiched between business districts, narrow lanes or alleyways which intersected and connected together in groups of four houses, each group sharing a common courtyard. As sightings of these four-house clusters multiplied, David turned and walked back toward the old man. He made a sweeping motion at some of the courtyard-styled homes they were passing and held his hands out questioningly.

The old man understood him and said, "Siheyuans."

"*Si-hey*-ones?" David pronounced the word slowly.

The old man nodded his head. "Siheyuans. Yes."

Soon they noticed entire neighborhoods formed by joining one siheyuan to another. When asked, the old man called these *hutongs*; one hutong joined to another, as building blocks.

David guessed by the people sitting, standing, or walking in the courtyards, that most were residences. Having heard that the Chinese typically housed several generations together, he wondered if all of these were used as extended family residences. But he could tell Western influence was spreading. A few siheyuans had been turned into business offices with signs outside announcing the enterprise within. The appearance, neatness, and regularity of the hutongs, he observed, improved the further north they traveled, suggesting the neighborhoods in the southernmost part of the outer city were more recent and indifferently built.

But everywhere they looked, the avenues, whether broad or narrow, were jammed with human bodies and beasts: Rickshaws, pull-carts, wagons, pedestrians, soldiers, merchants, businessmen, donkeys, and farmers with their animals of burden. Everyone was scurrying to be somewhere.

David even saw a few people on bikes, a Western innovation embraced as yet only by a handful of rich Chinese who had contact with American and European expatriates who were cyclists themselves.

"Aye, all these multitudes o' people, who have yet to hear the gospel o' Jesus," David clucked his tongue, turning his head this way and that. Ordinarily, the sights, sounds, even pungent smells of so many people—lost sheep in need of the Savior, would have made his evangelical heart sing. But now there was no time. He had three injured persons and three departed souls to deliver as quickly as he could.

Forty-five minutes later, after making their way down one crowded lane after another, the group finally stopped in the central northwest section of the outer city outside a brownish one-story building. David dashed inside; Edward had appeared more haggard and pale when last checked. He was in desperate need of a good doctor and hospital care.

"Is Reverend Baker in? I have a most urgent matter, and I must be seeing him immediately."

A slender freckle-cheeked lady who appeared to be several years older than David stopped typing and glanced up at the handsome man standing in front of her desk. It was obvious he was agitated.

"Yes, may I help you?"

The words tumbled out. "Aye, me name is David Adam MacDougall. Reverend MacDougall. I've been assigned to the Christ Is Lord mission in the city by the United Missionary Society O' Scotland. Reverend Baker was a going to make proper introductions and get me situated. But that can wait."

The intense expression on David's face concerned the girl. "I'm sorry, but he's not here right now. He told me you should arrive today, but we didn't expect you until evening. Reverend Baker had to go out on an appointment, and he's not due back for a couple of hours. Perhaps Reverend Smithers, his assistant, can help you?"

The girl looked hopefully at him.

"Aye, that'll be fine, but call him straightaway. I have three people injured in our traveling party. One person may die if he doesn't get medical attention. I also have three dead people whose bodies ought be reported and given to the authorities."

The secretary stared in astonishment at his words.

He stared back. "Do it now. Please, miss. We've no time to spare."

Startled, she leaped to her feet. "Yes, sir," she said, and hurried down the hall to find the good reverend.

A minute later, a chunky bespectacled man in his early thirties lumbered into the reception area, a slight frown upon his bookish face.

"Reverend MacDougall, is that right?" He hesitantly held out a thick clammy hand.

Tis like shaking paws with a shy miniature polar bear, David thought. *Cold, awkward, and a weak half-grip. Not a good sign. I need a person o' action else Edward may not make it.*

"How may I be of assistance to you?" Smithers said, still frowning. He didn't appreciate people coming in off the street and being sharp-tongued to their secretary, particularly fellow ministers.

"Aye, well, reverend, tis like this. Me party was attacked by bandits on the highway. We were forced to defend ourselves and wound up killing all eight of them, but not before they did their damage. I now have three corpses and three injured persons a waiting outside that need to be taken care of."

MacDougall eyed the shocked and pallid countenance of the man.

"One person needs a good hospital and a trained physician, the sooner the better, or he may die. A second person has bullet wounds to his shoulder and leg, and also needs attention. And the dead persons ought be turned over to the proper authorities along with identification, so that the next o' kin and any associates they have in the city can be notified."

"What? Where?" stammered the flummoxed man. "I mean, you have these people outside? Here? Right now?"

"Aye, me good man," David said, turning on his heel and walking briskly to the front door. "Where be the closest medical facility or doctor?" he called over his shoulder to the trailing Smithers, who was now visibly sweating.

"If you would be kind enough to give me directions there—*quickly*, please sir, time is o' the essence—I'm happy to be a taking the wagon with the injured parties. Also, me good reverend, I'll be letting your people handle the wagon with the bodies and luggage, as well as the other wagon with only the luggage, if you dinna mind."

Turning to the two women, one standing by the side and one looking down from the front seat of the ox-cart, and foregoing formality he addressed the ladies by first name. "Samantha, would you like to be staying here and making arrangements to find your address? I'm sure the Society personnel will be glad to assist you in any way they can. How about you, Emma? Are you well enough to stay here, or do you wish to accompany me to the hospital?"

By that time, the office secretary and two staff members had joined Reverend Smithers outside, all four gawking at the strange and shocking scene before them.

"Lord, have mercy," exclaimed the secretary, putting

her hand to her lips. "Every bit of it's true, then. Oh, you poor dears. You poor, poor souls."

"Candice, can you believe this?"

"Oh, my. This is terrible."

"I'll stay." Samantha answered with a clear strong voice. "I can be of more assistance here."

"And I'll stay with Samantha," Emma quietly replied, moving her long flowing hair out of her face and massaging her forehead as she spoke.

The old Chinese man watched the conversation with interest. He didn't understand but a few words, but somehow he gathered the gist of what was being said. No matter what, he had resolved in his heart to go where the young woman went to protect her from further harm. He had many distant relatives in the city, kinfolk he could stay with, but he intended to make sure the English girl was safe first.

He thought again of his beautiful innocent long-lost daughter. His dark brown eyes moistened and he stared off into the distance, remembering.

The good secretary had recovered from her irritation with David's abruptness. Having seen the urgency of the situation, she now took control with grace and efficiency. She went inside and returned with written directions to the central hospital eight city streets over to the east and two streets up.

Reverend Smithers felt a bit ashamed for his cool reception of David. To make amends, he took it upon himself to go with the man to the hospital. He knew the way. Plus, he thought he spoke adequate Mandarin, enough he felt, to speed up the process of getting the wounded Westerners registered and receiving adequate care. After the horrible tragedy of the recent Boxer Rebellion, latent bias against foreigners was widespread throughout the city. Speaking the language could only facilitate matters, he was sure.

The two men left immediately. David drove the two bound oxen forward as fast as he dared. He would have uploaded the cart of its cache of arms at the Society office first, but feared he had already lost too much time.

"Hang on Edward, both of you. We be almost there. Hang on just a little bit longer, lads."

MacDougall prayed silently under his breath as they hurried along. Smithers prayed out loud.

Edward's face was washed-out; he looked bad. Ralph lay beside him, swaying as the wagon rocked along, groaning now and then with every bad bump and twist in the road.

Meanwhile, Samantha helped Emma off the cart and the secretary led them both inside to plan their next steps. The secretary rousted a young trainee working in one of the offices, her voice crisp and authoritative.

"William, would you please go and watch the two carts. Just keep the beasts from wandering off. Make sure all the luggage and personal items remain where they are, if you take my meaning. I don't think anyone will be walking off with the bodies, though. Call out for me if you have any difficulty whatsoever."

William was an impressionable young man not yet graduated from seminary and was on a year's internship. He had only arrived in the city four days ago and was as green as could be.

He nodded respectfully. "Yes, ma'am, I'll be glad to keep the luggage and bodies safe. I'll...But wait! You said *bodies*?"

"Yes, William, there are three dead people loaded on one of the carts. Just kept them from wandering off, will you?" She patted his flushed cheek.

"Very good. I do appreciate it. Reverend Baker should be back in another hour or so, and he'll know what to do beyond that. "

She started to walk away then turned back around, "You don't mind, do you, William?" she asked in a sweeter tone.

"Oh no, not at all. Not at all," he repeated, shaking his head solemnly. "I'm happy to help, happy to watch the... ah, yes."

He ran his fingers nervously through his mop of dark brown hair. "Anyway, I was just writing out my practice sermon. It's mostly finished. I was polishing it up, and practicing to myself a bit, you know," the young man blushed.

"You're a dear. I'll bring you out some tea and a bite to eat in a minute."

Seeing the old man lurking by the front door, the secretary walked over and kindly guided him inside. She brought him and the women tea and English-style crumpets. But first, she led the three of them down the hall and made them all comfortable in the big meeting room.

Sitting in the chair across from them with a tea saucer and cup balanced in her amble lap, she smiled with genuine compassion and inquired, "Now ladies, tell me the name of the person or organization or business where you will be staying, who you wish to see, and what you've been told of their whereabouts in the city. We'll all figure it out together."

She took a sip of tea before continuing. "The Society will see to it that you get to where you want to go, as safely and conveniently as possible."

She smiled warmly again as Samantha began talking.

Chapter Twenty Eight

When they got there, Reverend Smithers rushed inside, leaving David to stand guard over the two injured men and the ox-cart at the street curb. Peering through the glass door entrance, David could make out Smithers' figure at the reception desk and could hear his muffled voice.

From what he could tell, he thought Smither's command of Mandarin was proving more of a hindrance than a help. However, the stack of currency the reverend had stuffed inside his coat pocket before they left the Society office ought to be a big help in getting quicker service from the Chinese. David grinned at the thought.

David had been in a real hospital just once in his life. It was during his university days. Brian Matthews Taylor, one of his best friends and the scion of a wealthy shipbuilding family, had broken his leg during a rugby game and had to be rushed to the Glasgow Royal Infirmary, with David and the rest of his teammates trailing behind.

The hospital had appeared enormous to players like David who came from poor, small villages. They'd watched in awe while dozens of efficient-looking nurses and doctors bustled by in the corridors, all in starched white medical uniforms.

Now, standing in sight of the ox-cart on the street, David continued to peer inside the front door.

"Och, not much to see," he grumbled.

He thought the facility was small and dingy compared to the huge, immaculate Royal Infirmary. In the days to come, when he visited the two patients, David would discover that the hospital was truly understaffed, and ill equipped, by Western standards. He would learn there were no European physicians on staff and that the five doctors and the nurses, aides and orderlies were all schooled in traditional Chinese medicine with limited knowledge of Western methods and with a distrust of modern surgery.

Watching now how the staff's attitude changed when Smithers pulled out a thick wad of money, David suspected the hospital catered to the rich.

If I had come by meself, a Westerner with two wounded Westerners, not knowing the language, all o' five Chinese dollars in me pocket, they probably wadna turned us away.

After a few minutes of watching Smithers fumble at the front desk, he knew it to be true.

At the admittance desk, Smithers enunciated each word carefully as the administrator, one aide, and two nurses leaned forward to decipher what he was saying: "The United Missionary Society," he waved vaguely in the direction of the location, *"jiāngyào jiézhàng ànzhào wěikuǎn ànzhào zhěnliáo,* will settle accounts according to balance due according to diagnosis and treatment."

He repeated the sentence, hoping they would understand.

David waited impatiently, keeping an anxious eye on the two men, the stack of firearms in the wagon bed, and the ox-cart. Edward seemed to be getting worse by the minute.

Finally, a band of orderlies came out. He watched them as they gently moved the injured men onto the gurneys and rolled them inside.

After the patients were gathered into the hospital, Smithers inquired at length about the method of treatment the doctors planned for each man, asking a question in his labored Chinese and frowning as he listened carefully to understand each answer. With his Mandarin vocabulary stretched to the limit and the inured men now inside receiving treatment, the reverend gave up. He said, *"Piānláo* Thank you for your trouble."

Bowing politely, he turned to go out into the street.

He explained what he knew to David as they guided the cart back to the Society building: what kind of medical remedies for each, the probable total costs, first-glance prognosis, and likely lengths of stay.

"Well, tis a sin the poor man has been shot and left a hanging on to his life by a thread," David said as they ambled along the slow-moving cart.

"Hey there, watch yourself, laddies!" he yelled sharply

at a trio of boisterous Chinese kids running and playing in the street. The lead boy was trotting backwards, facing his friends. He had his body turned to the oncoming wagon, making funny faces at his companions.

The other two boys broke out laughing, holding their stomachs in glee and pointing at their *xīlihútu*, silly friend, who barely saw the big lumbering oxen over his shoulder in time to leap out of the way.

The closest beast snorted a huge glob of snot and jerked its massive head with irritation at the errant boy.

David reached out and tousled the kid's hair and grinned at him as he passed by. The boy put his hand on the ruffled spot on his head. He stared with interest at the tall stranger, his brown eyes more wide with curiosity than alarm. His friends also eyed the two Westerners with inquisitive expressions.

David resumed his train of thought, "But Edward is a wealthy businessman who can afford to be a paying for his own keep. He's a proud man, at that. Ralph is a different matter. He's a poor beginner missionary just like me. He's got no money to speak o'."

"Not to worry, Reverend MacDougall. I'll discuss it with Reverend Baker."

Smithers placed his pudgy paw on David's shoulder in a gesture of reassurance. He felt bad about his initial unhelpful attitude and was determined to show he, too, was a proper Christian and a man of compassion.

"I'm quite sure he'll agree to use our discretionary fund to pay full expenses for both men. After all, it is solely because these men accompanied you that they were even attacked, and you are a member of the Society. So in a sense, their injuries become the responsibility of the Society. The same goes for finding the next of kin or otherwise making arrangements for the deceased. It's possible that none of this would have happened had they been traveling at a different time and with different associates."

He continued, "But since it *did* happen while they were traveling with you, I do feel the Society has a financial obligation to assist."

"Och well," replied David. "'Tis most generous o' you, at that."

Over the next few days, the Society office did everything it promised, and more.

Chinese assistants escorted the two ladies, Samantha and Emma, and their belongings to their respective destinations. Samantha confided in David that her second cousin lived in the main expatriate compound and had ample room for her. "I hope to find employment teaching English at the Imperial Capital University."

David already knew Emma was staying with English acquaintances for a few weeks before returning home. She explained her friends were very liberal and open-minded. Unusual for foreigners, her friends' home was outside the expat complex, a half mile away.

"When Anne and Robby Butler first came to this country, they decided they wanted to experience the real China for themselves. Without the entombing effect of life in the cloistered expatriate community. So after ten years here, they both speak Mandarin remarkably well. Their speech is understandable by the natives they came in contact with. They really are a fine couple; sweet, lovely, gregarious, broad-minded. You would like them very much. They now have two beautiful young children. They also have a number of good Chinese friends, several of whom sheltered and protected them from harm when the fighting started."

"Boxer?" he asked.

"Yes, I mean the Boxer Rebellion. Their brave Chinese friends risked their own lives and families to safeguard the Butlers. The English papers didn't tell the half of the violence and degradation inflicted on the poor victims at the time. There were many, many more Chinese casualties than foreign ones, you know."

Before they left the Society with the assistants, both women said farewell to MacDougall. Emma smiled her beguiling smile one last time. "You know, David, you've helped save my life twice now. I might never see you again after today."

Her eyes twinkled with a most mischievous look. "I think I owe you much more than a hasty hug and a quick handshake, wouldn't you say?"

Taking him by surprise as he stood there with an

audience looking on, she flung her arms around his neck, thrust her body up against his as tight as she could, feeling his hard muscles against her soft flesh, and planted a prolonged passionate kiss on his open mouth. Refusing to let go, she forced him to cradle his arms around her.

Her pent-up sexuality aroused David, despite his best efforts at self-control. She continued to hold him, kissed him again, and felt his growing firmness, despite the Oohs and Ahhs from the watching throng.

Samantha put her hand to her mouth in delighted shock and tittered. Smithers, a staid married man, turned beet-red at the scene.

The old Chinese man chuckled with satisfaction.

Finally, Emma let go, a satisfied smirk upon her lovely face. "Well, I suppose this really is goodbye, David. I'll think of you often, and I'll pray for you always. God bless you, reverend," she said, as their small group turned to leave.

David exhaled a deep breath and tugged on his shirt front to smooth it out. He could tell his face was flushed.

"Aye, well, God be a blessing the two o' you, too," he answered a bit stiffly, trying to regain what was left of his decorum.

The women waved a final goodbye and David waved back.

"Bye, Reverend MacDougall," Samantha sang out gaily. She grinned at him and turned to Emma. The two women immediately put their heads together in hushed conversation as they walked away with their Chinese helpers.

The old man went with Emma. He had relatives in the near area. But he was welcomed into the Butlers' home to visit the young woman whenever he wished. In time and with encouragement by Robby and Anne, he told them his own story, which they repeated to Emma in English.

Hearing his history from Anne, Emma blinked away tears. "He is such a dear!"

On his next visit, she gave the elderly man, whose first name she learned was Binjinguan, a lingering affectionate embrace, and had her friends communicate in Chinese her deep gratitude for saving her life.

"You are my Benny, my Benny Papa, my second father," she said, hugging him again. The elderly Chinese beamed when her words and his new name were explained to him in Mandarin.

"Mǎnqiāng! Nín shì Emmm-mahhh, wǒ cìnǚ!" (My heart is full! You are Emma, my second daughter!) He exclaimed merrily. Impulsively, he reached out a wrinkled brown-spotted hand, and softly touched the girl's cheek. In return, she reached out and took his other hand in both of hers and held it tightly.

The old man's eyes sparkled with fresh tears.

Then they laughed together. And laughed again, happy for the gift of life and of each other's company.

Chapter Twenty Nine

At the hospital, the combined effect of the ancient Oriental methods of treatment together with the resilience of the two men produced surprising results. Ralph mended quickest. His wounds were slight compared to Edward's, and he was much younger. He left the hospital on the third morning to complete his healing at the missionary compound.

Edward stayed a full week and a half. David visited him as often as he could.

"He's a former army veteran, a tough old bird, hard to kill," he observed.

Yet it had been touch-and-go the very first night and the next day. Working feverishly, the doctors were able to stop his bleeding, treat the infection, stabilize his system, and provide potions that relieved his intense pain.

However, they never operated, surgery being considered a Western practice. Until the end of his life, Edward Simpler would carry a perfectly shaped, undamaged lead bullet lodged between his stomach and his spleen. Why it had not exited the yielding flesh out the small of his back on the other side, neither the Chinese doctors, nor the English, the German, and the French physicians he later consulted could ever tell him.

The projectile stopped on its own accord, without hitting hard barrier or bone. Thereafter, on the coldest days, it caused a severe stabbing sensation whenever he stood up too quickly or leaned over. It also hurt worse during missionary sex. As a consequence, Edward became a late in life advocate of having the wife on top, much to the delight of Mrs. Simpler. "Oh, go on with ye, Eddie, you devil you," exclaimed the missus happily the first time they switched positions.

Upon his arrival back at the Society building late that first afternoon, Reverend Baker heard David's tale and Smithers' recommendation in the comfort of his office. He made soft utterances at various points in the story.

"My, my.

"My goodness.

"Oh, my."

Despite his exclamations, Baker listened attentively throughout, sitting straight-up in his upholstered dark-blue leather-back chair, left arm folded across his chest holding his right arm up with hand resting against the side of his face.

Once informed of the situation, Reverend Baker proved to be a man of action.

"I see. Well, yes, I do quite agree with you, Reverend Smithers. The Society should pay for all the medical expenses—help the two gentlemen get back on their feet. Also, you must notify the local government authorities and the British

Envoy's office immediately about the three unfortunates who were killed. Try as best you can to determine the next of kin, whether the bodies need to be shipped back to England under refrigeration, or if there are any associates or relatives locally who wish to inter the deceased."

Underneath Reverend Baker's refined exterior beat a genuine heart of compassion. David had been told the man's history by Reverend Johnston. Baker had sacrificed upper-class British wealth, connections, and ease to become a missionary. After eighteen years in the field, China, his current assignment, was by far the most fertile ground. He had earlier been a missionary to the wilds of Northwest India, attempting to evangelize across the border among the hostile tribes of Pashtun Afghans during the turbulent reign of Amir Abdur Rahman Khan. He knew deprivation and danger firsthand.

"As for you, my brave fellow, how can we thank you enough for saving the lives of the other five persons? You risked your own neck to defend theirs. '*Greater love hath no man than this, that a man lay down his life for his friends,*' John 15:13. You and Mister Simpler and Mister Harrison were all willing to sacrifice yourselves, if you must, to save others. Exemplary behavior. Most admirable of you all."

"Tis only what any red-blooded man, Christian or otherwise, would have done, sir," David replied modestly.

He stayed with the Baker family for almost a week, hoping to see Edward clear of danger before leaving. On the morning of his departure, he found a bright-eyed Chinese youth waiting in the parlor, eager to accompany him.

"We thought you might need a hand with your luggage. Also, the boy wants to see the Christ Is Lord church for himself," Reverend Baker explained, half apologizing.

The boy, he told David, had been persistent about going, and he'd finally relented. Besides, he felt the lad could be of some value to the mission. He'd been a volunteer helper at the Society office for nearly two years.

The teenager, who overheard everything, grinned, and said, "Yes, yes, I like go. Big help. You see!"

"Just give him a chance, Reverend MacDougall. He's a young Christian. He has no close relatives here. His mother died from the plague when he was ten, and he lost his father a year ago."

The young man, David discovered, liked to talk nonstop. Having learned English from being around the Society, he engaged David in a variety of topics. Inquisitive about all things Western, he was glad to be of assistance. He gave David a running commentary on anything that caught his eye or entered his mind as they traveled to the southwest part of the inner city where the Christ Is Lord mission church was strategically located two and quarter miles from the Foreign Legation Quarters.

The teenager, whose name was Jianming Zhou, had converted to Christianity at the age of fifteen. He still had a new believer's endless enthusiasm and boundless faith. David enjoyed the young man's personality. He was like a golden retriever pup—unlimited energy and excited all the time. David decided to nickname him Jimmy, the sound of which delighted the youngster.

"Jimmm–meee? Jimmm–meee. I like!"

He enunciated the words emphatically but slowly. "Da-vid, you...you call me Jimmmy, yes?"

He laughed. It sounded funny and Western to his ears, and he loved it.

Suddenly Jimmy saw something among the street scene. He grew quiet and his look became solemn.

He lightly bumped David's elbow with the luggage he was carrying. MacDougall stopped and turned toward him.

"*Yo!* Da-vid. *Yo.* See there? Tong mà, on door."

He struggled to remember the English words. "Red mark. On door. See there?" he jerked his head toward a heavy wooden door in the second shop to the left on the street they were passing. "Sell *dàyān* there, sell op-pee-umm there. *Ètú,* bad person. Must pray for him."

Jimmy's face was earnest and stricken-looking. "Pray."

"You say they sell opium there? Aye, Jimmy, we must be a praying for him and all others who need Jesus. We must tell others about the good news of the gospel."

"Yes? Pray?"

"You go right ahead and pray, lad, and I'll pray, too," he set his belongings down in the middle of the bustling street, and pointed at the boy. David put his hands together in supplication, and bowed his head, praying silently.

Jimmy nodded. He lowered the luggage and bowed his head, too. *"Zhùyì zhi lìdìchéng Christ-yun.* Help him stop. Help him stop do op-pee-umm and become a Christ-yun. A-men. *Amen!"* repeated Jimmy, heartily.

"Amen, me little brother." David clapped the boy on the shoulder in approval. "That's a very good prayer, a fine prayer." Jimmy's smile was ear-to-ear.

They gathered up the baggage and resumed walking. Soon, the street scene changed from the hutong-configured residences mixed among the many shops, neighborhood eateries, and other businesses, to several long blocks of open-air farmers' markets. Their stomachs growled as they sniffed the pungent aroma. At some stands, the vendors were cooking fresh vegetables with stir-fry meats: chicken, duck, beef, fish, and pork. At other stands, the vendors sold fresh-cut vegetables and fruits. Some sold exotic spices, seasonings, and teas.

"Hungry?" David asked.

Jimmy looked at him quizzically, shaking his head slightly. He didn't know that word.

"Eat! Food." David said, rubbing his stomach.

"Hungry means you want to eat." He put his fingers together with his thumb and made darting motions with his hand toward his open mouth.

"Oh, yes," the boy interrupted, before David could

finish his pantomime. Jimmy did know the English words 'eat' and 'food'.

David motioned grandly across the row of stands, letting the boy know he would get to pick the meal for both of them.

He chose the first vendor, and David paid the man in Yuan for the meals.

Jimmy watched in amusement as David attempted to gather up mouthfuls of the hot steaming rice and chicken using his chopsticks. The boy tried his best not to laugh, but his friend was so inept, he couldn't stop himself. Soon he was chuckling, louder and louder, covering his mouth with his hand. David tried again and again, only to have most of the food drop back into the bowl, or fall through the sticks and bounce off his chest into the street.

Westerners were so hilarious. Jimmy liked them, but they did such funny things.

Finally, the teenager could stand it no longer. He had to help his new friend. The boy said, "Da-vid, see?" Picking up his sticks, Jimmy demonstrated how to hold them and how to narrow the tips together to grasp a big bite.

"See?" The boy did it several times, watching David mimic his motions until satisfied he had gotten the technique down enough to eat without losing most of the food.

Finished with their meal, they picked up their belongings. Jimmy glanced over the avenue of stalls. He said in a quieter tone than usual, "Da-vid, see? Girls?" The boy looked sad.

MacDougall turned to where Jimmy was looking. They saw three young girls, not yet in their teens, across the street, working a sting. Although the conversation was all in Chinese, David intuitively grasped what was happening. In a stage whisper, Jimmy explained as best he could with his limited English.

Both hands on hips, one girl was loudly arguing with the man that her mother had purchased a meal there yesterday and had gotten very sick. What a dishonest evil person he was to be selling bad food and charging good money to decent hardworking folk. She went around to his side of the stall, her countenance combative and her voice fierce and accusing, to continue the tirade, face-to-face. She demanded a full refund for her supposed mother's supposed sickness.

Meanwhile, a second girl came around and stood at her left shoulder also shouting at the vendor he was a criminal and deserved to be whipped for his action.

Together, they kept the man angry, occupied and yelling back at them while the third girl stepped to the far opposite corner, behind him. She quickly pulled a weather-beaten leather schoolbag from under her skirt and began filling it with vegetables first, rice, and meats on top of everything. She filled it as full as she dared, than stuffed it back under her skirt. She turned and walked away down the street.

Seeing the deed done, the first girl waved her finger

at the vendor's furious red-splotched face, and threatened to bring her mother and the authorities there tomorrow. Abruptly, she and the other girl turned to go up the street, leaving the poor man apoplectic and clueless.

With the hubbub of the surrounding marketplace, and with their own customers engaging their attention, not a single one of the other street merchants paid attention to the brief episode. As long as it didn't happen to them, they didn't care.

David and Jimmy watched the two girls walk, unhurried, up three blocks. They turned right at the corner and disappeared behind the mass of stalls and buildings.

David's heart ached. "Och no. Dear sweet Lord. What can I do? The poor lassies."

He knew from his study of Chinese history that poverty and hunger were rampant in the country. Famine was common and cyclical. Every thirty or forty years some natural disaster such as floods or draught would plague the land and massive famine would break out, killing millions in its grasp. But to witness such young people, and girls, at that, broke his heart. He wished with all his might he could go after them, give them all of his money to live on, and tell them the story of Jesus.

He turned to the boy. Jimmy's eyes were wet and glum. For the moment, his perpetual happiness had escaped him.

"'Tis sorry I am, Jimmy. But there's nothing we can do, lad. They're already gone."

Sighing deeply, he reached down to retrieve the luggage, and signaled his companion to do the same.

They resumed their journey.

Life in China was very hard for the poor, David reflected sorrowfully.

Chapter Thirty

A short time later, they reached the Christ Is Lord Mission. It was located in a charming and well-preserved section of traditional siheyuan homes intermingled with a few inconspicuous business buildings scattered here and there.

"'Tis very lovely here, very peaceful looking," he said to Jimmy. Both of them glanced up and down the quiet street. They saw that many of the shared enclosures had small trees and other greenery.

To his eye, the neighborhood appeared older, almost historical, orderly, and unassuming. It was an idealized image, he imagined, of old Beiping as it might have been for the last four hundred years: tranquil, dignified yet unpretentious, and rooted to the wisdom of the past.

The CILM complex, he had been told, had two adjoining hutong squares along the street, each comprised of four houses sharing a common courtyard. Three blocks down on the corner, the Mission owned a large former warehouse that had been converted into a commodious church facility capable of seating twelve hundred souls, with standing room for hundreds more.

It was late Saturday morning, past first tea but not lunch time. David left the luggage with Jimmy by the street and strolled over to the first of the two houses that faced the road. He knocked on the heavy doorframe.

No one came. He waited a bit then pounded harder. Still no answer.

He looked over his shoulder at Jimmy, shrugged, and moved to the next house. MacDougall rapped loudly this time. Right before he knocked again, there came a sweet singsong voice from inside accompanied by the sounds of shuffling feet. Definitely female, definitely Chinese, perhaps elderly. That much he could tell.

"Nínhao? Shén merén shì nàr? Hello? Who is there?"

"Uh, tis Reverend MacDougall. From Scotland. To see Reverend Graham?"

"Oh, yes!" He heard the woman cheerfully reply.

Slowly, the heavy door creaked open.

David saw before him a tiny Chinese lady, elegant-looking, with kindness radiating from her lively eyes. She was clothed in a traditional qipao, or banner gown, that was loose and hung straight down the body. Her white hair, thinning but still beautiful, was combed back away from her lined face and wrapped into a graceful knot at the nape of her neck. He noticed that her once-bound feet, a lingering symbol of ancient Chinese culture, now splayed contentedly inside soft European-made slippers.

He later learned her story. Because she had been

fortunate enough to be born in Beiping of an industrious, liberal-minded family of third-generation merchants, her footbinding in her youth had not been as severe or as prolonged as inflicted upon many young girls of her time born in the backward rural areas of the country.

Taking delicate baby steps forward, she opened the door further to peer outside. Seeing the boy and the luggage, she motioned to Jimmy who stood in the street.

"Come inside. Please. You *shuāngrén*, you two. Come inside. Bring your *xīzhuāng*, your clothes. I make hot tea. Come. Sit. Be comfortable."

Her friendliness and warmth were comforting and contagious. *She seems such a nice person and a very refined older lady*, thought David, as he walked out to the street to help gather up the luggage with Jimmy.

She held the door for them, opened wide, bobbing her head up and down, smiling broadly as the men entered with David's belongings.

"Pastor Graham be back one hour. Lunch time. He at church working on sermon."

She waved them to chairs in the living room. The men sat as she disappeared with tiny yet energetic steps through the formal eating room into the kitchen area at the other end.

As they waited, David said, "I'm a thanking you for all your help this morning, Jimmy."

He clucked and winked in approval. "Appreciate it, I do. You tell Reverend Baker 'Thank you' for loaning you out to me." He spoke the words slowly so the boy could pick up the English phrases he knew.

"I want stay. Da-vid, I want stay. Help you. Here." Jimmy nodded solemnly.

"My new home. Here." He pointed at the walls, then to himself.

He nodded again, for emphasis.

"Well, I wouldn't mind if you be a staying. I suppose it's all up to Reverend Graham."

"I be big help. You see!"

"I'm sure you would be, laddie." His eyes twinkled at the boy.

Soon the old lady came bustling in, amazingly fast for someone taking such small steps. But each stride was so determined and rapid that, when she wanted, she could move almost as quickly as a young woman with unbound feet.

There was a low table situated in front of the two chairs. Upon it, she placed a tea tray bearing two ornate fragile-looking cups and saucers, an even more elaborate pot, and a large platter carrying a tempting array of small Chinese cookies.

Without waiting for the others, Jimmy took a huge handful of cookies—a big grin on his face.

David drank one cup and ate one cookie to satisfy the hostess. He was most anxious to see Reverend Graham at the church. Motioning for the boy to stay with the old woman, he rose to leave. "I'll just be a going now to visit pastor down the street. I'm sure we'll both be back shortly."

Jimmy was happy to see David get up. That meant extra helpings of cookies and tea for him. He reached out to grab three more cookies and piled them around the sides of his saucer.

The elderly lady sat and watched contentedly as the young man continued to eat and drink. Like all good cooks, it was a joy to see healthy men and youth and their voracious appetites.

With his mouth packed too full to say goodbye, Jimmy waved and watched David leave the room.

Chapter Thirty One

David stepped outside and pulled the heavy door shut. He stood there for several seconds, thinking. As he gathered his thoughts, puffs of warm summer wind mixed with the residue of dust off the streets washed over his face. He could smell the faint scent of flowers from the blooming gardens. He heard bees buzzing to and fro in the patios. So much had happened in the few weeks since he boarded the *Ayrshire* in early August; more feminine intrigue, more danger, injuries, bloodshed, and unfortunate deaths than he could have imagined.

"Och, Lord, I'm ready for the simple sheltered life of a missionary."

Or so he hoped.

He blinked and looked up and down the long avenue. It was silent and still in the neighborhood, except for the bees and a few birds—some of which he recognized: the pleasant singing of a Eurasian Blackbird nestling somewhere in a nearby courtyard garden; the fluted competing whistles of two Bullfinches; and the monosyllabic chirps of a family of Tree Sparrows.

Turning west, he walked toward the church-warehouse. Reaching the building, he paused on the bricked road and took in the size of it for a moment, noticing the broad signage atop the large double doors announcing the name in both Chinese and English.

David pulled on the right-hand entrance. Finding it unlocked, he opened it and stepped briskly inside.

The massive room was empty except for three wide columns of folding chairs which filled the large sanctuary. But for the bright outdoor light streaming through the raised windows on both sides, the auditorium was unlit, leaving the middle area lost in light gray shadows.

Once his eyes adjusted to the dimness, he walked around to the outermost aisle against the wall and went to the front. There he saw a long hallway to the left of the raised platform section. Only the first wall lamp had been lit, bathing the hall entry with a glow that faded into the blackness beyond. There was the tiniest gleam of light at the very end of the hall. Without hesitation, he strode toward it. He glimpsed rooms branching off on either side of the elongated passageway, but paid no attention to them. He went down the corridor, feeling his way with his hand touching the wall, until he reached the yellow reflection of a kerosene lamp shining through the partially closed office door.

"Pastor Graham?" he called quietly, rapping lightly on the doorframe. He moved into the doorway to show himself, opening the door wider.

"Tis Reverend David MacDougall, sir. From Scotland."

Unperturbed by the sudden knocking and voice, Graham looked up from his cluttered oak desk. "Well. Praise the Lord. It's good to see you so soon, Reverend. You made excellent time."

He smiled, yet David discerned his smile had sadness in it. Graham's expression, especially his eyes, had a faraway intensity, a deepness, which baffled David. He was usually adept at reading people, but there was something about this pastor's countenance he couldn't put his finger on.

"I understand you had great difficulties on your journey. Or so I'm told. Most sorry to hear that. Very sorry indeed. Tragic loss of life.

"Are you okay?" The words themselves carried concern; the feeling behind the words carried a virtual wellspring of compassion.

Reverend William Robertson Graham appeared to be in his late forties to early fifties. His medium-brown hair was graying around the sides and thinning in the crown region. He had a thick bottle-nose mustache that was now salt and russet pepper. The face was lined, tired-looking, yet the eyes were full of deepest sympathy. There was a profound measure of charity and understanding mixed with a large amount of melancholy about the man's visage.

David hesitated. Now that the heat of battle was gone, he found it hard to talk about his troubles.

"I'm fine, sir. Aye, we got attacked by bandits on the

road, we did. There were twelve o' us at the start. Three ran away including two Chinese guides; we've had no word o' their whereabouts. O' the rest, two were badly wounded; one knocked in the head; three killed; and three uninjured. All eight o' the robbers were killed.

"Frankly, tis not the type o' action I expected when I signed up to help win souls and work in the mission field, Pastor."

Reverend Graham said nothing, but gazed steadily at the younger man.

Tragic eyes, tis. The thought raced through David's mind.

David continued. "When I was 'board ship, we got attacked by pirates off the coast o' Shanghai in the middle o' the night. One sailor was killed, and the captain and several crewmen were injured. Four pirates were captured on ship, and an unconfirmed number were killed or wounded."

He laughed grimly. "Someone ought to have told this young whipper-snapper that church work on the foreign front could be dangerous to a man's health."

Pastor Graham said nothing, but stared at David and beyond. Half a minute passed. David began to get uneasy standing there, waiting, not knowing what to do.

Finally, Graham cleared his throat.

"Yes, being a missionary can sometimes require... extraordinary sacrifices." He continued to look intently at the figure before him.

Graham sighed deeply.

"I intended to tell you soon enough, Reverend. Better you hear it from me than get it sensationalized or embellished by one of the staff members. With what you've gone through on your journey, both at sea and on land, I think perhaps you'll understand my story without overreacting or false sentiment. Most people, when they hear it, treat me like…well, like an emotional leper. Even well-meaning Christian brothers and sisters tend to view me as some modern-day Job they must tiptoe around. You see, they look at me with mournful faces and act like they have to be careful of what they say in front of me."

David tilted his head a little to the side, curiosity and concern building up, wondering what in heaven's name the man was about to tell him.

"I'm sure you know of the terrible Boxer Rebellion that happened here in the capital city and throughout northern China a few years back."

David nodded he had.

"The insurgents, that is, the Boxers, Chinese Muslins, and many Imperial troops, surrounded a large collection of foreigners—businessmen, workers, educators, diplomats, soldiers, missionaries—as well as Chinese Christians, Chinese students, and other innocent natives inside the Legation compound. Most of the Chinese refugees, both Protestants and Catholics, were housed at first in the Su Wang Fu palace and homes. Later, school girls were moved into the British Legation away from the heavy fighting around the Fu.

"Outside the protection of the compound walls, throughout the city and all over North China, many dozens of Westerners along with thousands, perhaps tens of thousands, of Chinese Christians were slaughtered, women and children included. Battles raged daily all around the Legation grounds. Between the Chinese snipers and the constant barrage of artillery shells and shrapnel, a number of foreign civilians and soldiers were also slain."

He stared straight at David.

"My wife was a skilled nurse; caring, loving, utterly fearless, and sacrificial. She and our daughter, Julia, were outside the British building one day helping tend Japanese guards who had been wounded defending the Chinese Christians in the Fu from an Imperial troop attack. The number of wounded was too many to bring them all inside."

David held his breath.

"They were both…," It was still hard for Graham to say the words. "They were both… killed…killed by an exploding random shell. Their bodies were torn to bits. Both of my beautiful girls. Almost unrecognizable."

The pastor choked up. He gripped the edge of the desk to steady himself.

David swallowed hard and his heart stopped a beat. He gaped at the man. A minute ticked by, but it seemed an eternity.

Pastor Graham controlled himself and resumed his story. "On the day this happened, I was far away; responding, as usual, to another urgent plea. Once the rebellion had gathered steam, so to speak, there were calls for assistance all over the city and surrounding regions. We did what we could to save lives. I had assumed my own family would be safe behind the walls of the Legation."

His face flushed. He wiped his brow and coughed lightly.

"I had gone with a group of ministers and members of my staff to rescue the young children and teachers at a Christian school southwest of the city. The Boxers had already burned and savaged two schools in the area, raping, killing, pillaging. After spending an entire afternoon dodging marauding bands of Boxers, we eventually got the boys and girls to safety in the city before...before I found out...about my dear sweet wife Mariam, and my beautiful precious Julia."

Pastor Graham's countenance knotted with pain. He squeezed his eyes to block out unwanted tears. Composing himself with sheer force of will, he gritted his teeth and sighed heavily. "It's past. Done. Done and over with. They're now in heaven with our Lord. Someday soon I'll join them and we'll be reunited."

He glared at David with fierce determination. "But for the present, the Lord means for me to continue his work on earth. I don't want your sympathy or long face. We won't need to discuss this anymore. But before I close the subject, I want to also tell you about what happened to my very best Chinese friend. He's a good man who's been with me almost from the beginning and who does the translation of my sermons during the services for me. His name is Zhuang Li, or Brother Lee as we call him. He lost a son during the Rebellion. His youngest boy, Hui, was killed by the Boxers while attempting to defend a native Chinese pastor caught outside the Legation.

"Poor Hui and the pastor were stabbed, then their bowels gutted with an old rusty sword. Hui was still alive when...when they burned his body," Graham's steady voice suddenly broke.

"They took his life in such a brutal fashion. He suffered such a horrible, horrible death, as punishment...as *punishment*...for being a Christian. For taking sides with a person the Boxers considered a traitor to China."

"Och, me goodness," exclaimed MacDougall, his handsome face locked in shock. "Pastor, I had no idea about either one o' you. No one at the Society ever told me anything, not Reverend Johnston back in Scotland, not Reverend Baker at the branch. I'm so sorry."

His words were inadequate and hollow. What could he say?

"As I said, they're all now in heaven, in a much better place." Graham regained his composure. His expression was once again tired-looking but serene. "My wife and daughter can't come to me anymore; or his son, to Brother Lee. But both of us, I and Brother Lee, will go to be with them in heaven, in the Lord's time.

Reverend Graham continued.

"Ah, there are two other tales I want to mention to you. With the Lord's grace and strength, I have forgiven those responsible for killing my wife and daughter. As Jesus forgave on the cross, so I forgive too. In our church today, we have two of the Imperial officers who were in charge of the artillery position that fired the fateful shots. They are among our most faithful and loving brothers in the entire congregation. Fully repented, saved to the utmost, and filled-with-the-Spirit Christians. God is great."

David was awed at the story. "Aye, that He is, Pastor."

"The other tale is not so good," Graham's voice tensed and he had to fight to keep calm.

"After the Rebellion was quelled, certain men of the cloth, Protestant and Catholic alike, insisted on joining the victorious nations in extracting vengeance from the Chinese in the form of forced reparations. Naturally, I protested this monstrous injustice. The Chinese people had suffered enough, both Christians and non-Christians. Suffered more than we Westerners suffered, by far. These greedy publicans took what they wanted and literally stole the rest, often with little or no proof their victims were, or ever had been, Boxers. It was nothing less than sanctioned stealing, in my opinion."

He mashed his lips together in tight disapproval, then rolled his eyes to heaven and exhaled. "Well, I must forgive them, too, I suppose."

Chapter Thirty Two

Graham looked back down at the stack of yellow sheets containing his detailed hand-written sermon notes. The big desktop was strewn with a half-drunk mug of stale coffee, an inadequately sized in-basket overflowing with requests, two large opened Bible commentaries, a beautifully bound coal-black Bible, also opened, and various pads of paper and colored ink pens.

"Your timing is perfect. I think I've done about as much as I can for my message tomorrow, Reverend. We should be going. Madame Qiu will be expecting us for lunch."

Standing up, Graham stretched both arms and rolled and cracked his shoulders. Next, he leaned backward, forward, and to each side several times, loosening his torso. He'd been sitting and working for several hours and was stiff. Picking up the stack of papers on his desk, he tapped the sheets on the tabletop to straighten them, then folded and inserted the notes into his open Bible before closing it.

Graham smiled warmly for the first time, a thoughtful and reverent expression playing upon his lined face. Lifting the heavy tome, he remarked, "Reverend MacDougall, this is the only thing that lasts in this life and the life to come: His Word. All else is dust and ashes."

"Aye, sir. I fully agree. God's Word is eternal." David stepped to the side to allow Graham to exit first.

The pastor reached over to twist the knob at the base of the lamp shutting off the flame and flooding the room in darkness.

"Och, Pastor, I want to be a thankin' you," David hesitated, not quite sure how to finish his thought, "Not only for having me as part o' your fine church but also, for taking me into your confidence. Sharing with me the story o' your great loss and your wonderful testimony o' forgiveness. Tis a very personal and painful experience to be talking about, tis."

"Well, no need to speak of it further, Reverend. I appreciate your understanding."

Graham patted David on the small of his back as if he were the one who had lost a wife and child. Together, they left the room.

With his beloved Mariam and Julia deceased and his only son Robert and young Chinese bride newly departed to take a small Nebraska pastorate in America, Pastor Graham now lived alone in the second house fronting the street.

Of the seven other courtyard homes that comprised the two adjoining hutongs, one building was currently vacant; one house was occupied by the old Chinese woman and her middle-aged son and his wife; one house was assigned to Jianquo Wu, the church's assistant pastor, and his family;

one was reserved for visiting guests and speakers; and three were used as shelters for the unending stream of homeless Chinese youth and children who went to the church. There were two houses for the girl residents and one for the boys. The orphan homes each had an older unmarried female resident as house mother. All of the eight buildings had space for up to three formal bedrooms or sleeping areas. But in the children's homes, they crowded their pallets together on the floors in every room except for the house mother's bedroom, the kitchen, and the eating area.

There were twice as many homeless and unwanted girls, Pastor explained to David, as there were orphaned boys. There were many reasons.

"Boys represent strong arms and backs to work the fields and help bring in food. Girls represent mouths to feed. Boys are esteemed in China, while girls, as a rule, aren't. Not unless they come from an upper class family, and especially if the parents have embraced Western ideas. Boys are less likely to be taken into slavery. It is an abominable practice, but it is very common for poor farmers and even the poor in the cities to sell their prettiest daughters to the highest bidders just to feed the rest of the family."

"Och, pastor, tis beyond sad. Truly, tis."

David knew such things happened, but he still found it horrible to contemplate. Selling one's son or daughter into slavery was about as reprobate as one could get, he figured. He shuddered, causing Graham to look at him discerningly.

He thought of his own father and mother and how much they loved their children, and that they would do anything to keep their offspring safe, whole, and happy.

After a quick lunch, Pastor Graham and David returned to the church, and sat in his parsonage office, discussing many subjects. They talked about the present position, prospects, and plans for the Christ Is Lord church; the weakened state of evangelism in north China in the aftermath of the Boxer Rebellion; the suffering of the common Chinese facing never-ending famines, plagues, floods, earthquakes, bandits, poverty, abuse, and abandonment; the ceaseless turmoil, corruption, and ineffectiveness of the Imperial government; and the greed and interference of the victorious Western nations.

William Robertson Graham was as much a patriot as most fellow Brits and Scots, but his number one priority was the advancement of the Kingdom of God. In his opinion, Britain shared a portion of blame for the atrocities and harsh acts that had followed the defeat of the rebels.

"Reverend MacDougall, from a Christian perspective, the mood in northern China has taken a sharp turn for the worse over the past six years. In the countryside, the poor are still starving and dying without any relief. Foreign states treat the Imperial government as a lapdog, gobbling up resources and spheres of influence wherever they can. When the Alliance defeated the Boxers, they imposed severe sanctions on a nation already tottering on the edge of collapse. They may have crushed the rebellion, but they failed to crush widespread anti-Western bias. They only deepened the mood and made it go underground."

"I see," said David.

"The problem has been compounded by the fact that not all Christians have been pure in their motives and actions toward the Chinese. For example, during the siege, Chinese Catholics inside the compound were often denied food while the priests and Europeans rationed and shared among themselves. The Protestants did only a little better in that regard. But in the frenzy afterwards to collect restitution, several Protestant ministers were just as bad as the Catholic clerics in robbing the people."

David shook his head in disgust.

"Och aye, pastor. Tis a black mark against missionaries and churches everywhere, tis."

David leaned back in his chair and stroked his chin in thought. "The only way to combat it is be above reproach in one's dealings. We must conduct ourselves in fear and holiness, sharing the gospel in truth, loving the dear Chinese people as our own family, honoring their good laws, fighting to give them justice, succoring them with our bread, our money, our comfort, and our charity. They are our brothers and sisters." He pounded his meaty fist into his palm for emphasis.

"Yes, Reverend, I quite agree. We must exhibit true Christianity if we are to make headway against the hatred, bitterness, and mistrust. Love in action, over and over, every instance, every day, is the only way we shall overcome the suspicion and win precious souls to Jesus. Furthermore, I'm of the opinion that politics and patriotism should not enter into it. As far as I'm concerned, the native people and government have been interfered with far too much by the foreign powers."

As they talked, David perceived that the welfare of China and genuine Christian missions were intertwined. His honest heart hungered to be engaged in evangelism, sharing the love of God and the good news of the gospel to the lost. He couldn't wait to immerse himself into the daily fabric of the Christ Is Lord mission outreach.

Pastor Graham said, "Oh, by the way, we'll have you and Jimmy stay in the visitors' house for now."

"Whatever you want to do is fine with me," replied David. The church considered him as part of the permanent staff. Jimmy was another matter. His enthusiasm was boundless, but Graham needed more time to evaluate if and how he might utilize the boy's energy. The pastor thought Jimmy could possibly help as a youth leader.

The next morning dawned unusually crisp and cool for early September. A stiff breeze had driven away the street dust and early mist and rustled the leaves in the courtyard trees, but it abated. The sky was blue and scattered with small puffy clouds lined gray with the promise of sprinkles. The air carried a hint of the sea from the coastal direction, and when it blew, felt fresh, clean, and invigorating.

It was a fine day for a church service.

In the second house on the street, two people were

already up and bustling at first light. Now that their beloved Sister Mariam and Sister Julia were gone, the old Chinese lady and her daughter-in-law had taken over the household duties which included hostessing and preparing meals.

They both reverenced Pastor Graham. To them, it was an honor to help care for such a man of God.

He was humble to a fault, unassuming, undemanding, and always anxious that they might be overtaxed in their simple chores. Often, though, the two women had to resort to guile to take care of him and do the most basic tasks like getting Graham to take his daily medicine. It tasted bad and they had to hide it in a bite of food, as if he were a little child. When they discarded his old garments, they found he would often retrieve favorite shirts and other items from the trash after they had been thrown out.

The pastor had the habit of wearing the same things over and over without thought of laundering, and they had to constantly remind him to change into fresh garments. In tidying up his parsonage office, his recurring mountains of papers and stacks of books left them scrambling to clean underneath while remembering to put everything back exactly where they had found it. They had to use coercion to get him to eat and take meals on time. They had to search the house when it came time to polish his brown and black dress shoes because he left them scattered in various rooms wherever he remembered to take his shoes off.

On collecting the bed linens to be cleaned; the two

Chinese women were especially shy about going into a pastor's bedroom.

"Pastor, did you remember, leave bed things outside door for me?"

"No, Ginny, I forgot. I'm so sorry. I'm afraid I'm running a little late for a meeting with the board."

She looked at him sweetly.

He sighed. "Oh well, I suppose I can take time. Uh, just a minute, please," he mumbled and hurried back into the bedroom to collect the sheets and pillow cases. When done, the clean sheets would be folded and set outside the closed door on the floor in a neat pile. The two women were afraid to peek inside the room. They suspected the pastor threw the fresh sheets on the bed without actually making it up.

The truth was, after his wife and daughter passed, Graham had ceased caring about such mundane things. Saving souls, preaching, and serving the Chinese people, within his congregation and wherever he could, was what he lived for. It was all he lived for.

Today, Madame Qiu and Guangyansun Chou served a hearty Chinese-style breakfast for the men in the formal dinner room. There was strong black coffee as usual for the Pastor, plus green tea for David, Jimmy, and Chunghai Ho, Madame Qiu's middle-aged son. Chairs scraped inward on the bare floor, dishes and silverware clinked, and the table grew pleasantly noisy with the sounds of munching, sipping, coughing, and polite requests for passing the food.

"As always, thank you again, Madame Qiu and you too, Ginny, for a wonderful meal," the pastor said afterwards, pushing his chair back and bowing his head graciously toward the ladies. The two women smiled in return.

"Aye, thank you very much. Twas a wonderful breakfast," said David, nodding and standing up, his taut stomach near full to bursting. He had been ravenously hungry that morning.

"Yes, good. Good!" exclaimed young Jimmy in agreement.

Breakfast done, everyone walked together to the sanctuary; the men first, followed by the women. Pastor Graham liked to arrive forty minutes early to review his sermon outline and to pray for God's power and Holy Ghost unction upon the service. He unlocked the big double doors and turned toward David.

"Reverend, would you please come with me?"

Together they walked back to his office at the end of the long left-hand corridor.

Chapter Thirty Three

Entering the room, Pastor Graham took his place at the well-worn high-backed armchair while David went over to the visitor's side and knelt, resting his upper body on the flat wooden seat of the facing chair. Silently he prayed while Graham studied his notes and meditated on the main texts of scripture for the morning's discourse. Almost at once, David began to feel the peaceful gentle presence of the Holy Spirit in that small office. It seemed like a huge warm feathery comforter had wrapped around his physical body and soul, enclosing him in a cocoon of love and joy.

His prayer time was sweet and fulfilling. He couldn't wait for the service to begin.

Thirty minutes later, the two men retraced their steps down the long hall toward the raised speaker's platform. They saw the large auditorium was half-full, with most of the congregation packing the rows of seats closer to the sanctuary front. The place was buzzing with hundreds of muted but happy conversations in Mandarin, with individuals calling out greetings to those they hadn't seen in a week or two. There was a general feeling of joyful anticipation.

Whatever misgivings, resentments, and suspicions existed toward Westerners outside the four walls of this converted warehouse, inside it, David sensed an atmosphere of togetherness and brotherly love. *Such is the power o' God upon his committed church.*

On either flank of the pulpit were three chairs. Pastor took his usual spot. Graham, Zhuang Li (Brother Lee), the Chinese Translator, and Jean Paterson (Sister Jeannie) filled one side. Newly appointed Assistant Pastor Jianguo Wu and senior lay leader Malcolm Henderson (Brother Hennie) occupied the other side, leaving an empty visitor's chair for David.

Sitting between Pastor Wu and Brother Hennie, David watched with delight as little children were led by the hand all over the sanctuary down the long hall midway to the double room used for Little People Church, which was led by Aileen Colina (Sister Colie), with her Chinese assistants.

"Haowei. Over here, sweetie. This way. Come on."

Sister Colie motioned to an adorable little Chinese boy about five years old. His mother had stopped briefly to chat with a friend on the way down the aisle.

David could tell all of the kids were as excited about their children's meeting as grown-ups were about adult worship.

"So glad meet you," Pastor Wu held out his hand to David. "Pastor Graham very much praising you," he said.

They shook hands. David replied, speaking slowly,

"Aye, and I've heard many good things about you from Pastor Graham. I look forward to working with you."

Pastor Wu nodded and started to speak again. But just then, the choir behind them began to sing the first hymn, and Pastor raised his arms signaling the congregation to please stand.

David, standing with everyone else, turned to look, and saw the singers were divided into women and older girls forming one group on his left, and men and older boys on his right.

To his mild surprise, he also saw a band of musicians in the space between the two choirs. In the little village church back home and in the university chapel services in Glasgow, they only used a piano. *No wonder the singing sounds so rich n' uplifting*, he thought.

There was a lady of regal bearing playing upon a gleaming mahogany-brown upright piano. She was surrounded by a middle-aged trumpeter, who David learned had once played at the Empress Dowager's court, a second trumpet player, a young but highly gifted violinist, a female flutist, and a teen-aged boy who played Chinese-style clash cymbals.

Although the lyrics were in Mandarin, the tune was an old favorite that David knew, and it was sung up-tempo, much faster than typical, turning it into a celebration instead of a dirge. He sang "What a friend we have in Jesus" with unbridled enthusiasm, and somehow his English language blended with the melodious Chinese voices behind him. He concentrated on the words as he belted out the melody:

> "What a Friend we have in Jesus, all our sins and griefs to bear!
> What a privilege to carry everything to God in prayer!
> O what peace we often forfeit, O what needless pain we bear,
> All because we do not carry everything to God in prayer."

The choir sang five more hymns, each one livelier than the one before, as if the songs were building a crescendo of enthusiasm for the sermon itself. The last tune was an original composed by the piano player, Aimei Xu who was called Sister Amy. It was a great favorite of the other musicians and the congregation:

> "Jesus is my savior, my all and all, this morn-ing!
> And He can be your, all and all, this morn-ing!
> So jump up, hands up, open your heart up,
> Just let Him in, together you'll sup."

> "You can feast, too, at the Master's table, this morn-ing!"

Jack King

"Do you have shame, and darkness, deep with-in?
Would you like to be, finally free, of a-l-l sin?
So jump up, hands up, open your heart wide,
Just let Him in, you can be His bride."

"You can feast, too, at the Master's table, this
morn-ing!"

"Are you defeated, and hurting, with life's tri-als?
Do you feel weary and worn, in the journey's mil-
es?
So jump up, hands up, trust and believe,
Just let Him in, all cares He'll relieve."

"You can feast, too, at the Master's table, this
morn-ing!"

Eight years before, a seminary student from America had spent the summer as a missionary intern with Pastor Graham and his family. The young man came from New Orleans, a city noted for wild and jubilant passions, particularly in musical expression. A talented trombone player, he had often snuck off as a high school teenager to the forbidden French Quarters to sit in with the early rag-time bands of Papa Jack Laine, and Louis 'Papa' Tio. He had taught Sister Amy everything he'd learned of the snappy rhythms. Precocious herself, Sister

Amy soon incorporated the swing style into several originally composed hymns with hip lyrics.

All of the people loved the new songs by Sister Amy.

With every song, several people in the pews raised their hands to heaven as they worshipped, and many others clapped their hands in time to the music. The older children and teenagers in the congregation especially liked to clap hard and sing loud, grinning at each other across the pews to see who could perform the best.

Eyeing her cute boyfriend, Kangshi, dancing and jiving to the music in the aisle opposite her, pretty teenager Cai Lian started giggling so hard she began messing up the words badly, causing her and her best friend standing beside her, Dailanshu, to laugh even more.

Their parents frowned at the two girls, but they couldn't stop their mirth. The tempo of the last song was positively contagious.

Chapter Thirty Four

At the end of the last song, Pastor Wu stepped briskly to the pulpit. He spoke in Mandarin, his speech calm and crisp, more monotone in phonetics than the typical Chinese dialect. Pastor Wu had been a high level administrator in the royal government for many years before converting to Christianity. Liked and respected for his efficiency, he was widely noted in the church for being economical in words and action and for being intelligent and logical. The man was not verbose or emotionally expressive. He could be friendly and laugh at times, but he had no ability to engage in small talk, tell stories, or regale with jokes.

He was an exceptional organizer, brilliant planner, and a Godly man. Graham esteemed him for his management abilities, an area in which Graham admittedly had limited personal gifts. Especially after the loss of his wife and daughter, Wu's talent greatly complemented the Senior Pastor's diminished focus upon things of detail.

Although he understood only a few words of Chinese, David compensated by studying Wu's face as he spoke.

Brother Hennie, who had a decent command of

Mandarin, whispered a rough translation in David's ear as Pastor Wu spoke. "Sister Jeannie, Madame Feng, and Nancy Chou will be holding the monthly Bible study for ladies this Wednesday evening at 6:00pm at Madame Feng's residence, followed by a pot-luck dinner for all attendees. For more information, see Sister Jeannie or Madame Feng after the service. Brother Hennie and I will be leading the monthly men's meeting at church this Saturday morning. Also, I want to remind our deacons and church elected lay leaders of our mid-month prayer and planning meeting coming up. See me or Pastor Graham for more details.

"I am happy to announce that Brother Qinsong Yang, a long-time member of the church, is home from the hospital. We thank you for all of your prayers. He is much better now. For those of you who don't know, dear Brother Yang suffered a heart attack. His wife passed away two years ago, his daughters are married and live far way, and he needs in stay in bed for the next week. If any ladies can help by bringing meals in for Brother Yang, please see Brother Hennie or Sister Jeannie after the service. Also, Brother Alfred Chen was robbed by bandits returning from an extended business trip to Shanghai. He lost all of his suits, dress shoes, money, and many other valuables. He forgives the men who did this, but asks for prayer for God to bless his business two-fold to be able to replace what was stolen.

"Let us remember others in prayer who are sick or hurt or who have lost loved ones recently. Sister Tinglan Chen, who works in the children's church, threw out her back this week. She cannot stand straight, cannot walk except for short distances, and is in extreme pain. Pray for her. Sister Honghui Wan lost her mother, father, and uncle in a most horrible house fire. Lift up her and the rest of the family in their time of grief.

"Finally, just as our Lord Christ gave his life for all, those of us with plenty want to give to those who with need. If you have spare clothing your family doesn't use anymore, or if you can donate quantities of food from your household pantry, please bring those things to the church, so the pastors and helpers may distribute to those members who lack.

"And now, we come to the part of the service where God honors us by allowing us to humbly give back to him out of the many riches he has blessed us with. As the ushers come forward, please be seated and bow your heads. Pray silently to the Lord. Together, let us lift up these requests and believe our God for healing, for restoration, for comfort. After which, please continue to bow your heads as I pray over the offering. Ask the Lord what he would have you give this beautiful Sunday morning. Give not only out of your abundance, but like the widow woman, also give out of your need, and God will honor your gift accordingly.

"Let us pray."

Sitting on the platform, watching the service progress, even though all of it except Pastor Graham's sermon was in Chinese, David found he understood much of what was happening even without Brother Hennie's help. He was amazed. There was little difference he could see between the Chinese church and a big city Scottish church of the same size, except the people here had greater child-like faith and enthusiasm. Their eager hearts seemed more ready to receive and believe than their Western counterparts.

David was thrilled. He could sense the flow of the Spirit and the heartfelt worship. *Thank you Jesus! I'm home*, he thought happily.

Pastor Graham stood up to preach. David sat ramrod straight in his chair, eager to hear the sermon. As he spoke, Graham's message was translated paragraph-by-paragraph, pause-by-pause, into Mandarin by Brother Lee for the congregation's benefit. The overall effect of having a gap between phrases was that it gave the listeners, whether English or Chinese, extra time to digest and meditate on each glorious chunk of spiritual truth. David discovered it was an effective method to imprint the words into one's mind and soul.

Pastor Graham's mellow voice—sweet-sounding, strong, and sure—carried forth an immense wellspring of compassion and kindness in its very timbre. He was a man one wanted to hear.

"The text for this morning's sermon is found in Luke. Turn with me now if you have your Bibles to the tenth Chapter. We'll begin with verse thirty."

He paused for Brother Lee to interpret and also to let the people find the place.

All throughout the audience, one could hear the gentle

swishing of hundreds of pages being turned. It seemed as if almost every person, even many of the young adults and older children, had brought their Mandarin Bible with them. Those who didn't have their own Bible looked on with the person seated next to them. As he paged through his own Bible to Luke Chapter 10, David rejoiced at the sight.

"The title for my sermon is, 'Do you agape love your neighbor?'"

Graham repeated, "Do you show true *agape* love toward your neighbor?"

He continued to pause at each natural break to let Brother Lee interpret. "Many of you present today were here when we studied the subject of agape love in a series of lessons several months ago. For those who missed the lessons, let me digress and describe what agape love is.

"Agape is the love Jesus had on the cross when he shed his blood and died for our sins. Agape is pure selfless love that does not seek its own gain. When our heavenly Father extends unmerited grace to the sinner while he or she is yet in rebellion against him, this is agape in action.

"In the Parable of the Good Samaritan, we see two examples of selfish, uncaring, hard-hearted responses to a brother in need: A Jewish priest and a Levi. Don't forget. They were the spiritual leaders of their day.

"They passed by the poor wretched victim without so much as a word of encouragement or a second glance. He meant nothing to them.

"He couldn't give to them temple tithes or add to their riches. He couldn't help them enhance their positions of importance and power.

"Had he been robbed in a crowded Jerusalem street with many eyes around, they might have stopped to help... but only because they could have put on a fake show of their goodness and generosity in front of an adoring public.

"Then we see a stranger, a Samaritan who was scorned by all the Jews, who alone stopped and helped this brother in need." (Here he paused at length, letting the previous phrases sink in.)

"Let us read the story from the scripture."

As Pastor Graham flowed into the sermon, the wonder of his words made David feel as if he were an eye-witness to the events, so mesmerizing was the tale. "Tis like I'm seeing everything in person, and the Lord is a saying to me, 'Watch therefore and take heed,'" he said under his breath, as Pastor Wu looked at him and smiled.

At the end of the service, Pastor Wu came forward and gave an altar call for those wanting salvation as well as members wanting personal prayer from the church leaders for urgent needs. Out of a congregation of roughly four hundred souls, nearly fifty individuals crowded the front aisle for help.

Clearly, thought David, *God is at work in the Christ Is Lord mission church in the heart o' Beiping.*

Chapter Thirty Five

At the end of the thrilling message, David went forward to help pray for people. Without being asked, Brother Lee came and stood by his side to translate each person's request and then translate Pastor MacDougall's words back to the recipient.

The first individual was a middle-aged man weeping as though his heart would burst. Until today, this man had despised all Westerners with a great passion. His wife, Yan Ying, was a new believer, and very good at asking by faith for what she wanted. More than anything, she desired to see her husband saved, too. So, she prayed without ceasing and was relentless in asking Sunday after Sunday until the man could take it no longer. Simply to keep her quiet, he agreed to come to a church service, just the once.

Although the man had never been a formal member of the Boxers, he had joined with several bands of looters in the waning months of the unrest, and had rejoiced in the beatings and killings he witnessed. While most of his soul became more and more consumed with hate, a small window of his being felt contaminated by the growing rage. At times, he loathed himself for his constant black thoughts.

Pastor Graham's sermon on agape love broke through the darkness that morning. Freedom was close at hand.

Pastor Lee translated in phrases as the man poured out his anguish between his sobs. "I hated all foreign people... Everyone from the West. I wanted to see them driven out. Killed. Punished. Beaten."

He dipped his head in shame. "But I cannot live this way anymore. It's eating my insides up. I want to be *free* of this torment!

"I want the kind of love...*he* talked about," the man pointed at Pastor Graham.

David laid his hand gently on the man's shoulder and nodded. "Aye, by God's grace, you shall have it. Whom the Son sets free tis free indeed."

He waited for Brother Lee to catch up and then continued. "Repeat after me: Lord Jesus."

The man balked at saying the name.

"Lord Jesus," David said the words again, oblivious to the Asian's hesitation.

Brother Lee translated his words for the man.

"Lord Jesus..." David said the words yet a third time, his voice almost a whisper now, his blue-gray eyes penetrating the man's visage.

"Lord Je-sus," the man finally replied, his entire body trembling with release.

David continued, "I ask forgiveness for all o' my sins...I ask that you cleanse me totally...I ask that you come and live inside o' me...Be my Lord and Savior...Make me a new person inside...From this day on...I surrender my life to you...Fill me with your agape love."

"In Jesus' name, I pray. Amen!"

Not knowing any better, the man echoed each phrase after Brother Lee without first bowing in prayer. As he parroted the words, he stared with misty eyes at the lowered heads of the two pastors.

When Brother Lee and David looked up, they both knew instantly. All darkness was gone from the man's face. A different creature gazed jubilantly at them; a new creation in Christ. The Chinese man's eyes were positively shining with love.

He was almost dancing, he felt so light and free. His wife, who had been standing submissively ten feet behind praying and watching, now came joyously by his side and took his hand in hers.

The next person in line stood, quaking, wringing his hands in agony. He came to church for the free food and because he liked the music and singing. But he had stolen from an old woman out in the street that very week. He had beaten his wife over the smallest infraction. He had cursed at the government tax collector when the man and his armed guard had shown up to forcibly take a prized possession in lieu of payment. He felt ashamed, guilty, evil to the core, and he wanted forgiveness.

That morning, as he prayed in faith, he got it.

Now another person stepped forward to ask for victory over temptation and to rededicate his life to God's higher purpose. In turn, a fourth came to ask for blessing. Up and down the altar, David could see other exciting episodes of deliverance, of salvation, of freedom, of healing, of restoration, and of fresh commitment. People in the congregation were praying mightily for everyone who went forward.

Finally, the crowd at the front began thinning. Pastor Graham mounted the platform and took the pulpit again, with Brother Lee rejoining him to translate.

"For those of you who found Christ today...I want you to take time to talk with one of our leaders.

"Pastor Wu, Brother Lee, Sister Jeannie, Brother Hennie, or me.

"We want to give you as a free gift today your very own Bible, written in Mandarin, of course.

"We also want you to get connected to a person or family in the church who lives close to you.

"They will be your mentor and supporter as you grow in the Lord.

"Also, it is very important as a new Christian you come to church *every* Sunday.

"It has been a most glorious time in the Lord this morning, has it not? Can everyone say amen?"

"Amen!" shouted the entire congregation.

"Let us pray then."

Everyone bowed their heads for the closing prayer.

Chapter Thirty Six

Another life-transforming service at Christ Is Lord church was over. Outside, the noon day had warmed and brightened into a most gorgeous September setting. Inside, the atmosphere seemed just as beautiful, fresh, and radiant.

There was jubilation in the air.

His face wet with happy emotion, David surveyed the auditorium, watching the individuals gathering their things and departing in small groups, couples, and singles. *The power and presence o' the Holy Spirit is so strong*, he thought.

There was a quiet buzz of victory and anticipation all over the great room. The cheerful mood was reinforced by the strong sunlight now streaming down from the six large windows, three on either side, which had been built into the walls when the warehouse was first converted into a church building. Bright light also flooded from the front entrance as both doors opened and closed with people leaving. The natural sunlight made the kerosene-fueled lamps, affixed around the platform area in the wall spaces between windows, seem dingy and faded in the brilliance of the outside day.

On the edge of the platform, he saw Jimmy had already attached himself to Pastor Wu, eager to help in any way he could.

David smiled. He hoped the young man would grow to be a valuable assistant to the entire staff.

"So glad you here," said a middle-aged man, coming forward with his family.

Turning to meet him, David shook his hand, bowing when the little man bowed his head in greeting. "I am very glad to be here, too," he replied.

David bowed his head a second time and smiled as big as he could. He patted the man on the shoulder. "Thank you. Tis kind o' you to make me feel welcome." He bowed his head a third time as they left.

Now two older ladies walked up behind the man, waiting their turn to speak. "Pastor Ma-a-a-Doo-Gull, happy see you," they both nodded and smiled sweetly.

"I am very blessed to be here. God is so good," he spoke slowly, hoping they understood most of his words. When one woman extended her arm to shake, David gently took her hand in his and placing his other hand on top, he lightly squeezed, hoping she felt the sincerity of his joy in being with the Mission.

A cluster of teenagers, led by two athletic, nice-looking young men followed by a posse of four boys and five tittering girls, moved up next.

"Hello, I'm Kangshi, and this is my friend, Chenghui.

We are some, ah, younger people in church, and we want say, good have you as pastor."

Among the girls, Cai Lian elbowed her friend, Dailanshu, and giggled as her boyfriend spoke.

David gripped Kangshi's hand firmly and grinned. *I like this lad; he's bold.* He also shook the hand of Chenghui, and then reached out to do the same with each of the other boys in the group.

"Aye, lads and lassies, tis happy I am to be here at the Christ Is Lord Mission. I'm not sure what all Pastor Graham will have me a doin', but I look forward to worshipping the Lord with you youngsters as well as with the older folks."

Kangshi nodded again and gave David a little military salute, grinning back at him, causing the entire gang to break out laughing. "See you later, Pastor."

"Be seeing you," said David, amused by the liveliness of the teens. He saluted back, producing more chuckles and smiles. "Goodbye."

The lad's got a good sense o' humor, too. I appreciate that. Every church needs a dedicated group o' young adult leaders to fuel their growth.

Out of the corner of his eye, David saw Brother Lee approaching, accompanied by a Chinese lady attired in the latest European women's apparel, and a handsomely-suited man who appeared to be about David's own age. At the side of the younger man was an exceptionally pretty girl, clothed in a Bonne Femme-style dress that was corded and fully gathered round the waist. She had an expensive-looking silk Chinese scarf thrown around her slender neck and throat.

Three thoughts entered David's mind. *What a winsome, attractive Chinese family they be. And och, me goodness, but that lass is tall for her age, she is. Very comely girl, too.*

Only fourteen, he later discovered, the top of the girl's head reached the bridge of David's nose.

He couldn't help but notice her complexion; a heavenly creamy-pale brown. It looked as soft as baby skin. He saw she had full mischievous lips, an innocent yet seductive smile, and eyes slightly slanted, wide, and glowing with intelligence.

The girl's unusual height, intelligence, and beauty distracted him greatly. David had to force his eyes and attention back on Brother Lee as he walked up.

That first image of her burned into David's soul. He would remember that vision of loveliness for the rest of his life.

Part IV

Death and Love in Beiping

Chapter Thirty Seven

Since 1886, Zhuang Li, or Brother Lee as he was known, had worked in the inner city area for a large export firm owned by a wealthy British family of royal connection. Now semi-retired from this business, Brother Lee had polished his English language skills through hundreds of communications and face-to-face meetings with Western buyers, potential customers, venture partners, and the firm's senior management. Over time, he had become a trusted advisor and confidante to the owners on Chinese affairs, and even more so since he became a Christian believer nearly thirteen years ago.

His English was the best David had heard from a native Chinese, more formal and correct even than his own thick Scottish brogue.

The man's gaze was a bit inscrutable but gentle-looking. Wisdom emanated from his eyes.

"Pastor MacDougall," Brother Lee began.

"Och, please, sir. Call me David. Tis less formal," he interrupted.

"Pastor David," continued Brother Lee. "Allow me to introduce my family. This is my wife, Qiong Yang." She bowed elegantly. "This is my son, Wei Li." The two shook firm hands. "And this is my daughter, Xiu Li."

The father's eyes twinkled a little at the mention of her name. It was obvious that Xiu, as the youngest surviving child, was indulged by the other members. David later learned that in addition to the horrible death of their younger son, Hui, at the hands of the Boxers, Zhuang and Qiong had also lost a daughter, Mei Li, to the dreaded plague that had spread up to Beiping and the rest of northeastern China from the coastal Fujian province in 1901 and 1902.

Xiu Li looked with genuine interest at the tall handsome man standing in front of her.

"Hello, Dav-id!" she replied, with no trace of bashfulness or hesitancy. Though Xiu Li was still an adolescent, she was confident and candid. David found himself instantly smitten with the boldness of her personality.

"It is Pastor David," her father corrected her.

"Oh, right-o then! Hello, *Pastor* Dav-id!" she emphasized the title and grinned.

"Hello," he grinned back at her. *The whole family is a brick. No wonder Pastor Graham and Brother Lee are such close friends!* David liked everyone very much.

"What are you doing for lunch, pastor?" asked Brother Lee. "You're more than welcome to come home with us and share our humble meal." Qiong moved her head up and down in acknowledgement. The beautiful, spunky Xiu Li only grinned harder.

Warmth spread all over the reverend's body. He responded promptly, "Well, I suppose, I'll be a eating with you good folks."

They all exchanged polite goodbyes to Pastor Graham and the few staff and church members lingering in the large auditorium. The group strolled to their destination, enjoying the magnificent day. David found himself sandwiched between Brother Lee and his daughter on the way to their home. Xiu had quickened her pace to catch up to David, leaving her brother's side. Mother Wang and Wei trailed behind, mostly silent but observant of the conversation in front of them. The teenager talked as much as the two adults, interjecting into the discussion with random bits.

"Father, did you see Donghao standing up on the chair and wiggling his big butt, trying to dance to that last song?"

Zhuang grunted and replied, "It's called a hymn. Yes, I saw him, although I tried not to notice. Very childish behavior. We're supposed to be worshipping our Lord, not acting as if we're on a school playground. I'm glad his father made him get down."

"Well, I thought it was *so* funny. I laughed out loud." She looked up at the reverend. "Did you think it was funny? *Pastor?*" she emphasized the word again, feigning innocence.

The girl tis a pistol, and that be for sure. He grinned again in spite of himself.

"Aye, I saw it, lass. You be correct, too. The poor lad disna have a spot o' rhythm in his whole body."

"I'm sorry. What did you say? Dis-na?" Even her questioning air with her slightly impish frown seemed beautiful to David.

She caught her father's disapproving expression.

"Oh, yes, right. No, he doesn't have rhythm, Pastor, does he?"

Ignoring her father's continued stare, Xiu Li clapped her hands in amused agreement anyway. She was delighted their newest pastor was young, muscular, attractive, had a good sense of humor, and was not a stuffy kill-joy like other adults she knew. She glanced over slyly at her father when she thought this. She especially liked his strange Scottish pronunciation. She decided it was cute. She also decided she would not make fun of it to Pastor David when her father was around.

David discovered the residence of the Li family to be unusually large. It had spacious rooms throughout, new compared to other Chinese dwellings he had noticed, and was constructed in the Western style.

"Tis very luxurious, very impressive, tis," he said after getting a quick tour of the dining, kitchen, living areas, and Brother Lee's richly appointed office.

"Yes, I bought the home from a senior British diplomat, a Mr. Henry Wadsworth Weems, several years ago. He had the original building razed to the ground and had this built especially for his family when he first arrived here in Beiping in 1885. He was suddenly called away to India, and had to sell quickly. Most unfortunate for him but most fortunate for us. The Lord enabled me to purchase it at a very reasonable price."

The house was one of the few luxuries indulged in by Brother Lee. In a day and age of conspicuous consumption among the rich and the well-connected of the Chinese elite and ruling classes, Zhuang Li was very frugal; except for giving to the church, of which he made it a point of Christian honor to double-tithe unto the Lord, as David had been informed by Pastor Graham. He and his wife had scrimped and saved a lifetime to now enjoy a life of relative ease with their remaining offspring.

"Anpeng says lunch is ready. Please come to the dining room," called out Madam Wang, waving at everyone from the door.

Xiu bolted up from her living room chair and hurried in. She made sure she got the seat next to the pastor, ignoring her father's brief frown and her brother's raised eyebrows. She was beginning to like Reverend David Adam MacDougall, and didn't care a fig if he or anyone else knew it.

David noticed that lunch was more British than Chinese. Madam Wang had retained the Weems' Chinese cook, who had learned, during his time with the British family, to prepare passable English cuisine. The main course was a thick hearty beef stew filled with available fresh vegetables but flavored with Asian spices.

Och, after all the Chinese meals I've had, this'll go down a bit heavy, David thought. *I hinna had a Western dinner for some time.*

He knew beef was rarely served as a meat item at dinner tables in China; fish, pork, duck, and chicken for the well-to-do, and meat substitutes or no meat for the poorer. In his short time there, he had seen or heard of shark fins, seaweed, frogs, snakes, and even dog and cat meat, served at vendor stalls around the city. Various insects were also considered delicacies.

"Well, I hope you can stomach bad-tasting English food, Pastor. Anpeng didn't have time this morning to cook really good, healthy, tasty Chinese," Xiu quipped, flashing a dazzling smile at him while reaching to pick up his bowl for her father to fill up with stew.

She knotted her eyebrows in mock concern. "I know it's not what you usually eat. That's nasty fish eyes and old stale rice, right?"

David laughed in spite of himself, even while both her father and mother looked sternly at her. Brother Lee motioned to Xiu and she quieted somewhat for the remainder of the meal.

After that, the table talk was light, congenial, and bland. Brother Lee spoke only of the needs and plans of the church. Nothing was mentioned of his deceased children or of the turmoil of the government, and little of the past Boxer violence against Christians.

"Pastor David, the church wishes to reach out to all

classes of people: from the wealthiest to the poorest. All are lost sheep. We believe the good news of Jesus should be made available to all who have ears to hear. The...." he hesitated for the briefest moment, "*unfortunate events* of recent years have reduced our membership by half."

His eyes glinted. The corners of his mouth tightened with determination. "But with God's help, we will rebuild the church and add souls to the Kingdom."

"Brother Lee, feel free to be a using me in whatever way you wish. I'm a raw beginner and naught but a humble tool in the hands o' the church leaders. Me heart's desire is to win the lost, and grow the Christ Is Lord Missions to reach the mighty city o' Beiping and beyond."

An earnest zeal flooded his handsome face. "The Lord added to the church daily such as should be saved."

"Ah, Acts 2:27," gravely intoned Brother Lee.

"Pastor David," Xiu cut in before either man could continue. "Mei Ju, one of my good friends, was talking to Jimmy—he lives in the house with you?—after church today. Anyway, he told her that you know how to play Basket Ball? I've heard this game is becoming popular in Hong Kong and other big cities in the south."

Her father gazed disbelieving at his impetuous daughter. Mother Wang coughed softly. She delicately lifted her silk napkin up from her lap, and lightly touched the sides of her mouth. Here the men are speaking about serious things of the Lord, and silly Xiu Li brings up this frivolous subject.

She never knew what was going to come out of her daughter's mouth. *The young people today…*, she shook her head without finishing the thought.

"I would like to learn how to play." Xiu smiled brightly in the heat of her father's gentle scowl.

David cautiously glanced at Brother Lee and then back to the girl. "Aye, lass, when I'm not busy with the Lord's work and when you're not busy with your school and studying."

"Oh, I'm *very* smart. I always have my studies done early. My teachers are always amazed. I have much free time!" Her grin continued.

David looked over again at Brother Lee. "Aye. Well then, I suppose, ah, we'll have to see," he reddened a bit, "when there be time."

"I won't let you forget now." Her eyes sparkled as she said this.

David nodded in polite response, but Brother Lee put his hand up toward her in a halting motion as if to say, enough is enough.

Xiu quieted again.

David coughed in slight embarrassment, and the men resumed the original topic as if no interruption had occurred.

Pluck and sass! Pluck and sass! She's a handful, she is, and he chuckled to himself with amusement, glancing sideways at her from time to time.

Chapter Thirty Eight

From that moment on, David became like another son to Zhuang Li and his wife. He worked tirelessly with Brother Lee in evangelizing the Chinese communities and shops surrounding the church. Soon they began traveling to more distant parts of the city in their drive to win souls and rebuild the Christ Is Lord membership.

David felt they formed an excellent partnership: He with his fiery and passionate proclamations of the gospel, and Brother Lee's fluent and straight-forward translations to the listeners.

Occasionally, Wei Li or Jimmy went with them. But Wei was busy building his own business. He had inherited his father's talent for enterprise and industry. Besides, the son's heart was given to a young lady in the church, Ping Ling Zeng. The two were deeply in love, and planned to be married once Wei established himself. Jimmy, on the other hand, spent much of his time helping in the children's ministry and taking care of the orphaned children, a cause that was near and dear to his heart.

Evangelism was more difficult than ever. The Imperial government stayed in constant flux, swaying this way and that in its futile attempts to maintain equal footing with the foreign powers that voraciously surrounded the throne, a fact that only made daily life in the capital city even harder. Although public attitudes seemed to be softening, pockets of lingering resentment toward Western influence remained. Only by showing true Christianity, agape love in action, David knew, would the church be able to win true converts.

After a particularly futile morning spent visiting wealthy Chinese neighborhoods in the far northwestern section, Brother Lee and David halted outside a gray-walled army barracks housed in the inner city. In the side courtyard which was surrounded by a chain-link fence, they could see many Imperial soldiers and junior officers lounging, laughing, talking, playing games or cards, and smoking, all enjoying the unseasonably warm fall weather.

Brother Lee stopped an older soldier who was walking toward the fence gate and just about to go in. He expertly struck up a conversation. The man turned and listened politely at first. However, he became more agitated the longer Brother Lee spoke. Finally, the soldier grew angry. He muttered some words.

He's a cursing at us, David thought.

The man started waving Brother Lee away and thrusting both palms outward at David in a universal sign of rejection. Brother Lee remained calm and continued speaking.

"Taoshi? Wang Taoshi?" The soldier repeated a name Brother Lee had mentioned.

As David watched, somewhat amazed, the man's harsh scowl softened into a look of disbelief. He scratched his head as his mouth opened into a round circle. Now the soldier's eyes were wide and he appeared to be listening hard. His voice was less strident and more respectful, as he and Brother Lee engaged in animated conversation. He nodded his head several times, and at the end, made a little bow. To David, it seemed a bow of contrition.

After they walked some ways from the barracks, David asked Brother Lee what he had said.

"Ah yes, I told him Taoshi and Baoliang, the two officers responsible for killing Pastor Graham's wife and daughter, are now Christians and go to our church. He was in Taoshi's regiment that very day. His heart is hard toward Westerners. But I think he may be more open to talk about things of the Lord in the future now.

"He says he has been in the army a long time, and has many friends and knows many people. If he becomes a Christian, he can have great influence."

"Och, after all the rejections we got this morning a trying to talk with all the rich folk it would be a wonderful thing. And what's the man's name?"

"Chengning Yang."

"Chengning. Hmmm, sounds like the name o' a powerful Chinese evangelist to me. He might turn into a modern-day apostle Paul."

He grinned big, while Brother Lee gave him a solemn half smile in return.

"Perhaps so, Pastor. Perhaps so."

Chapter Thirty Nine

Of course David knew the ministry dealt with all aspects of life—the good and the bad, the sad and happy, the successes and failures. People were imperfect, in need of grace always. But somehow the man's tragic tale stayed with him long afterwards as a cautionary warning.

A most unfortunate situation had become public knowledge at Christ Is Lord shortly after David arrived in Beiping. A long-standing member of the board of deacons named Gangjie Huang, a handsome esteemed man with a lovely wife and three wonderful children, had engaged in a six-month long torrid affair with a younger woman in the church.

She was fairly new. Afterwards, people recalled seeing her only a few months before the whole thing must have started. In retrospect, they could see she had been targeting Huang all the time. They remembered her dressing somewhat provocatively and always sitting in the row right in front of the Huang family. Wherever Gangjie sat, she was careful to sit one seat over, so that he would be seeing her beautiful profile, her best side, as he looked up at the pulpit area. Even though it was forbidden for men to counsel women, or vice versa,

296

during altar calls, she made it a point to come forward every time there was an opportunity. She always made an excuse to the female workers who tried to talk with her, and found her way over to Gangjie instead.

Little did Gangjie know the woman's forward behavior was noticed, and he began being watched by his fellow deacons.

Soon, it was reported that Gangjie was having his wife stay home from church.

"You should spend more time preparing the meal," he had sternly told her in Mandarin. He began coming to services early, leaving his unsuspecting children to socialize with friends while he slipped away to meet with the other woman halfway down the unfinished right-hand back hall, ostensibly to counsel and pray for her needs.

The woman was unrelenting in her pursuit. Every time Gangjie's nascent guilt began to eat away at him and he made protest that he really should stop being with her one-on-one, she used her tears and wiles to play upon his basic compassion.

"If you were really concerned about me, you would stay and pray and help me. You have a stone for a heart. If you really were a Godly man, you would care for me."

It became harder and harder for him to say no.

"I do care for you. You're sweet and beautiful, inside and out, and you are—I do care for you. Please, dear, don't cry. I'll...I'll stay."

He bowed his head in defeat for yet another time. He

was weakening, and his flesh was taking over. Each time, his soul became more dulled to the spiritual danger.

He looked at her upturned face fresh-laced with tear streaks. She was incredibly desirable to him. He could not resist her.

Their relationship slipped beyond platonic and they began meeting secretly away from church, sometimes at her conspiring cousin's home where they were given complete privacy to be alone, sometimes at restaurants or parks far away from Huang's business office and his own home. Once they met at a friend's house who wasn't a Christian, and who thought it great sport to facilitate their romance.

Beset with other pressing issues, Pastor Graham had reluctantly spoken to Huang only after it had been brought to his notice a third time by concerned fellow deacons. The kindness of his heart and his spiritual desire to always think the best of people made it difficult to confront someone who had been such a stalwart supporter during the early years of Christ is Lord.

By then, the affair had been going on for many months. The other deacons and their wives had taken a vow of secrecy to not speak of it to Huang's wife, who remained clueless. The thought of her Godly husband cheating on her had never crossed her innocent mind.

They decided to let their senior pastor handle the matter.

Graham had sighed and looked with deepest

compassion at the tense figure of the man now standing in front of him with arms folded and glaring at him across his desk. Of all the vices Christian men could fall into, he knew sexual temptation was often the most devious, most destructive, and hardest to overcome—worse even than greed and money. During his twenty-five years in the ministry, he'd seen or heard of several good men ruined by sexual affairs.

"Brother Huang, I've been told that you are meeting with a certain lady within the church in...an inappropriate fashion." He held up his hand as Huang started to protest.

"I've no doubt that you had the best and most honorable of intentions in the beginning. But...I must ask that you stop seeing this lady alone. In fact, I must insist that you stop seeing this person at all. Don't have any more to do with her. If she has a need for prayer and guidance, I'll have Sister Jeannie help her. And if she refuses to leave you be, I'll have no choice but to ask her to leave our church."

Graham looked up at the drawn countenance of Gangjie, the normally handsome face mirroring the spiritual struggle within. The man didn't reply for several moments. A nerve twitched along the side of his mouth and cheek.

"No!" he finally blurted out. "No, I love her. And she loves me.

"I not give her up," he said, stubbornly.

Pastor held out his hands in supplication. He shook his head as a lonely tear streamed down the man's cheekbone. "Please, brother. You must be reasonable. You have your beautiful wife, Lanyun, to think of, and your marvelous children."

Pastor Graham had seen it all before. A Christian man falls for the charms of a calculating female. He falls so hard, it becomes like a sickness. In fact, it was a sickness, in Graham's opinion, a physical addiction, much like the opium so common among certain segments of Chinese society and classes. The more the man tasted of the forbidden fruit, the more he craved it, until the desire became an obsession, an unreasonable all-demanding hunger that took away the man's strength, his dignity, family, friends, and ultimately, his faith.

Now Gangjie's hands were clenched, and his features knotted. He shouted in anger. "I tell you I not give her up! I leave wife before I do that! I leave church!"

Shaking his fist in Graham's face, he leaned over the desk to get as close as he could without actually hitting. "She mean everything to me. No. No leave her!"

Pastor continued to try to talk with Gangjie, offering to let him take a sabbatical from the board of deacons to get his life in order. "No one in the church except for the staff and the board need know you're taking some time off. Your place on the board will be reserved for your return. All of us will be there to help—"

"I say no!" He slammed his fist upon the desk.

Graham calmly stood up, walked around the desk, and reached out to gently clasp Huang on the shoulder. "Brother, I know it's hard, the hardest thing you've ever done, but believe me—"

Gangjie seized Graham's hand and threw it violently away from his body. He stared daggers at the pastor he had known and loved for so long. For a second, Pastor thought the man would actually hit him.

Then Gangjie stormed out of the office, leaving the older man to bow his head in fervent prayer for his fallen colleague.

Pastor Graham took David with him twice to Gangjie's business office, attempting to convince Huang to return to his wife and his position in the church. The first time they went, he yelled at them in broken English and cursed at them in fluent Mandarin. The next time, he tried to push Pastor out of the room until David's mighty hands caught his thrusting arms in a vice-like grip that stopped him cold.

On one of Brother Lee's and David's evangelism outings in the business district months later, they saw him walking on the other side of the street with the woman. But he did not look happy. He turned his head deliberately to speak to her just as they passed by, ignoring their presence.

The sad sight only reinforced David's determination to remain celibate until marriage, and to remain faithful once married. No amount of short-term bodily pleasure, he decided, no matter how great it felt, was worth separation from God and the agony of continued guilt. He made it a point to make sure Jimmy included Huang's teenaged children in all youth activities. He went out of his way to be a friend to the two sons, as best he could.

Seeing the forsaken wife and family at church brought a fresh realization how fortunate he was to have such strong loving Christian parents.

"God, I be a thankin' you so much for me wonderful father and mother. Bless 'em both abundantly and keep me fully committed, Lord."

Chapter Forty

Days flew into months, and the months into a new season, followed by another. Slowly but surely the congregation grew.

Winter was especially hard the year after David arrived.

There were several soft knocks on the partially closed door of the last office down the left hand corridor. "Pastor Graham?" Pastor Wu opened the door and stepped in.

"Pastor, must talk. Urgent." He waited until he had the man's full attention. "We very low on food and clothes. Having to turn away many needy families in church," he said.

Looking up, Graham leaned back in the chair, distracted now from his sermon preparations. Absent-mindedly, he ran his hand through his thinning hair and sighed. There were always so many mouths to feed and bodies to clothe.

"All right. Let me contact the main office. Maybe the Society still has a little money left in the budget that they can spare us. Can you have Brother Hennie come see me, if he's not too busy? I'll have him personally go to the south office and speak to Reverend Baker about it." Graham thought a minute.

"How are Pastor David and Brother Lee doing in their efforts?"

"They help some. More and more coming in, all the time," admitted Pastor Wu, "but need so great, right now, Pastor."

"Fine, fine. We must do what we can. Well, do ask Brother Hennie to come see me."

In addition to daily evangelism with Brother Lee, David led the drive for donated clothing items and foodstuffs for the needy adults and families of the church, and for the rescued children living in the three siheyuan homes. Often, he and Pastor Lee would boldly ask for donations from wealthy merchants and individuals around the city after sharing the story of Jesus with them.

Although he had little practical experience yet, David was energetic, hardworking, and tenacious. He strove to be the best utility player he could be within the Christ Is Lord mission. He assisted Brother Hennie and Pastor Wu in the men's ministry and helped out with the youth whenever he had time.

David also did construction work, directing a volunteer group of carpenters and craftsmen as they finally built out the rest of the unfinished corridor on the right side beyond the sanctuary area.

The back one-third of the old warehouse was segmented into two rectangles, sharing a common partition down the middle and stretching behind the back wall of the speaker's auditorium on either side to the end of the building. The left side had long since been remodeled into a hallway populated with staff offices plus other rooms for meeting and teaching. Pastor's Graham's office was at the end of that left hall. The right side, however, remained incomplete with naked studs; there was but one finished office at the entrance. The rest of the rectangle was a vacant space.

As he and his crew labored, MacDougall often remembered Xiu Li's request to learn about the new sport of Basket Ball. He shook his head at the thought. *Och, where am I going to find time and energy to be a teaching her?*

Other people had approached David at church over the last few months, all asking about the sport. He knew Xiu had been busy drumming up interest among the youth. Much to her father and mother's disapproval, she had taken to frequently reminding him after church service or whenever he was invited to have lunch with the Li's.

He sighed and wiped the sweat off his brow. Even though it was late winter outside, it felt warm in the corridor with all the crew working and toiling away.

Tis busy as a beaver I am. Why, I haven't done any weightlifting or running or any proper exercise since, well, since way before Christmas. Indeed, he had not so much as bounced a ball or tacked up a basket since arriving in the city.

All the while, chaste thoughts of the saucy and stunning Xiu Li crept, unannounced and unwanted, into his innocent mind at inopportune situations.

Her lovely face drifted into his mind again, and he blushed furiously in spite of himself. He got angry this time, thinking, *No! She's barely fifteen, laddie. Don't be allowing even innocent thoughts into your mind.*

Passing by at that very moment with a two by four in his hands, Baojian, called Bennie, stopped, looked up at him with concern, and exclaimed, "Pastor Da-vid, you all right? Not feeling well?" David had clenched his teeth during his internal debate.

Embarrassed, David shook his head, a wry look plastered on his face. "No, I'm just a wasting time. Thinking too much about things I ought not be thinking about, Bennie. I ought be working, instead o' daydreaming, dinna I?"

He patted Bennie's shoulder. "Now, what was it you and Menghui wanted me to be helpin' you with in the center section?"

He walked with Bennie down the corridor as the man explained again.

A week later, David finally got the opportunity to teach the eager and impatient Xiu Li, her brother, and other interested youth the new American game of Basket Ball. They were fortunate in that the original owners of the warehouse had extended the leveled, smoothly-surfaced stone flooring well beyond the end of the building, as if they had intended to add a whole other section at a later date.

They were also fortunate in that it had not yet snowed that winter, allowing them to complete an outside Basket Ball court.

David guided the men in drilling out two eight-inch

wide holes through the hard stone and deep into the soft earth beneath, each opening positioned thirty feet from the back of the church, one for either side. Into these they inserted thick wooden poles. Onto each pole, the reverend fastened a heavy rectangle-shaped section of plywood, the bottom of which was nine feet above the ground. He then nailed into each plywood piece a sturdy apple basket, its top twelve inches from the bottom of the board. The lower half of each basket was cut away, leaving a bottom circumference nearly equal to the top opening. This made it possible for the ball to pass through unimpeded.

Finally, using water-resistant chalk, David measured and marked the out-of-bounds area, a half court line in the middle, and two free throw lines at either goal. Getting creative, he added elongated half-circles around each bucket to better designate the field of play.

There now! He thought happily, once he was done.

"Good job everyone! Give yourself a pat on the back." He looked around at his handiwork with satisfaction. *That ought to help all these new players know where to play and move so they can be a doing the most good for their team!*

It was on a late Thursday afternoon when the Basket Ball court was finished. The word spread and the following Saturday morning at ten o'clock, a total of eighteen curious people showed up to learn how to play this new game. Kangshi came with his best friend, Chenghui. So did Cai Lian and her friend, Dailanshu, to be with the boys.

There were three pre-teens, nine teenagers, four in their early twenties, and two over thirty; among the group were five females. Naturally, the feisty Xiu Li came. After much pleading on her part, so did Wei, her brother. Jimmy showed up, too, followed by a caravan of eleven younger children from the orphan's home that came to watch the big kids and grown-ups play.

David had Xiu Li and Kangshi help translate his instructions to the rest of the players, who gathered in a three-quarter circle around him.

"This is what we'll use as the Basket Ball," he said holding up a brand new European football. "The object o' the game is to get the ball inside the basket."

He walked over to the closest apple bucket.

"You can use both hands to shoot the ball, like this," he banked home a two-handed set attempt from twelve feet out. The crowd of onlookers oohed and aahed at the made bucket.

"Or you can use one hand, like this." He retrieved the ball, backed up, dribbled to the basket, and shot a lay-up.

"Or like this." He put his back to the basket, then dribbled left, and arched a pretty hook shot that swished through, hitting nothing but the bottom of the bucket.

"You can pass the ball to a teammate, like this," he positioned himself fifteen feet from Xiu and threw her a crisp bounce pass. She caught it and mimicked his motion, bouncing a saucy return to him.

"Very good, lassie!" he grinned, surprised.

She grinned back at him. "Oh yes, I'm always very good at everything I do, Pastor David!"

He laughed and then continued.

"You can pass the ball using both your hands, like this." He held the ball up over his head and turned with his back to the crowd, rotating around three quarters so everyone could see the position of his hands and fingers in gripping the ball. He then turned and faced Xiu.

"You want to be holding the ball close to your chest. Push off your back foot, take a step with your front foot, extend your arms, and follow through with your hands toward the chest o' your teammate."

He demonstrated a two-handed chest pass to Xiu, softening the throw as much as he could. He found out there was no need. She caught the ball with no difficulty, spun it in her hands, expertly positioned it with a proper grasp, and executed a hard pass to him, further surprising him.

Och, for a female that looks so dainty and pretty, the lass has real athletic ability, she does. Xiu Li was picking up everything as if she had been playing the sport for some time.

He threw the ball again to Xiu.

"Okay, now pass the ball to Kangshi. Then Kangshi, you pass it to Chenghui, who'll pass it back to me. Everyone be a watching, now."

Kangshi saluted, grinning as he said, "Whatever you want, Pastor, sir." He easily caught the ball from Xiu. He had no trouble getting the correct grip and motion. He zipped a hard pass to Chenghui, who fumbled the ball and dropped it.

Kangshi laughed at his friend. "That boy, all thumbs," he explained to David. *"Bèn shou bèn jiao,"* he said, shaking his head. "Pick it up, fool. Throw to Pastor."

Unsure of himself, Chenghui gripped the ball with his hands too close together and too far underneath the ball, such that his pass heaved forward like a poorly executed shot put. David had to step forward and bend low to catch the weak throw.

"Sorry," the teenager mumbled.

"Och. Well, tis a start. Tis a start. Now let's all gather 'round," he motioned everyone closer in, "and we'll try a doing some drills together."

A few of the Chinese played European football. They brought along their soccer balls, giving David a total of four to work with. He split the gathered crowd into four groups of four or five individuals each, taking care to include at least one taller and one older player in each group. He had them spread out on the court so everyone could see him. For nearly three hours, he drilled them on basic passing techniques, defensive movement and stance, handling the ball, shooting set shots, doing layups, making free throws, and getting into position on the offensive and defensive end.

By the end of the practice, he felt satisfied they had learned enough to be able to scrimmage and actually play a game or two the next time out.

"Well, what do you think?" he asked Xiu, Wei, and Kangshi after the long session.

"It is fun!" exclaimed Xiu Li. "I *love* it. I can't wait to play a real game."

Kangshi raised his eyebrows and nodded with exaggeration. "I like, too, Pastor. It's fun. Much better than games we play at school."

"Wei, what you think about it?" David turned to Xiu's brother.

"Well, I do need to do something for exercise." Wei scratched his head, a thoughtful look on his face. "I sit at a desk all day. It looks fun. I'll try it when I have the time to come."

"Good. That's good."

David eyed the group, his handsome features locked in concentration.

"Aye, I'm a thinking I may ask Pastor Graham to let us use the sanctuary on days when we dinna have services."

The others gasped.

"Say what, pastor?" exclaimed Xiu.

"You know the floor's the same as what we have outside behind the church. We could move and stack the folding chairs off to the side, and put 'em back once we be done. We could build portable stands for the two baskets, and the stands could be moved to the outside back when not being using. True, tis less than three quarters o' the length of a regulation court, tis, because of the walls, but would be inside, away from the bad weather. We could still run full court, just not the normal distance.

"Och, what do you think?"

They stared in wonder at his bold idea. One by one, they nodded in awed agreement.

"All right, then." David decided he would talk to Pastor Graham about it.

Chapter Forty One

On the Chinese coast, some two hundred miles past Beiping, strategic events were unfolding as the winter ended.

By early spring, the Russo-Japanese land war had been raging in Manchuria, far northeastern China, for over a year, with high casualties on both sides. The conflict began when the Japanese fleet launched a surprise attack and siege on the Russian naval troops in Port Arthur, known as Lüshun Port to the Chinese and Ryojun to the Japanese.

The outcome of the war would prove devastating in the decades to come for all of China.

"Did you hear the big news, Pastor MacDougall, Brother Lee, about the Japanese?" Graham asked them one Friday in late May, as the two men returned from the field to report in on their evangelistic and fund-gathering successes for the week.

Brother Lee gravely nodded. Being a good businessman, he made it his concern to know what was happening in greater China as it might affect his personal affairs and his family. His face showed a trace of apprehension. China suffered greatly through the years from foreign invasion and intervention, and he feared Japan's incursion most of all.

David replied, "No, I canna say I have, Pastor. Me Mandarin's not spruce enough to be a followin' the newspapers yet."

Graham laid out the details. The Japanese Admiral Togo Heihachiro finally got the decisive victory he craved, Pastor explained. His newer, faster, better equipped, heavily-armed navy had destroyed the aging Russian Baltic fleet led by the Russian Admiral Z.P. Rozhestvensky at Tsushima Straits. Many of the Russian ships were old, unserviceable, and manned by poorly trained crews, the news had reported. Further, beset by increasing domestic disturbance and political unrest at home, the Russian government sued for peace with the loss at Tsushima.

"I don't know what all of this means for China...but my heart feels grave misgivings." Graham frowned and shook his head. "In time, Japan may become a ravenous wolf in sheep's clothing within our beloved land. They have a lust for conquered territory and raw materials that won't stop with control of Manchuria, I fear."

Brother Lee nodded in stern agreement. He, too, felt a shadow of foreboding.

Although the other pastors and lay leaders at Christ Is Lord Mission gave the news serious thought, and certainly they had no way of knowing the future consequences of the event, the resultant Treaty of Portsmouth signed at summer's end gave Japan the foothold it needed to eventually turn into an oppressive stranglehold on the Chinese nation.

But for the moment, life at the church went on as usual, with all its ups and downs and daily challenges. David especially delighted in the Sunday services and in the outreach ministry.

On one of their evangelistic outings, David and Brother Lee stopped at the residence of Robby and Anne Butler, the same charming English couple with whom Emma Jones had stayed with during her few weeks in Beiping. David and Brother Lee had spent the morning talking to people they met within the mixed neighborhood. There they had found more progressive-thinking Chinese as well as more liberal-minded Westerners, all living together in relative harmony.

The Butlers, fluent in Mandarin, friendly and social, were well liked in the little community. Their two children, who also spoke excellent Mandarin and were known up and down the quaint little streets and serene courtyards, boisterously played with all the Chinese kids.

"Robby. Oh, Robby, dear. You absolutely must come and see! You'll never guess who's standing right here at our own front door."

A scholarly-looking man stepped up behind the woman, putting his arm around her waist and peering out of his wire-rim glasses. "So you must tell me who they are, sweetest."

"Remember the reverend traveling with Emma? He saved her from the pirates on the ship and from the gang of bandits in route to the city?"

"Well, yes darling, I do recall. Thrilling tales. Positively spiffing. David, I believe. David MacDougall, is that correct, sir?"

"Aye, tis."

David reached to shake his hand, even as his face was pinkish-red with embarrassment.

"How are you, sir? Mr. and Mrs. Butler, tis, right? Emma had very nice things to say about you two, she did."

"All lies, I can assure you. Scoundrels all, we Butlers are." The couple laughed together. David immediately liked them both.

"Och, and this is Brother Lee, Mr. Zhuang Li, to be formal."

"So very good to meet you," Robby said in precise Mandarin, giving a little bow.

Brother Lee bowed gravely in return, and replied in Chinese, "We are both from the Christ Is Lord mission church not far from here. We are telling people about our Lord and Savior and inviting them to visit the church."

"Yes, well, jolly good show. My humble opinion is that honest, true religion is the salvation of mankind. If we had more honest politicians and truer theologians, the world would be a much better place, now wouldn't it?"

The Butlers were non-practicing Church of England.

As with other issues, they were open-minded about religious topics, having Buddhists, Taoists, atheists, agnostics, and various Christian denominations represented among their many friends. They themselves believed in a higher power, but were unsure whether that higher power interfered directly in the affairs of mortal men. Nevertheless, they retained an open mind about the possibility of personal salvation and a personal God.

"Gentlemen, you must be tired from all your walking and talking this morning. Goodness, I know talking with Robby just wears me out," Anne laughed again and poked her husband in the side. He grabbed himself in the spot, moaned, and feigned a deadly injury.

"He just wants attention, as you can obviously see. Won't you please come inside? We can have some nice English scones and hot tea to unwind and get better acquainted." Anne held the door open wide and playfully pushed Robby behind her, while he continued to mimic a fatal wound.

Their children, Langdon and Georgina, frolicking down the street with friends, saw the unknown company going inside. They excused themselves and ran to the door, eager to be part of the grown-up fun, too.

David and Brother Lee stayed for over an hour and a half, listening to Robby talk about societal ills and ways to help others, and hearing the children tell how they brought home-cooked meals and medicines purchased out of the household budget to help this neighbor and that neighbor in need. It was obvious the entire family had a strong social conscience that showed up in practical, everyday demonstrations.

The six of them sat munching baked treats and sipping English black tea in the living room. David used the natural compassion and curiosity of the Butlers to ease the conversation into discussions of the various outreach programs of the church and describing in detail a typical service at the church.

Having forsaken formal religious attendance since before coming to China, Robby and Anne thought the description of a Christ Is Lord service sounded fascinating. The modern up-tempo music, the wonderful interplay between English and Mandarin languages, the realness of an altar call, the idea of specific prayer for individual needs, were all things they'd never come into contact with. The Church of England of their youth had been dull, filled with man-made traditions, and totally uninspiring.

"Sounds intriguing, doesn't it, Anne. We really ought to go at least once. You know, just to experience it for ourselves. Never let it be said that a Butler was afraid to try new things, righto, kiddos?"

"Never, father!" Both Langdon and Georgina answered loudly. They liked the idea of meeting and making new friends.

So the next service, true to their word, the four Butlers showed up and sat near the front row, eager to see what all the fuss was about. They continued to come, opening up a little more to the truth of the gospel message they heard each week.

Meanwhile, a watching Pastor, David, and Brother Lee prayed earnestly and the Holy Spirit worked His wonderful way within their searching hearts.

Five Sundays later, Robby and Anne, along with their children, went forward to receive Christ.

"I just feel something in my soul that I never felt before, Anne. It's like—*excuse us, so sorry*—it's like—*pardon us, please*—a hunger, like a void inside that must be filled up," he whispered to her as the whole family carefully made their way down the crowded row to the inside aisle.

"I know, sweetness, I know. I have the same intense feeling inside of me."

The deep spiritual longing awakened within was sated the moment each of the four Butlers made their personal decision for Christ. Robby and Anne's indecision whether or not a higher power actually cared about people, about individuals, was eradicated once and for all.

They now knew beyond a shadow of a doubt: God was a consuming, intimate, loving presence in their lives.

Chapter Forty Two

David's bold suggestion of using the inside floor for Basket Ball met with stiff resistance at first from the other pastors as well as the deacons. But Xiu mounted a vocal campaign among the youth and youth leaders, and eventually won over Brother Hennie as a second ally on church staff, and then her father as a reluctant third consenter.

After several months of vacillation, Pastor Graham relented.

"Pastor MacDougall, I have decided your group may use the back of the sanctuary for games on the following four conditions: One, there is to be no fighting, whatsoever. This is a house of God and that must be respected. If I hear a single report, just one, the games will be shut down for good. Two, you must sweep the floor, clean the area completely, and put everything back exactly the way it was, each time. No exception. Three, if any other church group has an approved need to use the sanctuary at that time they will have right of first refusal. Four, you must take special care to place these, ah, poles…what do you call them again?"

"They're the goal posts with baskets on them, sir."

"Right. Well, you must set these goal posts where there is absolutely no risk of a window being broken by a stray, whatever you call it."

"That would be the ball, sir."

"Yes. Right. The ball. Also, you must move the, ah, goal posts, to the far back section of the right hallway after you're finishing playing.

"If you fail to meet any of these preconditions, the arrangement is off. Understood?" he looked sternly at David, and then softened his stare.

"I know you'll do everything in your power to keep things in check." He reached out and patted David's shoulder.

It was determined that Thursday nights and Saturday mornings were almost always free.

As word spread of the fun new sport, participation grew rapidly. Many new players came, both youth and adults alike, exploding the average number of bodies to over sixty. David had to change the format to four-on-four, half court, so both ends could be used at the same time, and more people could play.

The two teams having the most wins for the night or morning session would then play each other for the championship, full court, five-on-five, by each choosing a fifth player from among the losing teams. However, when the weather was fine and not too cold, both the outdoor and indoor courts could be utilized at the same time, allowing David to return the format back into five-on-five, full court.

While most of the newer players didn't go to the church yet, a fair number began attending services, which added to the growth of Christ Is Lord. David used the games as an outreach tool, becoming a fervent evangelist for both game and gospel. It didn't take long for Pastor Graham and the staff to realize the value of holding Basket Ball games at the church.

"Och, hello, Guolong, how are you?"

It was Sunday morning. David recognized one of the newer Basket Ball players wandering among the gathering crowd, a bit lost, before service began. The man knew a little English. It was his first visit, and he seemed nervous and shy. David could tell he felt out of place being in a Christian church.

He saw David and bowed his head. "I fine. Coach," he said.

David reached out to shake his hand, "Very good to see you." He motioned for Guolong to stay where he was. "Ah, I'll be right back."

David scanned the throng for other players. He found Tiancheng huddled with Kangshi, Chenghui, Qiang, and Zhipeng in the far front corner.

They're probably all talking about Basket Ball, he thought, happily. Two of the men, he knew, were in their twenties. Tiancheng was older than that. But when it came to Basket Ball buddies, age, apparently, made no difference.

David hurried over.

"Kangshi, Tiancheng. Good morning, everyone!" he

beamed at them. "Excuse me, but we have a new visitor here. I think you all remember Guolong. He's been at the Basket Ball courts the last three Saturdays."

Kangshi translated for the other three.

"Yes, he's one likes foul hard, all time," laughed Kangshi. "But gets mad if *he* gets fouled."

"Aye, anyways, let's not worry 'bout that for now."

David looked over his shoulder to see where Guolong was. He jabbed his thumb in the man's direction. "He's a standing in the back there, near the front door, all alone. It would be a big help if some o' you lads could come with me and just make him feel welcome to the church. He doesn't speak much English, see, and he could use some Chinese friends."

He looked around at them as Kangshi translated.

"First time here, you know." David waited, smiling.

Kangshi, Tiancheng, and Qiang agreed to accompany David. But Chenghui stayed upfront with Zhipeng. Being a slower, awkward player himself, he was one of the ones who had been frequently fouled by Guolong. He just didn't care for the man.

David continued to preach the gospel of Christ and teach the game of Basket Ball with unbridled enthusiasm to those with open hearts and minds. A total of five other churches and three schools in the city developed Basket Ball courts with players of their own, each group trained in succession by David himself.

He absolutely loved the sport, and so did Xiu Li. Before she began working in her brother's office, she had accompanied David on his Basket Ball training missions.

"Aye, lass, you've got real Basket Ball smarts, you do," he had once told her with great admiration in his voice.

She had picked up the sport so completely, that in many ways she knew as much as he, and even came up with innovations of offense or defense on her own.

In addition to team games, they often played one-on-one against each other. He always won, but not by much, and only because he was stronger and able to bull his way to rebounds and his preferred shooting spots.

She was graceful and smooth in her movements and just as quick as David. Xiu had become an excellent set shooter, and handled the basketball as well as he. Her passes were harder and crisper than most men, and she had a knack of always being in the right place at the right time to make a play, whether cutting, curling, popping in, popping out, catching opponents off guard or out of position, using bodies as screens, or stopping suddenly then exploding to an open space. She instinctively knew how to move without the ball, a talent that many of the best male players never learned.

"Aeiii! I told you to watch her when she does that! You were supposed to pick her up," yelled one frustrated man in Mandarin to a teammate, after Xiu had back-cut for an easy layup.

"Fool. Watch her yourself. I had my hands full guarding Xuguan," hissed the other player.

Yes, Xiu Li was a wonder, in David's eyes. And not just for her Basket Ball skills.

Chapter Forty Three

Months sped into years, and several years went by. Slowly but steadily, the church grew. When the revolutionary thinker Sun Yat-sen became provisional president of the freshly-formed Republic of China in January 1912, the Christ Is Lord mission had reached eight hundred and seventy-two members, approaching its pre-Boxer zenith.

David liked the Chinese president very much. "Sun's a publicly confessed Christian believer!" he enthused to his colleagues upon hearing the news.

He'd read Sun had learned the English language in Hawaii, been baptized and later graduated with a medical degree in Hong Kong. His modernistic government broke away from old imperial traditions and seemed committed to what David hoped would be a positive direction for the strife-torn country.

Sadly, the previous year, in early October, Pastor Graham passed away suddenly. He had been working on his Sunday sermon in his office. It was suspected he'd died from a massive coronary, though no one knew for certain.

"Pastor David, I think my old friend died from a

lingering broken heart, one that never truly healed. I believe he finally refused to live any longer without his Mariam and Julia," Brother Lee had said at the time.

Lee sighed. "I know the feeling well. I, too, miss my son and daughter. Not a day goes by, but I remember them and grieve inside."

David had been the one to find pastor that sad morning. "Oh, no. Dear Lord, have you taken me dear brother home to heaven?" he'd whispered with a shocked voice, staring at the sight of the splayed body.

Graham was slumped forward on the desk, head turned to the side. His left cheek and eye lay smashed into the crumpled pages of the big black Bible on the desk, his right eye staring blankly beyond into space, the fingers of his right hand still touching the massive tome he had been reading, perhaps only seconds before.

Thereafter, Pastor Wu and Pastor David assumed the preaching and leadership responsibilities as co-senior pastors.

Mostly retired now from his business ventures, Brother Lee agreed to become a full-time pastor in charge of outreach and benevolence. He donated his small salary back to the church, in addition to double tithing on the earnings from his portfolio of investments and properties. He had been spending dozens of hours, week after week, as a volunteer anyway, so the move simply made his efforts official.

As David had hoped, Jimmy grew into a fine young man. He married a pretty young lady in the church, and was made pastor of the youth and the (orphan) children's home ministry, with his new wife managing the orphans' program. Sister Jeannie and Brother Hennie still labored as lay workers. But two years ago, the spinster Sister Colie had met a handsome and energetic middle-aged widower, Timothy O'Rourke, a Scotch-Irish minister. They courted, married, and moved south to Shanghai as a missionary couple. Consequently, her longtime senior helper, Lianyun, took over as the head of the Little People Church.

David felt that hostile feelings toward the West were subsiding, as Sun Yat-sen struggled to mold a lasting, stable republican form of government, more open to selected Western ideas of science and democracy than the old Qing Dynasty had been. But the brutal warlords, as the pastoral staff fretted over, still controlled much of the countryside, especially in the central, south, and far north of China.

At times, though, David sensed being a European was as big a handicap as it had ever been in his evangelism. After hard repetitive effort, he had mastered enough Mandarin to speak and understand simple sentences. But linguistics was not his cup of tea. Most Chinese he met put on a friendly, or at the very least, an ambiguous face. But he could tell resentment still lingered below the surface in many.

Then there was the delicate, continuing problem of Xiu Li.

What am I to do with meself? No matter where I go, in me mind and heart, she's always there.

David focused all his energy into serving the Lord, playing ball, and working out when he had a few spare moments. As he watched Xiu grow from a saucy schoolgirl into a confident young woman, David struggled mightily to keep a tight rein on his heartstrings.

She had begun working in her brother's booming business. Through that avenue, she had been introduced to a host of eligible men, both Chinese and foreign. She had casually gone on dinner dates with a few of them, but found no one interesting, and so, remained single.

Every time Xiu Li went out with another man, David experienced a flutter of nerves that could only be calmed by a grueling workout.

There were eight years between them. In truth, that seemed less of a real obstacle to David as time went on. As her pastor, though, he felt doubly constrained. He could control his thoughts but his heart was a different matter. Was it true love? Strong infatuation? Romantic inclination? He wasn't sure. He just knew he had a deep abiding affection toward her, and it wasn't just a 'big brother' mentality.

He fretted. He suffered. He agonized in his uncertainty of how to proceed. Or if he should let her know his heart. He prayed that the Lord would remove his tender regards for Xiu Li from his being, but to no avail.

Although Xiu delighted in joking and teasing with him, and was a frequent teammate or opponent on the court, he'd never quite figured out what her feelings toward him were. He'd always known she liked him a lot. But whether she felt anything more, he was clueless. Was he just an older brother figure? A sidekick? A teammate? A good friend and nothing more?

Was she afraid to get involved because he was her pastor?

Xiu Li, to me, tis beautiful beyond belief you are.

The loveliness of her face, her high level of intelligence, her immense confidence, her playful personality, lively conversation, unusual height, and dazzling smile...everything captivated him. She was exceptionally graceful in all her movements, too, especially when playing Basket Ball.

Finally, one Saturday late morning after almost everyone else had left the outdoor court, Xiu and David found themselves alone. She kept dribbling the ball back and forth between her hands, eyeing him mischievously. Suddenly, she faked throwing the ball at him, only to catch it at the end of her fingertips inches from his solemn, unblinking face. She had gotten very good at that, and made other players jump or throw up their hands up to block a pass that never completed. She loved their shocked expressions. Even those who guessed she was about to do it, still flinched every time.

"What's up, Pastor David? What are you thinking?"

She had already begun dribbling again, disappointed at his lack of response to her surprise attack. "You look very confused today. Did you not get your five cups of disgusting English black tea this morning to wake up?"

Xiu grinned at him.

He kept gazing at her with a grave expression on his handsome, chiseled face. A full minute passed. His heart was pounding in his chest. A small voice echoed in his soul.

It was now or never.

"Yes? Did you want to say something to me?" she stopped smiling and dribbling, and studied his face, with quiet curiosity.

David finally made up his mind and gathered his courage. "Xiu Li, I have to tell you a great secret. A secret o' the heart and soul."

"Oh, I *like* secrets," she said pertly, thinking he was about to share some big change in church leadership or similar unexciting announcement.

Breathing deeply, he rushed on before he totally lost his nerve.

"I love you, Xiu Li."

There was stunned silence. Off in the distance a few birds sang out. A warm breeze caressed the couple's faces.

"What, what did you say?"

Her gorgeous brown eyes opened the widest he'd ever seen. Looking into them, he became lost. It was like falling into the deepest pool of sweet emotion, and he didn't know if he would ever get out.

"I said," he swallowed hard, "I love you, lass."

He paused. The stillness seemed like an eternity to both of them.

"I guess I have loved you from the very first time I laid me eyes on you."

His temples were throbbing now and his stomach churned. He felt a strong burning tingling sensation like a shock wave rocket through his entire body as he stood, rooted and waiting.

"I love you," he said a third time, his voice almost a whisper now. He couldn't believe he'd finally confessed. He wondered if she would laugh or joke, as she so frequently did.

More moments passed. Her pretty face was flushed.

"I...I didn't know." She nervously glanced around to make sure they were alone. Her eyes were filled with surprise.

"I had no idea that you felt that way. About *me?*

She stared at him. "I always thought you thought of me as a little sister. Just a *tom-boy*, Father's little girl. I'm speechless, Pastor."

"Call me David. Please."

"All right, then. David."

She breathed out heavily, and her eyes narrowed as she became angry; at herself and at him. Impulsively, she slammed a curled fist upon his chest. "Are you blind?

"Don't you know? Couldn't you tell? I have loved you, too. *Always.*" She glared at him.

"But I didn't allow myself to think about it much when I was younger. I acted like the comic, joking, saying clever things. Just to help hide my feelings. I played rough and tough on the Basket Ball court, like a man would. Just to keep up a front.

"But the last few years, I couldn't help myself. I began wishing, more and more, that someday…Hoping, dreaming, even praying about you falling in love with me, seeing me for more than just a friend."

She slapped the ball on the court with great force several times, to drain off some of her pent-up emotion. She sighed and nervously moistened her beautiful lips with her tongue. She looked away for a moment and then looked back up at him, searching his face.

David was flooded with happiness. A tremendous weight had been lifted from his heart and soul. Reaching out, he gently took the ball from her hands and tossed it aside.

Hesitantly, the two of them edged closer together. Years of unfulfilled desire, waiting, watching, and wondering, were encompassed in their slowness of movement. Now his arms began to circle her slender waist, and she wrapped her arms around his thick neck. They leaned forward, both a bit shy, more than a little nervous, until their lips touched, ever so slightly. Instantly, pure electricity surged through their bodies.

They kissed harder, more passionately, then harder still.

Soon, their forms were pressing and struggling against one another so tightly, it seemed each body would merge into the other. Nothing in the world felt as wondrous to David as the crush of her full moist lips upon his, and the writhing pressure of her lithe figure upon his. Every cell in his being was exploding with excitement. Her long thigh pushed between his in urgency, and her taut eager breasts mashed against the top of his hard abdomen and his muscled torso.

When they unwrapped from each other, chests heaving and faces flushed with intense desire, the melody of singing birds in the background sounded like a love song.

Their own love song had begun, at long last.

"David, what should we tell my father and mother?"

"Well, we'll be speaking the truth, o' course. They both have eyes to see. And probably have been a seein' things more clearly than either o' us, all these years. Your father be a wise man, one o' the wisest I've ever known. He understands so much, more than I do. I'm a thinking that very little escapes him. I've a feeling they may have known all along, and been expecting such to happen, sooner or later, lass."

He put his arm around her waist, and looked at her upturned face. "Now's as good a time as any to be a telling them, dinna you think?"

"What did you say, Pastor David? Dinna?" She giggled.

It was an old, old joke between them, and he grinned back at her.

Chapter Forty Four

David was nervous when they met with Xiu's parents. Though he was now approaching thirty, having been a pastor for eight years at Christ Is Lord, and though she was twenty-two, he was afraid there would be resistance because of the age and cultural differences. Brother Lee had become almost like a second father to him, yet David had never confided his deep feelings about Xiu Li.

Brother Lee gave both of them a long knowing look when they told him of their announcement. He neither smiled nor spoke, but there was a twinkle in his eyes. However, Madam Yang clapped her hands together and exclaimed with happiness at the not unexpected joyful news.

"Jí lè! My sweet, precious, headstrong daughter! We couldn't be more delighted. We wondered when pastor was *finally* going to get around to it."

She lovingly patted David on the cheek and hugged Xiu tightly. "Yes, children, we always knew, always prayed, too," the dignified lady actually giggled. "One would have to be blind and deaf not to see the spark between you two.

"Almost an old man you are now, Pastor, and our daughter a fully grown woman."

For the second time that day, David breathed a sigh of equal parts relief and contentment.

When David reached out to shake, Brother Lee took his hand in both of his and held it firmly, putting years of unspoken communication, mutual friendship, and parental expectation into the gesture.

After several moments, he said, "Having lost a son and our other daughter, Xiu Li is doubly precious to her mother and me. Our very life's blood, our hopes and our dreams for the present and future are wrapped up in her being."

He continued to look deeply into David's face.

"Her eternal happiness and blessing is most important to us, Pastor. She can only marry a truly good man, a Godly man. One who loves her as he loves his own self. One who cherishes her as our Lord cherishes His church and watches over it."

David solemnly nodded.

A priceless gift was being bestowed upon him. It was his lasting responsibility to keep the gift safe, sheltered, comforted, cherished, and beloved, as she had always been.

"You have me sacred word of honor, Brother Lee. Tis a lovin' and carin' for her more than Jacob did for Rachel I be. All the days of her life."

"We know. We know." Brother Lee finally smiled.

The old couple had long treated David as a son. Other than the obvious fact he wasn't Chinese, he was perfect for their high-spirited daughter: Handsome, strong, Christian, faithful, disciplined, kind, respectful, hard-working, and intelligent. Plus he was a senior pastor of the church.

After their love was declared, when the Basket Ball games were over and if the weather was nice, David and Xiu Li would stroll the several miles to the Butler's eclectic yet warm, inviting home. There, once the general visiting was done, all four Butlers made sure the lovebirds had a lengthy period of privacy in the living room, the parents sneaking away to the far back office and the children excusing themselves to play outside.

The first time they had gone to the house as a couple, the worldly-wise Robby and Anne cottoned to the situation after twenty minutes or so of polite conversation. Their son did, too.

"Georgie, we need to go,"

Langdon snapped his fingers, waving his sister away from the sofa seat where she had been chatting away.

"Come outside with me. Let's play."

She arched her neck to look at her brother, but then turned back to the young couple. Langdon folded his arms in disgust and glared at his clueless sister.

"Let's go. Now!" he said in a loud stage whisper.

Finally, seeing her parents standing up with expectant looks on their faces, ready to leave the room, she caught on.

"*O-h-h-h.*"

She got up, smiled a huge smile at David and Xiu Li, and followed her brother out the front door.

Jack King

After so long a wait, David and Xiu's courtship was whirlwind and all-consuming. Both were still virgins. Both had high sex drives. Their chemistry was so strong that now, more than ever, David had to call upon his last reserves of rigid control to save the best—the ultimate ecstasy—for their honeymoon.

It was as if God had designed every lovely inch, every aspect of her exquisite essence just for him; to fit and fulfill his every desire. Every sweet, gentle curve seemed to melt into his rock-solid frame. She felt the same—they fit together as one.

"You are so amazingly beautiful, lassie. Just a few more months, a few more, and then you'll be Mrs. MacDougall."

"You got it all wrong, mister," she gave him a quick mischievous kiss. "I thought you were going to become Mr. Li," she laughed.

Though they didn't go *all the way* until marriage, they did almost everything else they could with their clothes on. It was a constant struggle. Time and again they came right to the edge of fulfillment, leaving their bodies tingling afterwards with pent-up desire. Barely keeping their raging passions in check, enough to avoid guilty feelings, neither could wait for their wedding, set several months hence.

That day seemed an eternity away.

Their discipline was helped by the fact there were few places where they could be truly alone for very long. Every avenue, every location, every spot seemed to have one or more amused observers. David didn't dare bring her into the courtyard house he still shared with Jimmy. Even if Jimmy allowed himself to be scarce, he was still a pastor and it was still church property. He had a sacred responsibility to be a Godly role model before the entire congregation.

"Darling, I canna possibly be more in love with you than I am," he said one moonlit evening, strolling back from the Butlers' house, his arm around her slender waist. "Aye, me heart would be bursting out o' me body, if I loved you one whit more. Och, I thought I was in love before, lass. But now I'm a knowing."

"Well, you can just forget, once and for all, about that other *awful* woman now that you're mine."

"Twas naught but child's play, a dim candlelight before, compared to the brilliance and heat o' the real sun."

"Why, Pas-tor Dav-id A-dam Mac-Dougall. I believe you're becoming a poet in your old age." She playfully bumped his hip with hers. They walked a few more steps before he turned in front of her, blocking her path, and enveloping her in his arms.

"Tis the might o' the West meets the mystery o' the East," he whispered, staring into her liquid shining eyes. "The brawn o' the West meets the beauty o' the East."

He leaned forward to meet her pouty moist lips. "Or something to that effect."

"You think so, do you? Well, I heard it was the other way around," she softly said, tilting her head back for his passionate, lingering kiss.

Chapter Forty Five

It seemed an eon to the lovebirds, waiting for their wedding date. Time slowed to a crawl. The four and a half months passed like four and a half years to David and Xiu Li. But finally the glorious day arrived. Co-Senior Pastor Wu officiated. The huge warehouse church was packed past pre-Boxer capacity with visitors as well as church members. During his years in Beiping, David had made many acquaintances and friends through both his evangelism and Basket Ball outreach.

All that long morning before the ceremony began, David felt a strange tightness in his chest. He almost had trouble breathing; he was so excited and nervous at the same time. But the years of discipline and waiting and wondering were over.

In Xiu Li, he'd won the woman of his dreams. She was everything he'd prayed and hoped for.

Xiu, on the other hand, was as calm and serene as a peaceful spring day. Her lovely face radiated complete happiness. The women tending to her thought she looked even more beautiful than usual. In her heart, she knew she was marrying the perfect man for her.

Now the much anticipated moment had arrived.

David stood waiting with his best man and groomsmen at the front, his heart and body settled and stilled in the magic of the moment.

As Xiu Li walked regally down the aisle with her father, heads turned to watch her pass by. Many women and girls exclaimed softly, so breathtaking was her loveliness in her angelic white wedding dress with lavender ribbon accentuating her slender waist.

David had requested that Pastor Lee repeat each Mandarin phase in English, so the wedding vows sounded even more solemn and sacred.

"Do you, David Adam MacDougall, take this woman, Li Xiu Li, to be your bride? Forsaking all others and faithful to her alone? For better or worse? For richer or poorer? In sickness and in health? To love and to cherish? Serving the Lord together? Raising all children in nurture and admonition of the Lord? Committed from this day forward, until death do you part?"

"I do," David said.

Pastor Wu repeated the vow for Xiu Li, who said her words in a clear, strong, confident voice.

Sister Amy and the church musicians played Highland Wedding, a traditional Scottish tune, followed by a Chinese wedding song of the bride's choosing. The gifted Sister Amy had composed a brass and piano rendition of the sprightly bagpipe-themed music.

Bride and groom said their vows to each other and

exchanged rings. Pastor Wu said, "You may now kiss bride," nodding at David.

"At last, me darling," he whispered, sweeping Xiu Li into his arms and forgetting the packed church filled with eager onlookers. They kissed long, hard, and passionately. All the teenagers in the audience gawked, whooped, and exchanged expressions of glee at the happy sight.

The couple finally broke away and turned with blushing faces to greet the glad church. After the service, the young adults who had grown up with Xiu, and those individuals who regularly played Basket Ball with them were especially boisterous, clapping their hands, hooting, calling out encouragements, having fun, and throwing their rice the hardest at the departing couple.

"You'll never catch her, Pastor. She's way too fast for you!"

"I hope all of your children look like *you*, Xiu Li," one girl said in Mandarin. "We both know Pastor MacDougall's so ugly!"

"It's about time, you two."

"I can't wait for you to become pregnant, Xiu, so I don't have to guard you anymore," exclaimed Cailan, in Mandarin. She was a relative newcomer to the church who sometimes drew the tough assignment of defending against Xiu Li, whenever her male teammates didn't feel like getting embarrassed.

Tightly holding David's hand in hers, face flushed with anticipation for the honeymoon to come, Xiu was the picture of radiance. As they left the church amidst a shower of rice and happy wishes from everyone, Xiu said to him, "Our new life is only beginning."

"Aye, tis the start of a wonderful lifetime together, me sweetness. Many joys and great happiness we'll be a havin'. With the Lord by our side, in good times and bad."

"Kill-joy," she laughed, and then kissed him passionately again.

Everything was incredibly romantic; nothing could stay their passion on their perfect honeymoon. Together they fulfilled all their fantasies, explored their bodies and their limits.

Chapter Forty Six

Jimmy had moved into the spare guest house two nights prior to their wedding, leaving the old home for the newlyweds upon their return. But before taking up residence, David and Xiu had traveled by railroad on the newly installed track to Tianjin. There, they boarded a semi-luxury ocean liner, the *SS Royal China*, for their honeymoon voyage. David's salary as co-senior pastor was modest, so the church had taken up an advance love offering to help pay for their trip.

Among other ports of call, they made stops in Hong Kong, and Perth, Australia, retracing some of David's original steps in his journey to China. They stayed in Australia for nearly two weeks, swimming in the crystal blue ocean, walking on the pure white sanded beaches near the city, and camping in the primitive yet picturesque wilds to the north and east of Perth, where the great outback began.

"Oh, David, it's so beautiful out here, so peaceful. Come and see."

Xiu Li had gotten up early to build a campfire and start the coffee. Behind her, one flap of their forest green tent was still open. She could hear him stirring around inside.

Xiu stretched her arms above her head, looking at the

gorgeous sunrise peaking over the rocky terrain. The shifting clouds above them and to the east were changing by the second, from night gray to raging streaks of violet-blue to deepest burnt-orange to lightest tangerine to brilliant yellow to intense white.

As it rose, the sun cast the sheen of a thousand tiny diamonds, catching boulders, pebbles, and reflective surfaces everywhere, sparkling across the unending horizon of red sandstone hills, gullies, bloodwood trees and miniature boab trees, scrub brush, and vast rocky landscape.

Putting her hands on her hips, Xiu arched her spine backwards as far as it would go; twisting her shoulders this way and that, to limber up. She yawned and smiled as David slipped up behind her, lightly cupping her breasts in his hands and gently kissing the nape of her neck. She leaned her head sideways, giving him more room to work his kisses up and down her neck and into her ear canal. Her breasts firmed in his hands as he brought his thumb and forefinger together to gently pull and massage her wakening nipples. She moaned, and twisted her head to the left to take his passionate kiss on the mouth, letting her tongue dart in and out, dueling with his, and then sucking his tongue deep into her mouth.

They roughed it in the outback, riding horses when they could, hiking when they had to, living off the land in some cases, and visiting the many little sheep herding and farming villages of the great western expanse.

When the couple returned to China on the decrepit

but highly affordable MS *Nippon Empress* they were tanned, fit, more in love than ever, and ready for the married routine.

With his gorgeous intelligent wife by his side in the ministry, David felt blessed beyond measure.

Two blissful years passed. David and Xiu Li settled into the married life with ease. Opposites though they were, they complemented each other in more ways than not, and together made a wonderful team as pastor and wife.

Much to her parents' dismay and against normal Chinese custom, Xiu Li had insisted that she and David get to enjoy their time as a couple. After they got back from Australia, she had used the rhythm method to avoid getting pregnant. It was fortunate her body had not been fertile during their torrent honeymoon.

"Sweetheart, I want us to have five years alone together," she had told David when they had discussed the topic.

"I'm sorry?" he'd asked.

"What I mean is I don't want to have children right away. I want it to be just the two of us. For at least four years. Maybe five. Yes, I know children are God's gift. And yes, I'd like both a son and daughter eventually. But I also know how much trouble they can be. I want us to be able to enjoy ourselves first."

In their hurry to get married they hadn't talked about such things before. She stared into his eyes then, hoping for understanding, but determined to get her way.

David studied her pretty face, his thick brows furrowing

a bit in his concentration. "Well, if that makes you happy, lass. If that's what you really desire, fine. I want me own children someday, and not *too* far into the future."

He smiled at her. "But I'm willing to wait a bit, if it makes you happy, wife o' mine."

He squeezed her hand. "The main things are, tis very much in love with you I am, and we're meant to be together, sweetness."

She breathed a sigh and then laughed. *What a good man I have.*

She was still young, and there was all the time in the world to have babies, she reasoned.

The two rarely argued. When they did, David tended to concede the point. It took too much energy to debate her—Xiu was so feisty and intelligent. However, they never disagreed about things of real importance. Despite her headstrong and spirited personality, Xiu reverenced her husband as the man of the house. For his part, David found Xiu Li's opinions to almost always be right anyway, and so it was very easy to agree with her.

One evening, David unknowingly gave Xiu Li new ammunition to use whenever she was slightly put out, or whenever she felt like it. They had taken a rickshaw to an expensive restaurant located outside the old Legation compound. The fine establishment catered to Western clientele as well as wealthy Chinese businessmen. The meal was exquisite and the service excellent. They'd had a wonderful time, and were waiting for an available rickshaw to return home, when David spoke.

"You know that me full name is David Adam MacDougall."

"Of course I do, silly," she smiled at him, wondering what he was about.

"Aye, well, the next time you get mad at me—"

She interrupted him, frowning a bit. "David, I never get mad at you for anything. There are times when I have to *convince* you that I'm right, but I never lose my temper at you. How could I, at someone as adorable as you?"

Ignoring the meticulously tailored couples around them, also waiting, Xiu Li moved closer still, pinching his bottom and putting her arms around his waist. One of the refined ladies who saw it, gasped.

"Och, as I was a saying, lass, the very next time you get a little irritated with me, you can just say, 'Dam, I'm right', or 'Dam, obey me', and I'll know what you mean."

"Damn? But that's a swear word. A profanity that Westerners like to use, right? I don't want to speak bad language at you." Her lovely face had a puzzled look.

"Do you know what an initial is, me beautiful mistress?"

She shook her head; she'd not heard of the English term before.

"It's the first letter of a word. What are the initials o' David Adam MacDougall?"

She pondered for only a second, and then exclaimed,

"D-A-M. Dam! It sounds like. Oh, I get it now. Very clever, *Pastor* David. Teaching an innocent young woman to use inappropriate language. You're a bad influence on me, mister.

"Hold on, that's incorrect, my darling. *Dam*, you're a bad influence on me, mister."

She broke into laughter, causing the several women with their men to look askance at her. She didn't care one bit.

"Well, dam, you didn't pass the ball to me enough, yesterday. Dam, you didn't hang up your clothes last night."

"Aye, I think you get the gist of it now," he said with a mild grimace.

"Oh, I'm just getting started, old man! Dam, you left me to do the dishes today, and it was your turn. Dam, you left the bedroom way too early this morning; I wasn't through with you. Dam, you forgot to scratch my back when I asked you to. Dam, you forgot to include that verse I told you to include in your last sermon. Dam, I don't want Jimmy and his girlfriend tagging along with us any more when we go out."

He looked at her, ruefully. He'd no idea she'd latch on to his silly jest so thoroughly.

"Very interesting." Xiu put her hands on her hips.

"You know this has real possibilities to keep you in line, mister."

She laughed again, squeezed his muscular arm, and to his relief, a rickshaw pulled up in front of the restaurant to take them home.

Chapter Forty Seven

More time passed. The Christ Is Lord congregation grew as never before, finally surpassing the pre-Boxer attendance record. Xiu Li proved to be an excellent administrator and formidable organizer. Although David was not forgetful or disorganized, she kept him on track for even the smallest details.

"David, did you talk to Rihui about getting Basket Ball set up at his school?"

"Rihui? Uh, no, I'm not sure I remember who tis you're talking about, sweetness."

Distracted, David had his head down, digging in the two drawers allotted to him in the huge oak chest they shared for their smallest clothing items. Of course, Xiu Li used five of the seven drawers. He couldn't find his dark gray socks to go with his handsome new suit that had been a Christmas present from the Li's.

He stood up and furrowed his brow.

"Och, now I remember. Mr. Tan is his last name. He's the principal at the New Chinese-Western School for Science, Arts and Literature. We met him several months ago when we hosted the Open Tournament."

"Yes, that's right. He was interested in learning more about Basket Ball and perhaps building an inside court at the school."

"Aye, I'll try to be finding time to visit with him in the next couple o' weeks." He looked up and grinned. "Does that meet with the approval o' the female head o' the house?"

"Possibly. It depends on how well you obey me in my other needs, slave."

It was another of their little jokes. Although she nipped at him all the time, she was only playing and respected his word in all important matters.

Just then, they heard a knocking at the front.

"Your turn," said Xiu Li.

David walked through the living area and opened the door.

"Pastor David. Pastor David, you must come to church. Quick! Something happened, Pastor Wu. Hurt *bad*." David saw Jimmy's anxious face surrounded by those of several men he knew from the congregation.

Xiu Li called out from behind him; she had trailed him into the room. "David, what's wrong? Did something happen?"

"Aye, I think Pastor Wu's been injured." He turned to her with a look of concern.

"Well, I'm coming, too."

Xiu Li grabbed a scarf she had slung over the sofa after their morning walk together. It was very blustery that day. Rather than subsiding, the heavy breeze had risen to occasional near-gale strength. She could hear the wind whistling around the corners and rustling the nearby treetops outside.

Joining the small crowd of men, they hurried the few blocks to the large building down the street, bent forward against the howling currents. Strong sudden gusts whipped their eyes and slammed against their figures as they pushed forward.

On the ground beside the far outside wall, David could see tangled wreckage and a limp figure beneath. On the mildly slanted warehouse roof above, he saw workers kneeling, holding on for security, and looking down with shocked expressions at the tragic scene.

"Och, no! Dear Lord, it canna be!"

David understood immediately. Leaning, he ran into the hard wind to reach Pastor Wu.

Xiu sprinted after him.

Only yesterday, he'd advised Co-senior Pastor Wu to wait until early the following week when he would have more time to assist him. The new modern steeple the church had ordered just came in, and Wu was determined to get it mounted in time for Sunday service.

In the opinion of many, including David, the old steeple was weather-beaten, a bit stained, and old-fashioned. Wu wanted the gleaming new, intricately-designed, metal pinnacle erected as a symbol of the exciting new growth and fresh direction of the Christ Is Lord Mission.

But the fierce winds had wrested the awkwardly-shaped spire out of the grasp of the men as they worked. They had watched in horror as it slipped off the old foundation block before they could secure it. It struck the lower portion of the roof once with its heavy base before flipping over the edge, hurling point first, aimed directly at the surprised figure of Pastor Wu below.

"Oh, no, David! This isn't real! This can't be happening,"

Xiu Li groaned at the gory sight, her pretty eyes staring in disbelief. She leaned against David's back and held onto him to steady her trembling legs.

The sharp point had thrust savagely through Wu's ribcage and exited the back, initially pinning him down, but popping back out of his body when it hit the hard stony ground beneath. The mass of twisted metal then somersaulted into the air, before landing on top of Wu's already mortally wounded body, the bloodied spike now facing outward across his convulsing chest.

"Jimmy, go to the Chinese Medical Hospital. It's the closest place. Run as fast as you can! Have them bring a stretcher or a cart. Anything. With a doctor, if they can spare one." David's face was tight. His jaw muscles clenched at he stared at the bloody scene before him.

Xiu Li repeated the instructions in Mandarin to make sure Jimmy understood. He raced off, head bent against the violent gusts.

"Longwen, you go to Brother Lee's house and fetch him here."

Xiu repeated this request in Mandarin as well.

David stooped, grabbed around the thick base and middle and lifted up the whole steeple, taking great care to not further injure Pastor Wu.

"Arghhhhh!"

Seething with helplessness, David took his anger out on the mangled piece of structure. He tossed the heavy object ten feet away into the storming winds, as if it were built of paper and not metal.

The other people gathered around them. David and Xiu Li knelt on either side of the still figure. Each tenderly took a hand to hold. They had no way to close his gaping wound, no bandages to staunch his massive bleeding, and no potions to ease his pain.

David bowed, "Lord, if tis your will, you can supernaturally heal Pastor Wu even now. By your stripes, the Word says, we be healed. We ask your touch upon him. Take away his pain."

They all prayed together, David in English, the others in Mandarin, some kneeling, some standing with heads bowed and arms folded. But everyone knew, unless God intervened with a mighty miracle raising him up from his death bed, that Pastor Wu would soon be in heaven with his Lord.

They watched his facial hue turn from pale to bleached to bone-white, and finally, to rubbery-chalk, the mask of death.

For twenty minutes, Pastor Wu's torn body had been racked with incredible pain and shock. He was unconscious at the very end. Wu died with unseeing eyes looking up into the gray afternoon stormy skies above.

Xiu Li began weeping inconsolably. She let go of Wu's hand, and reached out to David. It was a tragic accident. The church had lost a faithful man of God, a strong leader, a capable preacher, and a wonderful husband and father.

Yet the indifferent winds continued to rage and howl.

By the time Pastor Lee arrived in haste, Pastor Wu was gone. When the ambulance cart with its two attendants got there, it became a carrier for the morgue rather than the hospital.

Staring in utter disbelief, Pastor Lee knelt by his old friend, tears flooding his eyes. He took a pale hand in his own and bowed his head in fervent prayer.

Wearily, Pastor Lee stood up. He gave instructions to the men tending the cart and watched them pick up the broken figure.

"Easy! He is not a piece of wood," he snapped at the men in Mandarin. "Treat his body with all respect."

Wiping his cheeks off with the back of his hand, Lee looked off into the distant east horizon peering between the tops of the surrounding buildings.

"He was a good man, very dependable. Wu always gave sound practical advice. We will miss him greatly," Pastor Lee said, putting his hand on his son-in-law's slumping shoulder.

Xiu sagged against David's side, her beautiful cheeks lined with tear trails whipped by the raging wind.

Chapter Forty Eight

With Wu's death, David became the senior pastor, albeit with a heavy heart. After years of service as a dedicated layman, Brother Hennie finally consented to be a pastor, taking over the role of church administrator.

Although the Christ Is Lord had grown tremendously, there had been grave hardships and many disappointments in the decade since David had first arrived in the city. Life was still difficult for many members.

Outside the confines of the Christ Is Lord mission, in the world beyond, the bloodbath of WWI had begun several months earlier in Europe. It was now late October. Japan had already entered the war on the side of the Western powers and gained control of German possessions in Shandong, China, along with parts of Manchuria and Inner Mongolia.

Although the conflict did not directly affect the people of Beiping, David kept close tabs on reports of the war, getting English papers when he could, letters from home, and having Xiu Li read him the Chinese papers.

More time passed and the war deepened. Every week seemingly brought news of yet another bloody battle somewhere else in the world. Although no one from his own village had been lost, David learned of young men from towns close by who had died or been wounded or were missing in action. Two boys he had known while growing up.

The war brought a different kind of struggle within David. One day, he finally burst out his vexation to his wife.

"Xiu Li, I can hardly stand it." He had been praying about what to do, but with no definite answer from above.

"Seeing me countrymen fighting and dying, Scotsmen, too, and here I be, hiding behind a minister's license."

He rarely used her real name except in cases of urgent concern or great frustration. His usual loving nicknames for her were *princess*, *sweetness*, *mistress*, *darling*, and *glide*, the last one referring to her graceful athletic ability to escape opponents in Basket Ball.

He sat at the little dining table after breakfast, watching her sleek figure as she bustled around the kitchen area at the other end of the large connected room.

Immediately, she stopped what she was doing, and turned to confront him. Xiu frowned fiercely, a thing she rarely did.

"What are you talking about, David?"

He looked away from her without speaking; his manly face a mask of indecision and anguish.

"Answer me! What are you trying to say?"

She glared at him. She thought she knew what he meant by his words, and it made her very angry.

He didn't reply, but finally looked at her. She saw great agony in his eyes. Her breath caught for a moment at the thoughts racing through her mind, and then she reacted.

"Dam, you're married, mister. Dam, you belong to *me!*"

She threw the dishrag into the sink, ripped the pink apron off her waist, and marched over to the little table. She put her hands on her hips and stood before him. Defiant. Demanding.

"Dam, you have a church family that needs you. Dam, you have a home here with me. *We* are not fighting anyone here. That war does not involve *us.*

"It is *not* our battle."

David looked at her beautiful yet scowling face for half a minute more without replying. He knitted his eyebrows and bit his bottom lip deep in thought.

How can I be a puttin' it into words she'll understand?

His blood lust was up.

He was a natural born fighter, spawn of countless generations of warring tribesmen. He loved Xiu Li with every particle of his being. He delighted in being a pastor and caring for his flock. He esteemed his in-laws. He was very happy with his life in the little courtyard home in Beiping. But it troubled him. Made him restless; made him feel like a coward, to see the MacDougalls and countless other clans joining the military and him unable to help.

Give unto God what is God's and unto Caesar what is Caesar's, he thought. Caesar, Great Britain, was beckoning to her citizens and he hadn't answered the summons.

He sighed and looked at her sadly.

"Aye, I know, sweetness, I know. Tis very blessed I am. Tis my calling from the Lord to be a minister in China... but..." his voice trailed as he stared into space.

Suddenly she looked at him with new understanding. Her man was a warrior. Only the redemption of the cross had kept him from being a savage boxer, or a trained fighter, a mercenary soldier, or a career military officer. She put aside her anger, came around to his side, and sat next to him, her liquid eyes fastened on his face.

There was a hush. Xiu studied him as she collected her thoughts, what to say and how to say it. Then a bird burst into sound on the little tree in the patio courtyard outside the open kitchen window.

"David," she took his big hand in hers, "David, I'm ready to start thinking about children now." She nodded solemnly.

"We can start trying in another month or so. That would make our baby due sometime in August. You know that's my favorite month of the year. I've always wanted to have my first baby in August."

He felt she was capitulating in a sense, just because the war had released the martial side of his personality. He wanted children badly, but he stared at her with a doubtful expression.

"No, I dinna want you to rush things, all because me blood is heated up."

"Honest. I've been thinking more and more about it. I think it's time. Do you agree?"

David sat silent, mulling the question.

"Husband, do you agree?" her voice was softer than a whisper now.

After another moment of internal struggle, he replied, "Aye, I agree."

He sighed again. "I'll not be enlisting, princess. Although I could be a chaplain in the army and not have to fight, you know."

She shook her head emphatically.

"All right. Fine. I'll be a staying here with the Christ Is Lord."

He gave her a sad smile. "You and the Lord together make an unbeatable combination. Aye, we can have our baby."

He leaned forward to kiss her open lips.

David forced himself to stop following the war's progress, and focused all his energies on the church and on Xiu Li.

They tried for six months without success. Making a baby took much of the intrigue and spontaneity out of lovemaking. After one particular marathon session, David laid back, tiny beads of sweat collecting and cooling over his body in the warm spring evening.

"Lass, can we be taking a break for the next two or three nights? Tis worn to a frazzle I be. I feel like an old, old man."

"One night's rest, old man, and then we'll try again the next night."

There were occasions David felt simply exhausted, but Xiu Li carried a constant glow of happiness about her.

"I've been researching and thinking about names, lass."

It was another early Sunday evening and they were taking their usual walk about the neighborhood after the day's temperature had dropped.

"If we have a girl, I like Sarah a lot, because it's biblical and strong-sounding; a woman o' virtue and destiny. And I found a new word that I be a liking as well: Quanli. Your father tells me it means having all one's rights, empowered with all rights. To me it means a Christian has all their rights in the heavenly kingdom above and earth below as an adopted child o' God.

"So, what I'm a saying is her full name would be: Sarah… Quanli…MacDougall. What be your thoughts, princess?"

Xiu cut her eyes up to the sky, her pretty mouth twisted in a contemplative mood. "Well, perhaps. I like Rebecca better than Sarah. And I like Yue as a middle name."

"Maybe if we have two girls that can be the name o' the second one?" he suggested.

"Let me think about that."

They argued at length about a boy's name, since the male's designation carried more importance in Chinese society. They settled on Joshua Hao MacDougall for a son's name.

Finally in mid-May, Xiu became pregnant.

While her parents and friends rejoiced, she was

disappointed her baby would not be arriving in August, but instead in the dead of winter, her least favorite season. But in late January, 1916, David and Xiu Li had their first child, a big, healthy baby girl weighing eight and three quarter pounds and nearly twenty-two inches long. The infant was stout of build and even stouter of voice; her loud cries could be heard by people passing by the house outside.

Like David as a newborn, her cries were thunderous. She looked like Xiu Li in the face, but had David's strong body. It was obvious to everyone she would be a good-looking but sturdily-built woman when she grew up.

They named her Sarah: Sarah Quanli MacDougall.

It had been a long journey to the present for David; at times, treacherous; other times, tedious and tiring. He thought back to his childhood, his former fiancé Rose, his calling to the ministry, the many dangers of the voyage to China, and the years of effort and sacrifice that had gone into rebuilding Christ Is Lord.

He smiled when he thought about his other great passion: Basket Ball. In addition to his devotion to Xiu and the growing church body, it was part of his Calling, a cornerstone of his being. He delighted in teaching the game to eager devotees.

Yes, God had been good each step of the way. Now he had a church pastorate, a new home, a new country, a new people, a new sport, and a beautiful wife and baby girl. He wondered what the future held, but knew whatever blessings or perils lay ahead, he would rest in his faith.

The great adventure of life, love and leisure was really only beginning, after all.

End of Book One

ABOUT THE AUTHOR

Born in Tennessee to a military family, Jack King crisscrossed the country multiple times growing up. After obtaining graduate degrees in both business and history, he began a successful career in sales and marketing working for Fortune 500, mid-sized, and start-up firms along the way. *Game for the Middle Kingdom* is his second novel. Mr. King is currently at work on the next book in the Game saga: "The War Years".